PLAYING MADAME MAO

PLAYING MADAME MAO

Lau Siew Mei

SUMMERSDALE

First published by Brandl & Schlesinger Pty Ltd in 2000.

This edition published in 2002 by Summersdale Publishers Ltd.

Summersdale Publishers Ltd
46 West Street
Chichester
West Sussex
PO19 1RP
UK

www.summersdale.com

Printed and bound in Great Britain.

ISBN 1 84024 211 6

Cover design by Blue Lemon Design Consultancy
www.bluelemondesign.co.uk

For Esmi and Matthew with my love

About the Author

Lau Siew Mei was born in Singapore and now lives in Australia. Her stories have been broadcast on the BBC World Service, published in major international literary journals and several have won literary awards. *Playing Madame Mao* is her first novel.

Author's Note

I have used the pre-pinyin Wade-Giles spelling of names in the novel (Mao Tse-tung instead of Mao Zedong, which is now more common) because it reflects the way Chinese names are spelt in Singapore.

Acknowledgements

The cover page quotation by Roxane Witke is taken from Roxane Witke's *Comrade Chiang Ching* (Weidenfeld and Nicolson, London, 1977).

The cover page quotation by Chairman Mao, and the quote from Han Fei-tzu's essay, *The Five Vermin*, come from Simon Leys' *Broken Images: Essays On Chinese Culture and Politics* (translated by Steve Cox, St Martin's Press, New York, 1979).

Mao Tse-tung's poem, *The Golden Crane Tower*, comes from the translation into English by Wong Man in the book, *Poems of Mao Tse-tung* (Eastern Horizon Press, Hong Kong, 1966).

The song over the radio, which Tang hears before he dies, is the song the 81-year-old Mao reportedly sang as he went for a cataract removal in his right eye, and comes from Harrison Salisbury's book *The New Emperors Mao and Deng: A Dual Biography*, (HarperCollins Publishers, London, 1992).

Many thanks to my publishers, Summersdale, especially to my editor, Kelly Cattermole and commissioning editor, Liz Kershaw; my parents for love; Juliusz Maciej Zajaczkowski for numerous conversations; Yu-Li Hu and Marion Campbell for early faith.

I am grateful to Arts Queensland for supporting the writing of this novel in the form of a Project Grant, and the Eleanor Dark Foundation for a Varuna Writers Residential Fellowship.

Extracts from the novel have appeared in slightly different forms as short stories or within stories in *New Letters* (USA), *Overland* and *Australian Short Stories*.

'I realised how in her own mind truth and fiction, history and literature, past and present had blurred. Such synthesis was at the heart of the propaganda by which she lived.'
American journalist Roxane Witke on Madame Mao Tse-tung

'There is no construction without destruction, no flowing without damming and no motion without rest; the two are locked in a life-and-death struggle.'
Chairman Mao

'Comrades, you should always bear your own responsibilities. If you've got to shit, shit! If you've got to fart, fart! Don't hold things down in your bowels, and you'll feel easier.'
Chairman Mao

Prologue

Here I am. Here I come to the river in my yellow Versace jacket that hangs down to my knees, my body definite against the soft meandering lines of water and muddy banks. I stand firm, hair sleek, my words slipping out like polished stones, watching the ripples in the river widening, waiting. I am waiting, poised on the brink of my confidence, my sharp, modern cynicism. So maybe I will speak. I will say, 'Do you remember once here?' and words to that effect.

The wind weighs heavily, drooping the palm leaves into silence.

I face her in the reflected grey of the water. The old woman wrinkles her ancient nose. Such a one as she could have played the corpse desecrator in an act of *Rashomon*. Such a withered hag grimly pulling out the locks of those newly dead for material profit. 'Just a living,' her voice will wheeze, and the wind will leap about her head so her hair will rise wild and grey like storm-driven water.

Her eyes are bitter-lined, bitter as the pulped fruits of the putat laut fishermen used to stun fish in the waters.

'My husband is dead,' I cry, dropping my composure. She seems not to hear.

'I make my living upon the fortunes of the dead,' the old woman says. On the river the houseboats cling to the bank edge, unsteadily rocking.

Dance of the Red Machines

Opera posters are stuck upon ruined sandstone columns, where time's filigreed shadows dance in flickering movements. History falls in small chunks of crumbling stone, remnants of the time the Majapahit Empire reigned.

In an open-air space where the tombs of the Malay kings lie, and the angsana trees, giantlike, sprawl over the ground, and the royal ladies once bathed in a pool now dried up, here, among its ruins with the strangling waringin fig twining itself within the cracks, is a theatre.

The stage is bare planks laid down as floorboards, fronted by a big pink curtain of silk hung between pillars, the auditorium the cavernous darkness of night, seats rising softly up a slope. The opera posters display the anguished face of a painted woman against a starkly red background: the woman is me.

I play Madame Mao. The critics say I am the best enactment of her they have seen. My part is easy. Death is my familiar. On opera nights, I paint my face a ghastly white, and stretch my eyes with black grease till they touch the outermost limits of my face. I screech my killings. I chant the lines of her life that I make my own for a few hours on the lighted stage. I am the best substitute they have for a maligned woman, a murderess, who shut down theatres that denied her acting talents. They blame her now for the excesses of the Cultural Revolution, for the death of the arts. But who better than herself to know what the arts were about?

Chian Yi, a contemporary arts critic in the city, writes in his review: 'Chiang Ching, or to give her married designation, Madame Mao Tse-tung, persecuted theatre directors, writers, actors, singers, because she was a jealous woman. She knew they would never let her play, she, who thought herself the greatest actress who would ever step into an opera.'

I know better. She was afraid, and her fear that she was not the greatest actress, drove her to insanity, drove her, paradoxically, to play the role of death, the final and greatest play that can be written. For myself, because I know I am the greatest Madame Mao the stage has produced, because the applause of pundits still rings in my ear, I have no fear. Least of all of death.

This evening I sit on the balustraded balcony of my second floor apartment with some women friends from the theatre who have come round on hearing of my husband's arrest.

We slide our smiles around our glasses of translucent yellow wine, which we embrace loosely in our hands. The liquid sparkles coldly down our throats. The air is thick with the anticipation of monsoonal rains. The trees hold their breath. We sip and talk of this and that. We crack watermelon seeds with our teeth.

'Our beloved director says the government is not happy with the script. Some changes have to be made,' someone reports in the midst of our conversation rising lightly.

Some of the women frown. I cannot tell if they are unhappy with the news or simply do not want to hear it. Such news is not an issue to me. Many people I know in the theatre world argue or rebel even when their scripts are artistically bad.

'Hui,' I say, 'is an idiot.'

Which puts the government in a worse category for bothering with him, I think in my heart. No one speaks about my husband. A woman nursing her glass gasps as she watches the sky blaze, 'A beautiful sunset! How lucky you are to have such a wonderful view!'

Now that my husband has been arrested, my friends concern themselves with my ability to carry on with my performances. One of them leans over to pat my hand lightly, 'Darlin', you have shadows under your eyes! You have to look after yourself.'

'Try to get some rest,' they cry. 'Such marvellous reviews!'

It seems there is even a chance to take the play overseas.

I open my mouth and find myself speaking to them of death. Their pink powdered faces turn to me, showing signs of strain under the make-up. They wear their faces carefully and settle in their chairs. I fill their fluted glasses with more wine.

I think, *We in the theatre are like beings in the death realm. We are mirror creatures scattering light, catching now and again a nuance, a word that sounds like life.* In Chinese mythology, death is a watery realm. When I die my soul will travel to the Yellow Springs that run from the foot of the fu-sang tree in the east to the ruo tree in the west. When I die, I shall be as one of the creatures in a mirror world.

'One morning,' I begin, 'making up my face in the mirror, I see a line. An outline. Of a fish in the glass. Only a faint one. But it is the beginning.'

My friends are polite, they turn their heads to one another to judge the general reaction, glancing, shooting sparks from their eyes, as if to say, yes, we know, certainly.

'An outline. It's a legend. They are mirror creatures! In the time of the Yellow Emperor, they revolted and he imprisoned them behind the glass, to reduce them to slaves, to yes-men, imitating us. But one day they will break out.'

'The first to appear is the fish,' I shout into the sea of their faces. I shout myself onto stage, into the crowds forming a mass in the auditorium who come to witness, it is I, it is Madame Mao, listen! But their faces grow hostile.

The mirror creatures once lived in our world, in the time of the Yellow Emperor, though they were distinct from those of the real world. The mirror creatures mingled with us and had conversation. But the mirror ruler tried to take over, and the Yellow Emperor imprisoned the creatures behind the glass. He forced them to take on the identities of those who looked into the mirror, repeating their actions, as if in a dream. Some say that at a time in the future the glass will break. The mirror creatures will stir, with the fish awakening first. Slowly an outline will appear. More and more the outlines will take form, cracking the glass. The mirror creatures imprisoned throughout aeons will recover their true selves. They will act as those who walk freely.

The women are looking at me expectantly. One of them ventures, 'Ah? The mirror creatures! I have heard the tale. I remember hearing from my grandmother that they would return.'

'There will come another time,' I continue, 'when the world of men will suffer for their arrogance. That will be when the glass breaks.'

I believe Madame Mao knew the mirror creatures were akin to herself. Her being was of the substance theirs were. Their natures were reflective. Madame Mao, the great actress, had an understanding with these creatures. When she died, they were to take her body into their underwater realm. Upon the balcony, I close my eyes. The sensuous wine slides slowly down my throat. The reddening sun pulsates roundly against my eyeballs. I am walking upon a dark road to my end, but the dying sun-raven lighting the clouds in the sky, in defiance, extends prickly sun-ray claws to scratch my eyes. I open them wide.

'It is late! We have to go.' My theatre friends jostle themselves from my balcony, stepping back into my living room where I would leave time waiting.

I remain in my rattan chair on the balcony to sip the dregs of the wine. I am half-asleep. I murmur some lines from *The Golden Crane Tower*, a poem Mao wrote in the spring of 1927, and the thought behind the words comes to me – the heroes are gone!

Who knows whither the Golden Crane went
Leaving but a shrine for pilgrims?
I pour a libation on the foam,
My heartbeat upsurging with the waves.

When he wrote the poem, he was already an ardent Marxist,

but it would be some years before the Long March was taken through much of China, a journey that was to transform him into a legend for his people.

Chairman Mao's ambitions are reminiscent of the overwhelming desire of the First Emperor of China to control time and in so doing, also history. In a short story, *The Wall and the Books*, Jorge Luis Borges, portrays Emperor Chin Shih Huang Ti's two famous actions – the construction of the Great Wall and the burning of books of earlier ages – as a need to control history. The despotic emperor who was sole ruler from 221–210 BC, a mere eleven years, had wanted time and history to begin with him, which may be why he appropriated to himself a name that has its roots in Shang Ti, the High Lord of the Heavens. To put it simply: I will build this wall. I will be remembered. I will tell the world of the exact moment the Middle Kingdom began, the first unification. I will define space and territory. I will say this is mine.

Mao wanted to be the father of modern China, to have time start from *his* rule, I think. During China's civil war, Mao's army situated itself, oddly enough, within the bend of the Yellow River in northern Shensi, north-eastern Kansu and south-eastern Ninghsia. This region almost corresponds to the original confines of the birthplace of China. It is near here the Chinese first created themselves as a people, four thousand years ago.

And in a closed Party session in 1958, Chairman Mao purportedly remarked to his colleagues: 'Well, what was so extraordinary about Chin Shih Huang? He only executed 460 scholars; we've executed 46,000! I said that once to some democrats: you think you are insulting us by calling us Chin Shih Huangs, I said, but you're wrong, we've done a hundred times better than Chin Shih Huang.'

The Arrest

The evening, which was to be the last before his arrest, I remember we went to the Esplanade. I think of the last walk we took, the warm wet breeze that rippled the dull face of the water, the silver fish glimpsed in glints of light, and the river bank with the lantern-shaped fruits of the putat laut, dangling like beacons, summoning us to a fate we did not know awaited.

As we walked, I sniffed the light attar of the evening. Behind us, his shadow beside mine was long, thin, and somehow absurd. I laughed, pointing out to him the way he walked, like a stick bobbing along the river! What was left of the daylight wrapped around us. A moth flew into my face. There were many moths in the twilight, attracted to the trees' fragrant flowers. By morning the putat laut flowers would fall. We sauntered along the embankment, watching the waves hissing at the base.

The night the men in white clothes come to take my husband away, we are at supper. Ah Mui, the old amah, enters the dining area, her pigtail swinging to her knees like a hangman's rope or a bell-pull to toll the hours passing. She comes in wiping her hands on a striped dish-cloth.

'Two men to see master,' she mouths. She rounds her eyes.

'Who are they?' I ask impatiently. I dislike leaving porridge to go cold on the table.

'Don't know. Important men. Government men,' she bleats. My husband raises his eyebrows at me. I get up and go to the living room where she has left them waiting. I see two men, neat and polite.

'Is Tang Na Juan, your husband, home?'

'He is coming now,' I reply, as I hear the sounds of Ah Mui clearing the dishes, and my husband running water in the bathroom to wash his hands. Then the news comes.

'Why are you here? What have you come for?' I plead, tugging their white-clad arms, as they prepare to lead my frightened husband to their car.

'Idiot!' I shriek at Ah Mui as she closes the door after them. 'Why did you let them in, you pig?' I pinch the fleshy part of her skinny arm nearest to me. I burst into hysterics as she watches me, her mouth falling open, her eyes red-rimmed and rounded.

They say he is an enemy of the state. My husband has been arrested for plotting against the government. For being too concerned with the welfare of others. 'Your husband opposes the authorities for no reason. You know that those who oppose authority without cause will be torn apart by wild dogs in the seventh court of justice in the death realm!' I hear the men cry.

MIND YOUR OWN BUSINESS. It is written upon my forehead, everyone's forehead. The business of the state is not to concern me, only basic necessities like how to earn enough money to feed my belly and put a roof over my head. I am not to make comments on things I can have insufficient information on. 'You people are fools,' they declare. My scholar-husband wrote the articles that brought us down. He gave his two cents' worth of criticism in the Catholic journal he helped to found.

'I am not someone who shoots off his mouth for no purpose. I am a nation-builder,' he wrote. 'This country is the place of my birth.'

'Is your stomach full? If it is filled, keep your mouth shut,' I said.

'We are living in a chicken coop society,' he wrote. 'Even if the door of the coop were to open, we would remain because here we are given food and shelter, we have grown fat. We have traded in our freedom for bread. We are kept people. We let the government do our thinking for us.'

But then he would despair and say, 'What is the point? Well-fed stomachs do not make good revolutionaries.' He was right and he had forgotten. He too was such a product of the society. I read the newspaper item that appears the next day:

Communist agitators have infiltrated the Catholic Church, using it as a shield for their subversive activities, a Ministry of Home Affairs spokesman said last night.

In his brief statement, he said the recent arrests of twenty-two persons under the Internal Security Act was an attempt by the government 'to put the lid on the situation before it reaches a critical point'.

'The conspirators infiltrated the church. We have spoken to the Archbishop … who has promised to look into the cleaning up of his church,' said the spokesman.

According to his statement, the ringleaders of the alleged group of communist activists are lay pastors working in the Justice and Peace Commission, an outgrowth of the Catholic Church.

The Commission, set up ten years ago, has upon its agenda complaints of social injustice and poverty, which it aims to correct.

The detainees are said to have accused the government of certain inequalities and injustices within the country's social and political system.

Among other things, they claim that a large proportion of the country's population is being ignored: those with a lower level of education, the lower-income earners, and migrant workers.

The government alleges that the detainees have tried to stir up the people against them.

The spokesman said further details would be disclosed by the government at a later date.

At the end of dreaming, it is only a little room with cream walls that I wake up in. The curtains flap in the dust and smell of city living. It is a narrow area, and I am driven by desperation to look for a space beyond. Looking in my mirror of retribution, I see that I look an old woman, my hair rising as if driven by the wind, like the grey waves in monsoon season, but if my years are counted, they will say I am still young enough for beauty and coquettish smiles, too late now, such a time for me has passed; my spirit has been a long time dying. I do not fear my physical death. There is a moment when to have one's life thread cut, to live out a time of dreaming, of non-existence, seems more comforting.

With my husband taken from me, all I have left now is revenge. Hui has asked me to help him redraft the play. I will play a dominant role, going over each word, taking the actors through the rehearsals, making sure each intonation, each gesture, each movement, betrays a hidden intent: to satirise Them. My husband was arrested by a government of white clothes, led by a man I will call the Chairman. A great man, apparently, but a man born under the sign of the Virgo: intellectual, meticulous, a tough opponent. But not one to look too deeply into matters of the heart. His hirsute attributes are rather diminished near the temples. He reveals a grand sweep of forehead, a pockmarked nose, and thin lips. Some women claim his ruddy complexion indicates a virile nature. That may be so. What is more certain, it reveals a fiery temper, a cutting tongue and an intolerance for fools. Fools, he believes, compose 99 per cent of the population he rules.

Across the sky a shooting star. It is May, 1987. A light breeze comes in eastwards over the cemetery, whispers through the trees, lifting tired leaves and reviving the coloured flowers. In the air, a whiff of the neighbours' burning joss sticks. A funeral wake is being held, the burnt ashes fly shivering in the wind, to crumble on my lap. The weight of bearing up alone terrifies me. Even my old servant has left. I may have my evening meal on the balcony, and watch the night shoppers like dolls in the distance amidst the bright hard lights.

From where I sit, I oversee the city itself: mini-America, some say, lighted towers, shopping complexes, neon advertisements and traffic lights. Upon it are written the slogans: progress and excellence. Beyond the sea, if I stretch my imagination, an arc of small jungle-ringed islands surrounds this tortoise-shaped city. The city is famous for its unique positioning, at a fork for incoming ships from Europe and India in the west; China, Japan, Vietnam, Laos, Cambodia and Thailand in the north; Borneo, and the Moluccas in the east; and from Java and Australasia to the south. It has survived because it is on a crossroads. Its face is traversed with tourists and peregrines. Here is a meeting place. In more than one sense.

It is also a place where a meeting of people is suspect.

I think of making the Chairman appear like a figure in a Theatre of the Absurd. I write down his common nickname: Hairy. I pretend he is not the demigod he is in reality, presiding over our lives; he is an unkempt rock star who keeps the masses in slavish adoration. A good explanation for his prolonged popularity among the populace, who return him to power every election with the highest percentage of votes. How else can I explain this phenomenon?

At a rally, where the Chairman is campaigning for election, a rock fan speaks, 'Nothing he does can be wrong.'

A rebel is overheard, muttering, 'According to himself.'

The rock fan looks around, 'Who said that?'

The rebel backs down, 'I meant nothing.' *Pause*.

The rock fan remarks idly, 'Next time, watch what you say.'

I espy him, the rebel, sitting in his soft plush chair high in the auditorium, shouting out jeers and whistles that he would not dare pronounce were it not for the darkness of the theatre that hides him. He is mocking me. On the stage, I, as Madame Mao, re-enact her tragic miscalculations, my face painted and wild, my eyes stretched to outermost limits, my voice set up in a wail.

Only yesterday, Ah Mui told me as she helped me into my operatic robes that she wished to leave my service. That wizened frog had been with me for five years but with the trickling smell of official unpleasantness seeping into the air she would disappear like water sucked by the sun. She claimed she wanted to retire from service, and live with her son and daughter-in-law in their small two-bedroom Housing Development Board flat.

'I am old, *lah*,' she excused herself, as she tightened the cloth belt binding my small waist.

I replied curtly, 'I will find a replacement.'

Ah Mui's eyes widened and narrowed, she was lost for words. When Ah Mui had left the room, I was alone with my face before the mirror. I surveyed the outlines of the mirror creatures gradually forming. The fish was almost there.

This morning I hear the singing outside my window, the sound so bright it seems effulgent, breaking in waves of light as my consciousness slowly rises from the depths of sleep. It is the music of the finale. It is the moment I hold the audience enthralled. It is as the old woman, the fortune-teller, told me. I am the greatest Madame Mao who has ever stepped onto the stage.

When I was a child, my mother carried me to the fortune-teller with her makeshift stall by the side of Cluny Road. The woman studied my face, my skull, the length of my ears, the shape of my hands and my palms; she told my mother that my life would be filled with sorrow, that I would know the death of those I loved, but that I would redeem my life with a song. My mother, poverty-burdened, was too awed to ask her further. Only when we reached our home and she had settled me on the floor to play, she sighed, 'Useless child! A song, what song? Will you be a cabaret girl?'

Today, I am celebrated, lauded, and my mother is long dead.

The director yells from the auditorium, 'MOVE! A little more to centre. Where's the Red Guard chorus? Haven't you heard your CUE?'

On a good day, I get maybe six curtain calls. I get flowers in my dressing room, among the grease pots. A strong scent of jasmine and roses. The director smiles and all are pleased.

MY DEATH COMES FOR ME, A PETRIFIED MASK THAT LINGERS AFTER MY LIFE IS OVER

The day after they take my husband, I stand before my face in the bedroom mirror and paint the black outline of a fish without a tail onto the rims of my eyes. I run white foundation onto my cheeks, plastering them into a semblance of death. I line my lips with dark red gloss. The face of a warrior woman, which I turn to the audience. This is where I hide. The crowd cheers and boos. To confront them, I raise a stern hand and cry, 'I am.' But the singing of the chorus drowns me. Slowly I arch my blackened eyebrows. I make my eyes wide and staring. I pull a grimace in the mirror. As if in a dream I see the woman in the mirror follow my actions.

Do they think I am afraid? Yes, the mind hides from the memory of fear. I wear a look of blankness. This is a mind that grew up with fear, with feeling stunted and undernourished, without warmth of air and light to spur its growth. A wall hems in my thoughts. Today, I fear too much sun. Darkness is where I am safe to think my thoughts in peace, to hold my bellyful of dreams, to rock in the embracing coolness of stars. Then I am infinite. Then my fear becomes a tiny part of something unseen. Most times, I deny I am afraid.

I stand in the middle of my lines, my mouth agape for noiseless sounds to wind their tortured way up my larynx. I see them coming. The Red Guards coming for me. Why should Madame Mao be able to fight off demons? They have always been there. My head splits open, the waves of fear emanating from the stage.

Cang! A resounding clash of cymbals. The director yells, 'RED GUARD CHORUS!'

Tock, tock, tock … cang!

Husband's voice: They have taken me and stripped me of my clothes, and made me wear a pair of thin cotton pyjamas. My feet are bare on the cold floor. I stand. Before me, they shine lights, brilliant spotlights trained onto me. I am centre stage. Unlike my wife, I am not used to such a starring role. I play to an audience of bodiless, faceless voices that cry out my misdeeds. Confess! Repent! Sometimes out of the light, a hand emerges to strike my face. Sometimes I feel something hard land on my stomach. I throw up my supper.

Voices of the Red Guards: TRAITOR! Beat him. Kill. Burn. Crush.

Voice of a Red Guard: Listen. We don't have an easy job. We have to feed our stomachs too. Don't judge me harshly. I'm your friendly neighbour.

One of our neighbours played informant. After talking to my husband, he took a few copies of the journal in which his articles were appearing, and brought them to the attention of the authorities. The entire staff of the Catholic journal has been arrested. The editor faces charges of sedition.

Voice of husband: Look, how long are you going to keep this up? I've told you I know nothing about the conspiracy … stop blowing cigarette smoke into my face.

Voices of Red Guards: Oh, shut UP.

Voice of husband: When am I to be released? I want a lawyer.

Voices of Red Guards: No one can get you out. Confess and be done with it. You could be here forever.

Laughter. An imprecation muttered. Cigarette butts crushed underfoot. A door swings open. Light from outside. Eyes blink.

Voice of Red Guard (indifferently): How long do you think anyone will care what happens to you?

I prepare for my finale. This afternoon, I visited the tombstone makers deep in the wilder parts of an industrial suburb, where the Christian cemeteries lie. I wanted to ask if any could carve for me an epitaph.

'I want it to be written that she died majestically. That her death meant something,' I said.

I had found the tombstone maker's workshop hidden down several narrow lanes. Outside in a tin shed, the blocks of stones lie scattered in dusty abandonment. Some of them bear inscriptions to the dead. It was an old man to whom I spoke. A small, sturdy man with a thin wizened face, and the narrow, delicate yet strong fingers of the craftsman. He chuckled, and clutched his engraver's tool. He held a block of stone steady with his other hand. Still squatting, he replied, 'You must be important lady, ah. What you like? A poem? In stone? You have money?'

Then he winked, 'Many think death important.'

He shook his head, laughing at the foolishness of mortals, this man so near death himself.

Money speaks in this glistening city. In China they would say, 'Ah, your streets are paved with gold. If I had a job as a sweeper in your city, I could live a luxurious life. Only give me a passport and I will go.' And their eyes gleam with the promise of a Golconda.

I left him with a monetary deposit and a promise of further payment. He will make for me such a tombstone. I will look a martyr in my death.

It is the night of my final performance. My cloth slippers pad over the coarse grain of the stage, the curtains are great wings behind which I hide, the yells from the audience resound in my ears, my robes go *swish swish* over the floor, my arms are hidden in voluminous sleeves. A scent of jasmine whiffs from my hair.

The water rises. In front of me ripples stir, breaking the levels of air between me and my audience. I catch my breath. The currents grow stronger. I see it. A fish, black tail, black outlines, darting like a shadow in the auditorium. The crowd is applauding vigorously. The music is dying away. A last crash of cymbals. My voice has fallen to a murmuring. I am spent. My hair loose and wild. They have come for me. They haul me to my feet. They bind my arms in chains and lead me before the crowd. I whisper through misted eyes. I close my lids and let death come to me. I watch my soul enter the mirror realm.

After Performance

I sit in my chair on the balcony, watching the stars, waiting, till time collapses and history rewrites itself. In the aftermath of his televised confession, release, rearrest, further confession, release, he has become moody, upset. He begins to cultivate bonsai, stunted trees of a warped beauty. He accepts membership in the ex-political detainees' club when a letter from the government arrives, asking if he would like to join.

'Is it not a way of keeping tabs on what we are doing?' I ask him.

He shrugs. He is indifferent. I spend my time absorbed in redrafting my play. My play, I call it, because I have taken over from Hui.

PART ONE

1

Ching

He will send for me and I will be ready. I will comb my hair into a black sheet and stand at the window looking out. I smile, turn and catch sight of my flushed face in the dressing table mirror. My face and yet not mine.

I look around the room with quiet satisfaction. It is luxurious but not extravagantly so. I sink into a mother-of-pearl chair. I myself chose the red silken covers for the four-poster bed, where I now spend my nights. A black lacquer screen patterned with slim flowing maidens shelters the bed modestly from one side. My thoughts turn to the Chairman. He would be in the garden waiting.

Holding my hair up in both hands, I pull it forward over my face, then fling my head back. I run the comb down the length. It is strange … I remember something different. I struggle to draw breath and as I inhale, the warm air outside seasoned with the scent of jasmine and roses penetrates my lungs.

The white filmy curtains at the window balloon into the shape of a pregnant woman. I rise and place a hesitant hand on the windowsill.

The strangeness of the place extends to the inhabitants of the garden: an ageing man in a rattan chair under a tree, and several servants in loose cotton pants passing in and out of the house.

Under the spreading branches of a rain tree, there, the Chairman sits. A teacup on a small cane table by his side is filled with Dragon Well tea. Puffed biscuits lie on a white porcelain plate. The *pon piah* have sticky coatings of maltose surrounding the void at their centres. Sparrows rustle among the trees.

In the mornings the garden is rosy with a clear light and birds wake me with their songs. I trace a path from the window to the horizon and back again. In the afternoons the garden sparkles with a hard glow – it is still and flat, pasted into cardboard humidity. Later, nearing evening, in that hour before dark – that is the time I anticipate, when the sky is only just turning grey, the Chairman will take his seat.

'Go, go,' he tells the manservant who has helped him to his chair. He is displeased by the signs of weakness.

I continue at the window watching the birds in the trees preparing to roost. The wind whips up from the grass and circles the house. So slow the storm that's brewing. So cold this space. I hug myself, trying to keep something from slipping, from lying in broken wreckage like flotsam in the sea.

Despite many years of training – of wearing a mask, conquering the audience – despite the smiles and the holding high of my head … I look at the earth and imagine the red worms wriggling and crawling, half-blind, for light.

Before the garden is dark, I will join the Chairman in a last cup of tea: a ritual. I take a seat beside him and watch the leaves fluttering down and the sun sinking.

'Tomorrow,' I chirp. 'Tomorrow I'll do this and that. I will go to the market. To the shopping centre.' And lay down my plans. He nods and chimes in with his deep-toned remarks. The uncertainty cannot have escaped him – he is bound to notice it, if not in my face, then in the faces of the servants. I should say, 'Fate willing, I will be going to the market.' I should tell him how they are watching me.

They watch me. I sense their presence with me. As I sit with the Chairman, they appear to me heavy and sluggish, like the heavy weight of the air around. Sunlight cartwheels across the garden, taking with it colour, definition and light. In the sharpening shadows, *they* leave imprints. The shape of a foot. The colour of a dress. Scent of jasmine. I overturn my glass, for a drowsy fly has stunned itself in the drink.

The Chairman murmurs, 'It turns dark quite soon. The servants should turn on the lights in the garden.' He claps his hands and a manservant slides up quickly. He gives his instructions.

I look at the Chairman. He is calm and proud, his thin lips protrude. He has a high colour in his cheeks. He frowns, 'Soon, maybe even tomorrow, I will be gone.'

There is an instant of electricity in the air. I shift uneasily, 'You are talking nonsense. I will not hear such talk.' I rifle the pages of the woman's magazine I am holding in my hands, and frown.

'*Suttee*?' he says, leaning towards me. His eyes, mockingly bright, interrogate mine. I glance down at the article which I have unseeingly read. Then I say, 'Yes. Amazing. To expect that a woman should follow her husband to his death!' And laugh to show my unconcern.

The Chairman is still and absorbed in himself. He is like a rock. Then peace is broken, he flicks away a noisy fly. His movement is quick and sharp.

'Well?' I demand.

He shrugs his shoulders to discard some pain, 'As she pleases. It is not my will.'

A cold wind strikes my back and I hear the unspoken words, *But when I am gone, beware.*

He looks at me.

'Are you thinking of it?' he suggests. 'Widow burning?'

I reply, forcing a smile, 'Not as long as I have you.'

But I know. *They* expect me to cast myself upon the pyre. Tang's dead. I know they think me selfish, brutal even, but how do I explain … that I am not responsible. I could not have known.

But all this I see: the fall of the curtains, the shadows in the wings, and the darkness overtake the light. I hear my audience breathe in sharply. Around me, I feel the gathering force of murmurs that would rise and fell me to the ground. Sharp hisses steal in. They break the fabric of my rapt silence.

No, I am not a good Christian like my friend, Roxanne, who I am to meet shortly. Although I must, to preserve her good opinion, act with some semblance of one. Act, yes. She used that word on me. Perhaps she is right, perhaps I do not know who I really am. Perhaps I only act, try on different skins and then wait for the reaction. Perhaps I always have my audience before me, and the light and dark of the stage is the real and shadowy world I inhabit. I think they expect me, like a good woman, to leave the Chairman, for my being with him at this time seems indecent. I wish to leave him. He has become impotent. He wobbles as he walks with the help of a stick. Hours alone, he spends on his rattan chair. How old he looks. How sickly. Branches drop leaves upon his head, but he stays in their shade, hiding from the sun.

There – he takes a sip of his tea and then another, unconscious that around him the shadows dance a ghastly round.

*

She looks at her image in the mirror and rubs her forehead. Yesterday she had looked and seen no one in the mirror. She had stood before it running the comb down the length of her hair, and the thin plastic spines caught and tangled; she did not cry out, but her palms were wet. She dropped the comb onto the dressing table, and leaned her face against the mirror's cold surface, and she pressed as though to peer through a window. In the silvery depths, she seemed to find movement and faces. Faces that stared back. They threaded their ways at the bottom of the glass, and she could hear fading the sounds of singing.

That was yesterday. The woman swiftly plasters her face with cream and powder, and lines her lips.

She tells herself, *I do not wish to go out but some urge impels me to do so; I cannot be still. It seems the walls would enclose me if I stay – stupid of me, I know they might shield me.*

But on this humid day, with the sun overhead, her friend Roxanne will find herself walking along the path to the river. She has come to the conclusion that every Madame Mao will have her Roxanne, the faithful scribe, the loyal admirer. They were at school together but their paths diverged. Roxanne called two years ago to ask for an interview. She is a journalist with *The Straits Times*. They met in a coffee shop at Boat Quay. Roxanne called again to clarify details of the interview: a profile on the woman's work as an actress. It came out in the papers the next weekend. The woman was pleased and thanked her with a phone call. Such is the nature of friendship that it should be a mutual admiration society, or perhaps one admires and the other grants her favours for her admiration.

The woman thinks, *On such a day, Roxanne, will walk to the river. I have received a premonition. In the morning just before waking, I heard a voice say to me, 'Today, go to the river.'* My room appeared a cream box, the translucent curtains billowing, my startled face in view in the dressing table mirror. Beside the bed the radio clock broke into sudden raucous sound. Time to get up. I left the door to the bathroom open and brushed my teeth. In the kitchen, I opened a new pack of rice cereal, shook some into a bowl and poured cold Nestlé milk over it. I stirred my spoon through and watched the patterns emerge.

Dressed and washed, the woman makes her way down the river path. The path is neat and tidy, with most of the stray and fallen leaves carefully swept into large storm drains. Hot asphalt crackles under her high-heeled shoes. Sunny pathways and paths in shadow: one may lead to the other, and life is never certain. Sunlight dapples the fallen leaves. On the path are little lizards that slither to the dark roots of bushes after sunning themselves. On rainy days the path is lovely and wet, but not so lovely are the huge toads which sit obstinately in the way. Sometimes the woman sees these toads dried out and flattened by passing vehicles when the unfortunate ones wander off the path and onto the road. They look like laboratory specimens then.

Heels go *tap-tap,* her Gucci pair, black and elegant. She is making her way to the river when confusion descends. She is standing in a place that has been buried. The ground turns and she feels nothing below. The air she breathes in is as insubstantial as … a snowflake, *ten thousand miles of snowflakes*, as alien to her as ten thousand golden daffodils. She is standing in a drowned world. She hears sounds of laughter. She sees a mangrove tree, its thickened arms creeping along the ground by the river. Two butterflies are mating, jerking awkwardly through space. As the woman takes the path towards the river a lizard appears, sharp head darting. Its body wriggles in quick scuttling movements. It grows a frilly collar around its neck. She watches the lizard till her eyes water. Around her the palm leaves droop their heads. The sun is high in the sky when she reaches the riverbank.

The woman senses the life growing near the water: the putat laut trees, coconut palms, pong-pong trees and the worms that burrow deep in the earth and reappear at their feet, the seething life of the vegetation that maunders silently in the midst of constructions. Like a ripple in space-time, an uneasy commingling of earth and unearth, the woman sees her, a mirror woman, on the riverbank. The mirror woman is standing like a lost soul. Her voice calls out. It is a sound light and reedy, like the thin shriek of a mouse. The mirror woman is summoning a monk.

'Kapila,' she calls. Kapila. The name of the Brahman monk who in the course of his life uttered one hundred foolish words.

'Ape-head! Dog-face! Pig's bottom!' he insulted his students who had travelled from far to learn from this man of wisdom. 'Dog-head! Horse-brain! Asses! Sons of pigs!'

When he had passed from this earth, his soul had garnered his thousand insults, drawn to him like sticking magnets. In one wild gesticulating outburst from the water, the monk had been reborn as an orc with a hundred heads. His hundred insults had taken on life. They came to him as his karma. He hid in the river where he breathed the shallow waters and prayed not to be attacked by fishermen. But in these parts, a strange sight such as he was more likely to be revered than disdained.

The fishermen offer mandarins and chicken by the waters to draw him out. Once in a while, he may emerge to answer the riddles of life.

'Kapila,' the mirror woman calls again.

Sometimes, one or another of his heads will break through the water or he may rise with all hundred heads showing.

After calling for some minutes, the mirror woman seems to grow tired.

The woman, who is called Chiang Ching, approaches the bank. Against her eardrums a pounding of waves. The face of the mirror woman turning towards Ching changes shape, hovering between forms and time until it is a face lined and frail, skin thin as tissue, brown as wood. Hair tight in a bun. An old woman. Over their heads, a tree flowers, white petals begin dropping. The sweet smell of frangipanis fills Ching's nostrils. The smell grows stronger and she starts to choke.

'Tell me,' Ching says, 'what … I know you are not of this earth.'

But the old woman/mirror woman screeches in return, 'Ai, child! Earth is my habitat. River is my element. Chiang Ching! My dear Green River.'

'You know me,' Ching cries.

Before Ching's eyes, in the sky appears a black-haired woman, wind blowing her hair into a fan, a comet-driven thing, driving ten suns across the sky. Bright clean suns with scrubbed shiny faces. The sky is a blazing vault of inexorable light. The heat is intense.

She is momentarily blinded. She covers her eyes with her hands and falls down. The earth moves and settles. When Ching opens her eyes, the sky is a peaceful cerulean, and she is lying beside the river.

Vaguely, she hears the sounds of laughter. They seem nearer this time. They come from some tables where diners are sitting drinking wine. They seem very cheerful. The men are in open-necked shirts, the women in cool summer dresses. There are more tables than Ching has thought. In fact, the entire bank is lined with tables.

Behind the tables is a long row of restaurants. Their names come slowly to her: New England Seafood Bar and Restaurant, Hot Stones, Thai Paradise, Quayside Lounge. Ching rises to her feet.

'A table, ma'am?' says a waiter in black bow tie.

'What?'

'Would you like a seat? Waiting for a party?' he says.

'Thanks,' she says. 'I'm waiting for a friend.'

He goes away. Ching takes a seat, her mind dizzy. The smells are appetising. She waits patiently. The waiter appears again, menu in hand.

'Like to make a choice, ma'am?' he says. 'Our specialty today is the grilled fish. A very special sauce to go with it. The chef's own.'

She considers. Roxanne has not yet come. She is hungry. *Roxanne will not mind if I begin my meal*, she thinks.

'I will have the grilled fish in *sambal*,' she decides. The price is $18.90. A glass of complimentary wine accompanies it. The waiter brings it to her as she sits enjoying the view of the river and perspiring in the humid air. It is a light dry wine. She takes it in slow sips between parched lips. It runs long cold waves down her throat.

The table next to hers is full of merrymakers. Laughter breaks out at regular intervals, like a ground swell. Black water breaks against the stone steps of the bank where families and couples sit. The heat is oppressive.

By the time her fish arrives, night has fallen. A few bright stars shine. The light from the candle on her table is reflected on the white flesh of the fish on the plate. She picks up her knife and starts slicing. The waiter appears with a jug of iced water.

'Are you enjoying your meal, ma'am?'

'Thank you, yes.'

Ching enjoys her meal. When she sees the waiter again out of the corner of her eye, he is juggling the silverware. The diners applaud when he stops. A dog appears, sniffing about the bare or trousered legs of the diners. A stray dog. There are shrieks and curses from some tables. An odd scrap or two is all he picks up. Growling in his throat, the dog gallops off.

Ching, picking up her wineglass, takes a sip, and eyes the dog disappearing round the corner, its feathery tail waving. She is too hot to move. Perhaps mechanical fans should be installed to cool the air. She has a vision of a long line of waiters and waitresses waving large palm leaves while the diners sip and eat.

A loud noise startles her from her reverie. A pile of plates has crashed to the floor. The manager disappears.

Silence returns, but the interruption has left a stir in the atmosphere. Something has changed. Subtly changed. The diners are lifting their heads sniffing. The earth has moved and even if by a fraction, things are no longer as they were a moment ago.

Even as they sit, the earth is tilting slightly more off-course. *Perhaps*, Ching reflects, *we are nearing the end of* kali-yuga, *the age of destruction*. As she continues sitting, something is added, something taken away.

On the street, there is an old man selling *kachang puteh* from his makeshift stall. He shouts, 'K … a … *chang Pu … u … teh …*' He pushes his mobile stall towards the diners, who ignore him.

Ching, hesitating over her meal, looks towards the river, and thinks she sees an old woman making her way down. The old woman's skin is burnt brown, her head is balding, her feet make splashing sounds. She can hear the burden of the old woman's song which comes upon the air. The old woman is singing, '*La, la, the world is a fine place. I am the madwoman of Chu roaming where I will, singing my songs in a dying world.*'

Ching thinks she dreams of the old madwoman of Chu (madman in Li Po's poem of that name). As the old woman quickens her pace, the soft mud catches at her feet. Translucent shoals of fish glide through the water. The fat droplets of water fall in little splashes as her feet make their way down the river. The water stirs in widening ripples. Upon reaching the banks, the old woman squats by a kerosene lamp, and waits patiently. Soon the darkness around her stirs and falls into human shapes that gather close. The old woman begins to speak. She spins a tale for an appreciative coin or two, which drop into a small copper bowl by her feet. Up in the branches overhead, a white-collared kingfisher flashes by. Home is a nest of fishbones in a hole in the riverbank. The river water darkens, and as night descends, the listeners sitting, squatting or leaning against the river trees find their edges blurring, their hard definite shapes losing their sharpness. Only the whites of their eyes can be seen shining in the dark.

The storyteller has no name. She is known only as the old woman, *Po Po*. No one knows where she has her home or if she is a creature of the river. You can see her often squatting by her kerosene lamp, her shadow broached by a gathering semi-circle of listeners. The trees stand back in the darkness and that little circle continues unbroken till dawn.

The voice of the storyteller speaks out of the darkness. The words come to Ching as if from within. The old woman is still speaking in harsh gasps of Foochow, which is a dialect Ching understands. The audience listens, mouths open. The old woman tells an old Foochow tale of the maiden of Hsing-chou, whose destined husband sought to kill her when she was a little girl of three, because he was ashamed that her only guardian, her grandmother, was without wealth or connections. The listeners delight in the old story with a moral that fate is stronger than all human endeavours: that marry the girl he must for the red thread that binds her little finger runs to his and nothing may undo the thread. Indeed love does come to him in the end.

In the hush of evening, even the fish are listening. The fish come dancing to the shores of the river; upon their tails they twirl and bow, for the storyteller is revered as a dragon mother, and fish are subjects of dragons, as are all water creatures.

Sitting, sipping her glass of wine, Ching experiences a sense of imbalance. She feels a sudden longing to see a familiar face, hear the voice of someone dear, to give her anchor in a shifting world. But darkness hides the faces. The waiter comes to clear the table.

'Ma'am,' he says, 'we are closing.'

It is almost midnight and the river rats are scurrying to look for leftovers. Ching shakes her head to clear the wine fumes. Roxanne has not come. She has an uneasy sense of things going wrong. She is like a general abandoned by her troops.

Ching can scarcely believe it. She invents excuses for Roxanne, which she does not believe.

It is around this time that Ching first starts thinking in a serious way of leaving the city. She stares, till her eyes hurt, at the black waters. The ships are twinkling. A cold wind blows inwards to the land. Across the river is a long line of high-rise apartments lit like dynamite that is ready to go.

Time to go. The signs are there, visible. Some ignore the signs, clinging to a vague hope that ultimately they will be justified, that in their fantasies the city embraces them, thanks them for the services they have rendered, accepts them as total people – *oh, the fools!* – they live only with their regrets and bitterness. She will leave behind her city. She feels the monsoonal wind at her back creeping cold fingers. She will leave behind the lush vegetation, wet grass which forbids sitting down, hookworms, ringworms, nut grass, lalang, mangroves, tiny houses glued together, high-rise apartments and the buildings ever-rocketing skywards as the city burgeons into the sea.

2

Long before the feeling came that she needed to emigrate, Chiang Ching was enjoying considerable success as an actress. She had a growing reputation and roles came readily to her. The peak of her career came with her role as Madame Mao in an opera. During that period of triumph, her friend Roxanne would visit her on a regular basis as she lived not far away, and if Ching sometimes used Roxanne as a mirror for her ego's expression, so too did Roxanne gain from Ching a sense of entering another world, one removed from her tiring daily work, and providing an escape from the home she shared with her husband, Jeff, who left her much to her own devices, while he entertained his business clients.

Perhaps Roxanne, who was diffident with regard to her own charms, found in Ching a refreshing boldness. Roxanne was a Plain Jane with a name that spoke of romance – a name rather exotic in the city. Those women who bore Anglicised names were usually called Catherine or Audrey or Karen. Her mother had chosen the name from a baby book.

There are giant flowers blooming by the roadside, lush in their wanton fragrance, running over the graves of the cemetery across from where Ching lives, overwhelming Roxanne with a sense of life's tender fragility and the poignancy of each moment as she cycles up to Ching's apartment on Sixth Avenue. The flowers remind her of Chiang Ching. Her wild eyes and high complexion, the way she has of seeming to lure, yet repelling any closeness, any real intimacy or knowledge of herself. Her munificence, the gifts she buys for those she favours.

From her, Roxanne has received bedsheets made of the finest silk, a skirt imported from Paris, Estée Lauder lipstick and a cosmetic case of ivory. Ching has little need of make-up. Her perfume is constant: Chanel No. 5. She is, Roxanne finds, and many others will admit to it, not beautiful, but arresting. This makes her almost ugly in photographs, but face to face her charm and intelligence transform her into something out of the ordinary. Roxanne told her this once as they sat talking in Ching's living room. Ching was playing idly with a tassel, the red silk cushion on her lap, her inevitable pair of sunglasses hiding her eyes, and smiling vaguely as if she was thinking of great things.

She had a manner about her as though she was only partly living in the current world, as if she was saving herself for the things she would some day do.

Stopping her bicycle at the guardhouse, Roxanne hops off, thinking of her friend as she wheels the bicycle into the compound – Ching has faith in one thing: herself. She sees her destiny quite clearly, I believe, as written by herself upon the palms of her life.

'I will be your mirror,' Roxanne had said to her, inspired. 'Look at me. Tell me if you see your own fate.'

Ching laughed in that girlish way she had, dangled a foot from the velvet-upholstered armchair she was sitting on, and leaned upon a cushion.

'I see,' she said, 'that you are kind to my faults. You will not do. Such a mirror!'

'I am not blind. I have eyes,' Roxanne insisted.

'Then you see here a woman. A woman playing Madame Mao.'

Roxanne looked startled, for she went on, 'On the stage. You see, I am modest. I ask for little, outside of the unreal world: the theatre. Only a stage.'

Ching was then waiting to receive word from Hui, the director, as to whether the changes she had made to the play were acceptable.

Roxanne would later muse, *How was I to know what would come between us? How was I to know then how my feelings would change, how I, her faithful follower, would start to see her not as an empress holding court but as a monster? I could not foresee, and she was so much a part of me, who was her mirror; I was quite, quite blind.*

Roxanne gives old Encik Ali, the *jagar* at the guardhouse, a wave.

'Ah,' he says, with a nod. 'You come again, ah? Going to see your friend?'

'Yes.'

The old man wipes sweat from his forehead with a big hanky, 'Today, very hot.' This exchange of pleasantries is like a code, a password to be given before Roxanne can enter the magic kingdom.

The magic kingdom, however, is not always as pleasant as it can be. Occasionally, quarrels break in. Chiang Ching has a way of thinking which Roxanne finds strange: to her, life is really quite easy – it is an endless power struggle, and to live means being free. Free in other words to impose her will. But is it really so clear? Is there another way of looking at something or someone?

Because it is the only barrier between them, as Roxanne fondly imagines, she tries to tear it down.

She is talking of wanting children, when Ching says, 'You wouldn't want them after you have them.'

'Oh, I would. Never seemed to work. Jeff's so seldom home till late, and I keep falling asleep when I think I ought to wait up. That's when I feel like having one or two.'

Roxanne feels something uncoil itself at the base of her brain, some tingling of remembrance.

'Didn't you …? You did …?'

It was some old research she had done or something Ching had told her, which she had forgotten. Roxanne thinks, *Oh.* She feels like she has said something out of place – she remembers now that Ching had once been pregnant, but had lost the baby.

Roxanne starts to stammer about the politics of the day, what was happening in the news. Ching, moody and withdrawn, jumps on a remark Roxanne has made about the Chairman.

Ching sneers, 'He is so patriarchal, and you support him.'

Roxanne says to Ching, a little righteously, remembering sermons she has heard, 'There is the way of love.'

The way of love means seeing beyond what constitutes an unjust universe.

Roxanne looks into Ching's eyes. Ching is almost a stranger when she speaks like this, her eyes glowing inwardly. But she is right, of course. Roxanne thinks: *I can try to explain that I do not support him, only that she has to agree his policies have brought success to the city.*

Dimly it flashes across Roxanne's mind what Tang once said of his wife – that she carries a lot of anger. He knew her, this mild man with the intense heart. Yes, Ching is right in what she said. Right in part but not in the whole. For the whole man belongs to something other, and *that* cannot be understood.

How Tang loves her! She is indeed lucky.

Roxanne feels inadequate in voicing what she is thinking, so she examines her ink-stained fingers, scratches an itch nervously and says, 'You're right. Shall we go for dinner?'

3

Roxanne

Chiang Ching and I – we are not entwined souls, but mutually reflective selves. I struggle to be completely in tune with her, to walk in her shoes, but I often fail; we stand facing each other as if looking into a mirror.

We sit at an oaken table in a restaurant, The Ship, in the heart of the Orchard Road district. The restaurant's interior plays on the theme of the sea with anchors and nets stretched from hook to hook on the wooden walls. In the dim light from the candle on the table between us and the swaying lanterns in macramé hangers above our heads our faces are ghastly and pale.

I glance at her but cannot think of anything to say that will not trigger some conflict. Of late it seems all we say is at cross-purposes. So we eat our baked oysters with relish, and drink some wine. Putting down my fork, I say, 'You know Lui's wife? She's run away with a man.'

'Lui? That millionaire? She's the second wife, I think. Very young and very pretty. I met her at a party. She can't be more than twenty. I thought she married for money. Lui is rolling in it.'

'So's the other man.'

'Who did she run off with?'

Because we pretend that nothing has changed between us or in the world at large, we talk of trivial matters. After a discussion on the merits of Lui compared with the new man, a silence falls between us, then, 'Your hair looks lovely. Where did you get it permed?'

'Oh, at the Pavilion.'

'Has your director heard from the Ministry yet? Are they leaving the play intact?'

'No, no word. I suspect some things will not pass the censors.'

I reach for my glass of wine, and sipping it, look at the other diners. A young couple sits beside our table. The man is leaning across to whisper to the woman, his hand plays with her fingers. The wine makes me drowsy. I say, still watching the young couple, 'I bumped into an old friend the other day. I was covering the story on illegal betting at the racecourse. He has his office in that area.'

'Who's this?'

'Sorry, I'm talking about William. Remember William Chee, the one with owl-glasses? School prefect. He was the top O-level student.'

'William, yes! I think Tang knows him.'

'They know each other?' I am surprised. 'Do you see him then? You didn't tell me.'

'No, I don't see him. He's one of Tang's acquaintances. I think he's written some articles for Tang's journal.'

'I see.' I don't know why but my stomach contracts suddenly. William Chee cannot be called a close friend of mine. We have not kept in touch all these years, but seeing him on the street that day gave me a sense of deep pleasure. It was so easy. So easy to fall back into an old camaraderie. To assume the old selves we leave behind when we emerge into the working world. I saw him as I had seen him all those years ago, as the gentle and bright young man who offered to carry my books on the way to school. It took him out of his way to accompany me to the entrance of my convent school. St Joseph's Institution, which was his school, was on Bras Basah Road.

'You don't have to,' I would say, struggling to conquer the thrill of pride that a boy was willing to walk me to school. But he always did. He would wait at the bus stop until I came along and we would walk together the rest of the way.

The girls teased me about my boyfriend, but William was never that. I was comfortable with him. I was also a little shy. The subject of romance never arose between us.

Some people remind us of home. William's character is like

home. I can't explain it but he is familiar in a way nothing in the outside world is familiar.

I sip some water and have a feeling creep into me that Ching and I have vastly different ways of looking at the world. The fact strikes me afresh. It is not so much the contents of what we have said to each other during the night but that we have uttered them, which frightens me. I try not to admit it, it makes me uncomfortable. Have you ever been with someone very close, and then suddenly become aware that you are staring into a gulf?

'Eat, you have only pecked at your food,' I say, knowing that neither of us have in our possession a tightrope to throw across the gap, and that neither will risk crossing at this time. I make a show of cutting up my piece of medium-rare steak, showing an appetite I lack.

Ching says, 'Well, how about the bombe Alaska for dessert?'

Once Ching had said, 'If I were to be completely myself, I would be like *this*.' She hunched herself and stayed absolutely still like a stone.

I have often sensed that she dramatised herself. She is really charming. So terribly artless and naive in her remarks, yet so dangerous. I believe Ching spends sections of her time talking to herself in the mirror, acting out the part of the ingénue, which it pleases her to play.

I think she is not at ease. No matter how far Ching goes, how far away from her home, and the people who remember her, no matter how she tries to recreate herself, hoping to find in another soul her rest, she will never know rest. She will never know peace.

I remember a hymn that was sung at the convent school that we had both at one time attended.

Man is lonely by birth / Man is but a pilgrim on earth.

'It's true, isn't it? No matter how much you search for someone

47

to understand you fully, you find you are alone,' I once heard her say.

Chiang Ching had sought in me a confidante, a silent unquestioning disciple.

★

Ching is beginning to suspect that her friend is not with her. No longer is she the ardent listener, the dependable admirer. In a wave of panic, she realises that her Roxanne has a mind independent of hers.

Did you think it was going to be different? the voice whispers inside her. She rocks her pain inside herself. *Will I have no rest?* Why does she feel she is walking on the edge most of the time, that beneath her feet a tightrope is fraying?

Ching thinks, *When I was thirteen I went to the circus. I saw a little man on a tightrope up in the tent. I wondered what he would do if I were to climb there and slowly cut his rope. Would he fall gracefully, his arms outstretched in a swooping arc? Would he tumble like a clown in a somersault? Or would he sprout a pair of wings and fly upwards and out of the tent? And I did not know what he would do then, for the rope had started to give way ...*

Ching says, slowly, 'I don't remember him much.'

'Who?'

'My father. Mother left home when I was only little. I know he drank and he beat her. Sometimes he hit me too.'

She shrugs.

She says, 'We were living with his relations. They supported him. He was only a little man to look at, my mother's height. She was terrified of him.'

Roxanne studies her face.

'Like I said,' Ching repeats, 'I don't remember him much.'

Roxanne suspects Ching makes things up to tell her. If she were to believe her, the actress's father had been a brutish man.

The actress's father had been a much older man than her

mother. 'Never trust men,' Ching's mother said to her. Her mother told her that when she had been pregnant, her father had found himself another woman.

'You don't depend on a man for your happiness,' Roxanne tells her, as Ching stares out of the paned window into the lighted street.

The role of passive weeping woman, so common in a classic like *The Dream of the Red Chamber*, is not for her, though it is obvious to Roxanne that Ching has assigned this role to her mother.

'I won't be a victim,' Ching declares.

The actress grew up with a distorted idea of what it meant to live. To her, living was uncertainty. She could not begin to comprehend other people, even herself.

Roxanne

'So what will you write of me?' Ching says abruptly, in the middle of eating.

The actress in her keeps asking me to write about her. She keeps on saying, 'Have you written about me yet? When are you going to do it?' She seems to imply, *I have allowed you to get this close to me, so you can write about me.*

She brings me a gift: silk sheets to sleep upon.

She buys me a skirt.

She thinks that once written about, she can look at the printed page and have a stable sense of her self and her life. She thinks that words imprisoned in the white cage will pin her down somehow, she will be both released from having to analyse herself and trying to make sense of her living. She wants to be pinned down. She wants to see her soul *there*. There it is, like a gorgeous butterfly.

Then she will know who she really is.

Ching says, 'Once as a child I dreamt that I was in a cell, lying on a narrow hard mattress. I had forgotten why or what I was doing there, and then I knew. I knew everything. I knew who I really *was*. Then a woman, whose face I cannot place, appeared. She smiled sympathetically, *"It's time. You know it's time, don't you?"* That was all she said. I knew then that everything I had learnt in that flash would disappear from my conscious memory. That was it. It was all gone.'

'Sounds silly,' she says.

I comment, 'Not at all. Perhaps you are seeking perfection. Which is impossible. The dream reminds you how impossible.'

A woman feeling the weight of perfection sitting on her decides she would rather be a fish, which is the symbol of perfection. And what is Ching talking of now? Stage musicals. She starts humming a tune from *The Sound of Music*.

4

Ching

Until I turned fifteen, all the life I knew was within the narrow walls of my home. I lived with my mother, and after the early years saw my father rarely. My mother went out to houses to wash clothes, often coming home late.

The sky was cold, flat and grey, and no one walked the street at that time of the morning except people of a certain stamp. The ones that society rejected. Women like my mother. In such light the slatted windows were like eyes watching her slow steps as she weaved her way to one of the houses in the row of wooden terraces.

A door opened.

'Ma!' And the woman, smiling in half-sleep and half-drunkenness, bent and stumbled against the door frame. She cursed.

I took my mother's hand and tried to lead her to an inner room, but she spat on the floor and pulled away. Muttering, my mother slumped to the cold floor. I stayed for a moment staring down at her face, which was as grey as the floor. I touched her eyelids gently as if to awaken her. Her breath heaved. Reluctantly, I backed into my own room, to my own little bed, where I lay under the coarse blanket and tried to shut out the sounds of my mother's breath.

The bed I slept on was uncomfortable, for my mattress was made of cotton and my fine bones could feel the hard planks beneath, so I turned and tried to angle my body so my hip bone did not press too hard against the planks.

My mother's late homecomings were only part of the problem. There were too many men. Far worse were the nights they lurched in through the doorway with their arms around my mother. These men came and went in my childhood.

I hated their smells, the flowers they brought, the way they behaved as if they owned our home.

I pressed my cold feet to the floor, and went to the kitchen to boil water. My mother was still asleep on the floor, her luxuriant hair in disarray. I tiptoed past her.

My mother often sighed for a husband. She appeared romantic in a way many of the women in our vicinity were not. Auntie Yee, a neighbour whose business was dubious, and who ran a house full of ladies, clucked over her, saying, 'Featherhead! No cow-sense.' Mother was vain and not practical. Sweet words could win her. She let the men use her, and got little in return, Auntie Yee said.

Mother would stand, with me clinging to her, by the open window and breathe in the salty air.

'Little Ching, one day your father come back. Then I no need to work so hard.'

Mother fondled my hair with hands reddened by constant scrubbing. She stood in thick shoes, her legs still slim but the work she did had caused varicose veins to appear. Sometimes, when I massaged her legs and feet at her request, I would trace the veins with my fingers. I tried to smooth them away.

'Ma, ma, don't marry, OK? We are happy together.'

'Ma, ma, you don't have to look for husband.'

It would be enough for me. But men continued to come. And my mother would buy rice and fish with the money they gave.

Some time later, my mother began to see one man constantly. This lover had plenty of money. He brought mother home in his Mercedes-Benz. He came laughing and pushing in. He brought with him a single stalk of an orchid on each visit. A china vase stood at the centre of the otherwise dull wooden kitchen table, and from the vase one proud stalk would stand. I saw how the orchid bent thickly at its stem, with its purple petals held out.

The man himself would be in my mother's bedroom, from which emerged light giggles and light talk, accompanied by the scuttle of rats into their underground labyrinths, if I listened hard. His shoes coming off with thuds. Shirt buttons popped. Gently now. What would they be doing? A window flung open. The salt smell of the sea in the distance.

I imagined he would be naked. Crumpled sheets between his legs where his genitalia rested like baby birds, suspended in an agony before my mother began with her hands then her soft lips.

My mother would hold his roughened soles between her small breasts, nibble at his toes, lick the square edges of his toenails cut bluntly. I never liked going into my mother's room afterwards. There would be the smell of his sex rising from the wet sheets. My mother looking vague.

The man said 'Hello' when he came out, rubbing his eyes like he was tired. The backs of his hands were bony, his knuckles straining out of the skin. He was not particularly handsome.

I could smell his genitals. A salt smell like black shrimp paste.

They sat down afterwards at the table and ate the simple rice and salted fish, which I had prepared and served. My mother ate, as was her habit, in silence, and quickly, barely tasting the grains of boiled rice, which she shovelled in with her wooden chopsticks. She would not look at me then. I would lift my head to watch them. First one silent face, then the other.

Sometimes, he tousled my hair. Once alone he had looked at me with a strange expression, so my heart leapt, and said, 'How old are you?'

I lied.

I disliked orchids. They fascinated me. I could lean my cheek against their surface and imagine my mother sliding her cold body from beneath her lover's, pulling back her hair with her large flat hands to pin it tidy. With a finger I touched one petal. It felt fake. The shape of its outline. The difference between the need of the flower and the heat of my small finger. I ran it round and round the petal's edge, compulsively.

He would leave. Mother followed the man to the front door and watched him go out into the cold morning. I looked at mother's back in the doorway, standing just beyond the multicoloured bead curtain. Only a thin cotton housedress sheathing protruding shoulder blades. I leaned against the sides of an open window, and felt the air prickle my skin, and then I thought, *I will get out of here. I will be someone.*

Then I drew in a deep breath, tasting the cold bitterness of the air. Stars slowly disappeared from the sky. When my mother returned, I avoided her eyes.

'How you like to have new father?' my mother spoke self-consciously.

I did not reply. I fiddled with my dress.

'Ma, ma. I will go away.'

I realised I was betraying my mother.

'You don't have to miss me. I will visit you.' I spoke low, and because I was upset, I clung to her. My mother, catching her hair in her fingers, coughed as the cold air lingered in her throat.

There would be no husband for my mother. No wedding as she had dreamed, nor a house with a garden and a car to ride in. They remained dreams, for something unforeseen came into the equation: death. I had not anticipated death. When my mother began to cough, I ran to get her water, but my thoughts did not stray to the furthest reaches, never imagined that my mother's soul was ready to enter the watery world. But the dragon-king sent rain and wind, which brought ill health, and whiteness to the cheeks. When the doctor arrived, he said she had pneumonia.

The day mother died, people came into the house. They talked around me, and occasionally asked for answers. The doctor left. People came and took the body. If they expected me to cry, I disappointed them. I watched them from my post in the kitchen. Someone spoke to me. I made out her words vaguely, 'I have a bed in my house. If you work hard … you can stay. Your mother was good to me. Many nights of mah-jong we played.'

'I have made my mother's favourite dish,' I said, 'and I have put too much rock sugar in it. I hope it will not be too sweet to eat.'

'You poor girl,' she said. 'I always said you were good girl.'

I realised then it was Auntie Yee that had just spoken to me and left. How different she looked with her hair in a bun and a long plain dress. When the house was once again mine, I scooped some rice into a bowl, washed my hands and my face and sat down at the kitchen table. On the table was a dish of braised and very tender pork leg that I had specially prepared early in the morning, but which my mother would not now be sharing with me. I ate my share, covered the rest, then stood at the sink.

A cry! *N … iang!*

I paused. The soapsuds slid off my hands. I listened and again on the breeze I heard a faint cry. A cry of heartbreak, of loss.

N … iang!

The *wayang*, I thought, suddenly. They are playing not far away.

I began running water.

I had stopped going to school when my mother fell ill. When mother died, the principal came around one day.

'What are you going to do?' the principal said.

Her plump arms quivered as she raised them to pat her hair. I watched the principal's fingers coming down on the tabletop. Thick little fingers against the wood.

'I could arrange for you to stay at the convent's orphanage or do you think your father's relatives will take you?'

Mother had no living relations. I considered the orphanage. It was within the school compound. I would be able to continue with my studies. The nuns would look after me.

There were walls around the convent, high walls with shards of glass protruding from the top. The orphans were mainly invisible. They stayed in and sewed and cooked and cleaned the toilets. I would sleep in a dormitory. I blinked.

'My aunt from Perak is coming. I have to speak with her. I cannot know what to do,' I lied.

'Let me know your decision,' my principal said as she got up to go. 'I will come again tomorrow or send your teacher.'

The principal walked swaying down the road. When she had gone, I dragged a wooden stool from the kitchen and went to the opera troupe's site on a field. Something in the exaggerated gestures, the sway of the hands, the little steps or the wide sleeves flapping, had a charm. The faces were whitened and opaque, unrecognisable. It sent a thrill through me. This power of being able to express great emotions and yet to hide behind a mask. The *wayang* had me enthralled.

'Uncle,' I caught an old man by his sleeve, when it was over and the crowd stirred to leave. 'Do you know who owns the troupe?'

'You talk to that man. Mr Tan. Over there.' The old man pointed. I looked at the man he pointed at. That man held my future.

5

Ching

I tremble. My legs feel weak, unable to carry the weight I must bear. This weakness strikes me all of a sudden as I gaze into the face of the Chairman. The light whitens his face. I turn from him to my husband.

Tang Na, I think with a wrench of the heart. My husband. Who loves me.

I hold aloft a pole with pennons fluttering. My robe whips around my legs. I charge forward. We walk in a great round of the stage, one behind the other, such a journey, such weather and travails, and then we arrive.

In the city. At such a time. I come in the midst of chaos. I stop a young boy running past to enquire, 'What is going on?'

He wrenches himself away from my grasp, 'You don't know? They have arrested him.'

'Who?' I say, aroused. I wish to shake him, as he stares at me bug-eyed. 'Who?'

'The President.'

I watch the boy run off. I stop at the Indian *mamak* shop to pick up the day's newspaper. The sun-warmed newspaper rustles in my grasp as I unfold it. Only a short paragraph concerning the arrest. Perhaps the media people know what really is going on, but they report very little of it.

I fold up the paper. I want to ask Tang if he knows. Tang will know. He will be able to tell me. My way home is filled with shoving pedestrians, crowds scuttling like wounded gazelles, but silent, unnatural. They breathe of fear.

Tang is troubled. I find him sitting in the living room, gazing out the window. His expression is an absent one.

'Home already?'

I hold up the newspaper. 'Yes,' he tells me, 'but there are

more people. Many more involved who will be arrested before long.'

'How do you know? Is it an upheaval? Is this a crisis?' I exclaim. I drop into a chair.

Tang manages a laugh. 'Don't worry. Not yet.' He pats my hand.

But that night more are arrested. It appears in the newspaper the next morning. Tang flips open *The Straits Times* and there it is on the front page. The editors unable to refrain from commenting on such a big event. In subdued accents the article reports that so far fifteen people have been accused of anti-government activities. They represent a surprising cross-section, rich, poor, young, old, male and female. The youngest is a seventeen-year-old female student at a polytechnic. Lawyers, actors, politicians, the clergy. A purge begins.

The Red Guards march upon the streets like demons from the dark. In my nightly dreams, a phalanx of soldiers, crashing wavelike.

The sound is immense. It engulfs me. When I look again, I see the Red Guards in their uniforms, threatening, encircling a mirror woman. They spit at her. Jeer. Around the mirror woman their moving lips clamour. As one, the guards suck at her silence. Words. Their words. Falling upon her. Stoned by the din and trapped in a circle, the mirror woman cowers. In her mind she is shrieking, *Lies!*

Insinuatingly the Red Guards taunt her, 'Take off your clothes! Put this on.'

A short halter-neck dress.

The mirror woman's lips tighten, determined that no words should fall, but they begin to pull at her. Their hands paw, clutching at the folds of her clothes. Afraid, she protests, 'It is cold. I will not wear it.'

But in their eyes is no mercy. They cry, 'But why did you wear the dress on your visit to the Captain?'

She shrugs, 'A warm day.'

The Red Guards sneer, 'We will keep you warm, take off your clothes and put this on.'

Their voices circumscribe, enfold her within the warmth of their bodies and words. They drop upon her like her guardian angels, entwine into her like snakes. She has only her naked self to protect.

I find myself outside that circle of Red Guards. When they have finished jeering and pause for breath, I begin to mock her spitefully, 'Did you think you were the greatest then? Did you think you were beyond the law?'

A wordless hatred fills the space between us. The taunted woman looks up and into my eyes. She says quietly and bitterly, 'Your time will come.'

I throw back my head laughing, 'It has come. It is now.'

The mirror woman crawls fast beneath the white light, her kowtowing knees scraping, carpet-burning, she is going as fast as she can, while their rifle butts and the thick leather points of their boots nudge her pale belly, exposed. She is lying like a fish upon the cutting board where she is peeled and sliced, soft flesh falling away, her skeleton of bones laid aside. She is probed with the tips of stinging knives, tested by forks, her thighs are wedged open, she is salted.

They rise from their knees, laughing coarsely. They are tugging their trousers up, pulling up zips, adjusting their belts. The light shines upon her body, lying on its back. It is like one dead.

From the sidelines I watch my victims. In my time I too have bent to *them*, turned for them, as they turned luckless fish upon their plates. I have been shipwrecked upon the shores of their directions. This time I write the scripts, rehearse their lines. In my hand the whiplash snakes out. I am a quiet figure, a spectator of their ecstasies, seeing their buttocks uncovered, like white maps, their bodies melding with the prisoner's cries.

They have always had the power. Upon big-character posters a woman's name is written large. She is caricatured as a loose woman, a devil's consort; that she has been the wife of a high-ranking official, now demoted, is forgotten. Her husband's name and hers are trampled in the mud. There are others who fall: those opposing the Chairman. These he roots out ruthlessly.

There is an order issued. The President is required to attend a meeting. In truth an interrogation. He is in his pyjamas, still hazy from the last evening's drinking bout at some grand party. A large white sedan whisks him away.

The President's speech is slurred and he speaks with some effort, 'Who is it? Who has asked for this meeting?'

The man in white clothes sitting beside him in the upholstered car, replies languidly, 'The Chairman.'

The President sinks back into his seat and closes his eyes. When he opens them, he murmurs, 'I was his friend.'

The man in white clothes is silent.

The President pictures himself naked before a crowd of spectators, and stares with disturbed eyes out of the car window for the rest of the journey. The streets are dark and mainly empty of people. The President tries to recall all the events that have led to this ignominious moment. The news spreads fast through the city.

Tang claims the President's arrest equals persecution. The President has supported many democratic reforms. He has criticised the government for its autocratic rule.

At the breakfast table, Tang says to me, 'He wrote some articles for the papers. Do you remember what he said of the government?'

I say cautiously, 'He is a drunkard. The doctors have said so. At the party, he molested the wife of a dignitary.'

'She has not complained,' Tang cries.

I widen my eyes. 'But of course, she would not. It is not diplomatic.'

With the President removed from power, the city is in a

shambles of suspended sentence. No one knows to whom they can turn, where they can look for help and guidance.

A few days later, a new President is sworn in. A clean-living decent man of grandfatherly years. Nothing for anyone to protest against. But a crack has opened. I sense the city waiting. Years of sleep, of simple existence, years when the city people thought little, felt little, wanting only to be fed and looked after, seem at an end.

It is on the evening news. I sit on Tang's lap and we watch the news of the President's resignation on the television. The President looks shaken but otherwise his message is clear. He has let the people down. He is sorry.

I get up to shut the door to the living room and see Ah Mui lurking in the passageway. Her own black and white TV is at the repair shop, she too is curious for news.

'Ah Mui was listening in the doorway,' I announce to Tang, resuming my former position.

'Good, let her,' Tang says. 'She has a right to know what goes on in this city.'

And then Tang thinks, *She, like the others of the city, has felt the build-up of events.* And he feels a great sorrow.

6

Roxanne

Look how the light glitters on her skin. Her pale face. Her neck slender and frail like the stem of an orchid. The heat of the overhead and footlights makes her perspire. The sweat creases down her powdered white mask. Her eyes are staring at some point beyond the lights, towards someone.

The stage is her friend – the coarse woodgrain beneath her tread, the reverberations that follow her pace, the echo after each wail she utters. The echo lingers in the audience, like something half-remembered, half-forgotten.

'Roxanne,' she cries.

'You're cold,' I murmur. I massage her hands.

Her slender hands weigh lightly in mine. Suddenly I cry, 'Are you afraid?'

I do not know why I should have asked her that question. I am not someone who is superstitious.

She withdraws her hands, with a laugh. 'No. What should I be afraid of?' She pauses. 'What can you be thinking … to think me afraid?'

She stares at me out of darkened eyes. The audience walks to and fro past our two selves, held as we are in a lariat of unease. I reassure her and give her my wishes for luck. Then I am back in my seat between an old man, coughing, and a *samfoo*-clad woman, who breaks into interminable intervals of gossip with her passing acquaintances. Seated on her other side, her children stuff their mouths with prawn crackers and roasted peas, and giggle. I have left Ching, there, alone on the stage, subject to the stare and mutter of the crowds. It is right that it should be so. To me, she takes her place among illusions.

The old men and women, housewives and children, blue-collar workers, gather. They flock to see this woman on Fort Canning Hill. They pull out wooden three-legged stools from under their kitchen tables. They sit under the flocculent clouds and hot moon. The performers on the *wayang* stage move in graceful stilted motions, their air-filled sleeves flapping, so they resemble so many birds. Chiang Ching's white masklike face is impassive, her eyes swivel. She raises her voice to a high sing-song, to a denunciatory pitch, threatening. She seeks revenge. *Pao Chou!* Repay the bitter!

Ching

I have always been an independent woman. Perhaps too much so for the men of my city. To them, an independent woman is something of a whore. The city cannot contain me. My destiny is wider than its narrow confines. Hardly surprising when you consider that I share the name of the woman whose life I play so well upon the stage: Chiang Ching. The enigmatic Madame Mao.

It is with her face now that I turn towards the crowd. The audience has become a faceless beast swimming out of reach beyond the lights. I do not know what it is they want. Is it to devour me with their eyes, their sniggers, their laughter and applause?

I am conscious only of my feet. Yes, my feet planted firmly upon the stage. *Here* is my refuge, this stage I am upon. The one solid thing in the midst of a shifting kaleidoscope of colours and sounds and people coming and going and shouting at me. I draw in my breath, and let out a wail.

Roxanne

On the stage a woman sits in a cell with a damp floor, and a smell of decaying walls, her head bent over scraps of paper. That head is greying. When she lifts her head for a moment as if to think, I see the face with white paper-thin skin, creased with age, crow's feet around the black eyes. A frail woman. Just a woman. No different from the millions outside her cell. Who would think she has held their lives in her cold palms?

Ching

The lights have begun to fade. I am conscious no longer of them or of that great beast hiding behind them. I huddle in a spotlight. Within the circle of light, I am captive. My head is bent over pieces of paper. I scribble busily. When I have written thus far, I wrap the pages around myself. The damp cell I sit in, fifteen square metres of space, is all my world. The single hard bed. The flat pillow. The solitary twenty-five watt bulb hanging from the mould-crusted ceiling.

'I want more paper,' I announce to the guard who appears abruptly into my space, holding in his hands my evening meal: a plate of steamed rice, strips of chicken fried with *choy sum*, a mug of water and two sweet dumplings for dessert.

I look into his face anxiously. I lay aside the paper, which are the beginnings of my memoir, stuff food into my mouth. Try to hide the dumplings under my pillow when the guard looks away. For a late-night snack.

'*Wei*, mistress! Give them back,' the guard orders.

'What?' I pretend.

'You don't want to eat, it's OK with me, but you put them back on the tray and we take them,' he says relentlessly. He is stern in his uniform. He has eyes in the back of his head. He waits. Ashamed and anxious, I fish out the two dumplings and sullenly drop them onto his open palms. When he is gone, I unwrap myself, peel off the sweating pages, stare hard at the fine print in the dimming light … The stage is scattered with stalks of wild orchids. Madame Mao loved orchids.

7

Ching

A successful performance. I arrive home with my arms full of bouquets, ready to unwind, but the amah is waiting for me.

'Some men come here,' Ah Mui peers at me out of curious black eyes. She looks frightened. After a pause, I guess whom it is she speaks of.

'Tang?' I say, quickly. 'Is he home?'

The men in white clothes. They have been to other homes before ours, looking, they say, for evidence. Tang has caught a whiff of where things are heading. Ah Mui negates my query.

'What did they want?' I ask, wearily. I draw off my Gucci shoes which are pinching my toes miserably, and toss them into a corner of the hall. Ah Mui scurries to pick them up. Standing there, holding them, she stares at me with such intensity that I feel a wave of irritation.

'Well?' I snap.

'Only papers,' she says. 'They say they only want to look into master's writings.'

'Of course,' I reply calmly, though my heart is pounding. 'And did you show them where his study was?' She nods. I walk to the study, and nearly jump. Shelves of books are missing. Everything left is in a mess. They have been thorough.

'What is this? What is going on?' I shout, my eyes hovering over his desk and accusing bookshelves, where the remaining book spines face me. A book sprawls at my feet. I bend to pick it up. I see it is one of Tang's scientific books that he has been reading recently on quantum physics.

Ah Mui comes up behind me. 'Letters and photographs also,' she remarks. 'They say they take important papers.' Her narrow eyes cast down, slyly, it seems to me. I instantly suspect her of some collaboration.

'Some of his files,' she says. She draws back a little when she sees the way I am looking at her.

'But the books? Where are his books?'

'I don't know, *Ah Yi*,' she begins sobbing. 'They take them. I only wait in the kitchen. I cook. They look.'

I have a sense of distaste for the whole matter, so I dismiss her and turn back to his study where I examine at length what remains. What am I to tell him when he comes home from work?

'They burnt them. I know. These things can be felt in the heart.'

We sit at supper. We discuss what has happened. Tang shakes his head.

'In here,' he says to me, laying a hand on his heart. 'They will burn the books of scholars because in our history thought is more to be feared than weapons. It is safer to turn us to making money than to let us think.'

'Do you think it means anything?' I ask him.

'I wouldn't worry,' Tang comments. He picks up a piece of fried fish with his chopsticks and puts it into his mouth.

'Are you sure?' I say.

And then that night the men in white clothes return.

8

Ching began wearing sunglasses around the time she started playing the role of Madame Mao. She said it was to get her into the part. Madame Mao often wore sunglasses. Ching said it was because they were fashionable, and Madame Mao was a vain and self-conscious woman. It didn't explain why Ching had to wear them in the house even when she was playing host to Roxanne. But then when Tang was arrested, the glasses perched on her face took on a tragic significance. They were the blind eyes of the mourner, and Roxanne stopped teasing her about wearing them.

When Ching became the suffering wife, Roxanne started to accord her even greater respect, although there were times she could not understand her, and even times when she thought Ching quite callous. But suffering suited the idea Roxanne held of Ching, and Roxanne sympathised terribly.

9

Roxanne

It's no use telling Ching to pray and wait. The government has now detained twenty-two persons. A large number of them are Catholics or lay pastors. They are accused of involving themselves in a conspiracy to subvert the government. Social issues, poverty, injustice – it is part of the Catholics' creed – to right wrongs, to care for those oppressed and suffering. But *Communists!* the newspaper headlines roar each day.

At the office, some of the journalists appear wary of their Catholic colleagues. It is hysterical the paranoia that has spread through the Catholic community. What if I am next? Who will speak for me? These are questions I and others ask ourselves. We examine our lives, our behaviour. Have we stepped out of bounds? What are the limits?

On Sunday I attend church as usual. The priest devotes his sermon to the plight of the detainees. He prays for the truth, whatever that truth may be. He prays for peace. The choir begins to sing:

> *It is better to light just one little candle than to stumble in the dark*
> *Better far to light just one little candle*
> *All you need is a tiny spark*
> *If we all say a prayer then the world will be free*
> *What a wonderful dawn of a new day we'll see.*

Some people in my pew are crying. I add my prayer for those detained. The church is packed with newcomers. These are people who have gathered for the mass said for the detainees. In the sky the clouds hang fat and low. The cross and steeple mark the landscape.

This is the way.

And by the wayside, in patches of matted grass that rise

defiantly in spite of the paved-over walkways and asphalt roads, there are the pulut-pulut, the twelve o'clock flower, the snake's tongue, the yellow wood sorrel, the shrew bean, the elephant's foot, the veronia, the star of Bethlehem, the wild purple orchids.

The heavy bell in the tower chimes deeply.

In the name of the father, the son and the holy ghost …

This is the church where the Virgin herself appeared to the women selling flowers before the gates. Thus it is said that the church is blessed. The Virgin had bought flowers from one of the women. The woman had known her straightaway, for in her heart a light had entered, and a calm she had not known before filled her. Then a miracle, for the Virgin, with a radiant face, ascended to heaven. When they returned home, all the women who had seen her had a similar radiance in their faces.

When I left the church that Sunday, I was sweating and tired. There had been a crush of people attending. The mass was long. And then the scene before me seemed to swell as the chorus began to sing. In the midst of so much pious and suffering humanity, it seemed angels would visit.

'It's not ready.'

The editor stands at my desk.

'Hurry up with it,' he says.

Back at work on Monday, and the editor is harassing me. Before he turns away, I say, 'I was thinking that if I interviewed the Chairman …?'

I can see him considering. He is one of those in the office whose behaviour to me has not changed. He is a Catholic, although not a practising one. He is divorced and remarried. He likes me and he approves of my work.

'If you can. If he agrees. Go ahead,' he says with a shrug. 'Good luck.'

10

Ching

I do not know why Madame Mao's ghost is to haunt me. Perhaps it is the collected karma within my self, the hunger to assert an identity, the unreasonableness that only builds ego walls around the soul, indeed … it is hard to be an empty boat.

I paint my eyes and lips and stretch the curve of my smile around my words, hanging onto the edges before they fall.

I whisper her name, *Chiang Ching*, which is also mine.

'What do you think is the purpose of all this living?' I address her.

'Do you think I know how to live?' she replies.

I have to admit that she is right. She, of all people. The question becomes rather absurd.

I turn to her, a woman who strangely enough wove pettiness, melodrama, stupidity and cruelty into a persona that was at once larger than life and smaller. She was neither the heroine nor empress she tried to make herself. When the time came, the public ravaged her like wolves. They hated her. Deservedly.

When one considers, it is so easy to hate a woman who is not in line, while Mao, that waxen old man, lies in glassed immortality in Tian An Men Square.

I study my face in my mirror. But the mirror is only a slave, and can do no more than reflect the face of the beholder. I have long known that in the mirror I have my friend, my audience to whom I perform my smiles, lines and gestures. A false self perhaps. I learn nothing more than what I tell it.

Is it me – or you – I see?

Madame Mao. From her later photographs I would not call her beautiful. But in her youth, men have said she was beautiful. Till the end she remained careful about her looks. And at the height of her power she drank double-boiled chicken soup daily to revitalise her skin. She had a woman in her entourage make her a paste from bird droppings and rice bran, which she smeared over her body. Three times a week she had her feet massaged so her blood would circulate freely and keep her in good health. Even when she was clad in ugly Mao jackets, she would make an effort to look stylish, by adding a touch of colour with a kerchief at the neck or arranging her cap at a more rakish angle.

11

Ching

Tang is brooding in the living room.

'What is it?' I ask.

'I'm waiting for Keng to call.'

But when no calls come from Keng, who, with Tang's help, edits the Catholic journal, I can see that Tang is anxious. He plays with the remote control, switching channels on the television, and watching flashes of sitcoms.

'Why doesn't he call?' He has given up the pretence of watching TV and is pacing the living room. His footsteps reverberate through my bones.

'Ching!'

I reply cautiously, 'Perhaps nothing has happened. But why don't you call him to find out?'

'Oh, it's probably all right. On the news today, there were two arrested, two I know. I don't want to disturb Keng.' Tang stands helplessly next to a white vase on a stand.

'He won't be in bed yet,' I say, helpfully. 'Call. And then you can be sure.'

Tang refuses to call. Perhaps he is afraid of picking up the phone. There are people who find it hard to live and Tang is one of them. My husband is caught in a labyrinth and is unable to see his way through. I find his look pitiful and look away to avoid sentimentality. Sometimes I find it hard to comprehend life's dark forces or to understand the impact on our lives, and it is hard to describe how events begin, what causes them, why at such a point there is a meeting of explosive elements.

True, the city is going through a recession, following the stockmarket crash. Perhaps all that happens is a distraction the government cooks up for the people. Few of us speak openly of what we think. It would seem, in fact, that we do not dare to think. Maybe we simply accept it happening as we accept all things, just and unjust, that occur in our little universe.

Tang makes a gesture of helplessness, 'We have appointed our gods and we live as they dictate. I wonder if Keng has heard anything.'

The two men arrested were fellow contributors to the Catholic journal.

'Do you think I should call him?' he mutters.

I say, 'I don't know. Perhaps wait.'

'If there is trouble – I will wait. I do not know what else to do,' he cries. He cradles his head in his arms.

It would seem that only fools dare to stand up in opposition. I remember one year, during the campaign for elections, an opposition party put up an ice cream peddler, two former mental patients and a road sweeper. In other words, those with little to lose. The professionals hide away. Perhaps they are wise!

'Go to bed. You don't have to sit up with me,' Tang orders. I lift a surprised head to gaze at him before dropping the magazine I am reading.

'Sleep,' he says, in a gentler voice. I slide onto his lap and we kiss, then I say, 'What are you going to do?'

'I won't call him now. It's too late. I'll see him tomorrow. I'll drop in at his office.'

'They might be watching it.'

'No! Why would they?' He pauses and seems to struggle with an inner fear. 'It's all right. I'll go. Maybe I'll be able to reach him at home if I call early.'

He pushes me off his lap. 'Go now.'

12

When Ching began travelling with the opera troupe, she carried no vision of her future; she sought only to escape. Nine years passed. In that period of time, she grew into a woman. She lost the roundness of her cheeks, the awkwardness that accompanied her movements, the shyness of her manner. Her hair she kept long and swinging to her hips. She liked to talk to men in a pert and teasing way. She was considered pretty and was not often left alone. She was no prude and enjoyed having a good time.

In one season, the troupe set up their platform under a block of Housing Development Board flats in Lakeview, close to a row of provision shops.

Hock Hua Sweetshop. The red banner welcomed the customer. The customer entering the gap in the folding metal doors was besieged by huge biscuit tins and glass containers, with their maws pitted with various preserved plums, mangoes and olives.

In the dimly lit interior, the sweetshop keeper weighed the sweets and pulled down the change in a rusted tin bucket dangling on a string from the ceiling.

Laid out in rows were the plastic squares of hot ginger to chew and get one's teeth stained with artificial colouring. In cane baskets: sweets in yellow and red and white rabbit candy wrapped in edible transparent paper, with pictures of white rabbits, ears aloft.

The sweetshop keeper was an old man. He ran his shop mostly from the five-foot way, judging from the amount of time he spent in his rattan chair placed strategically at the entrance to his shop. When a customer appeared he would uncurl himself without haste and follow her inside. But these were mere interruptions to his real job of watching people pass by and indulging in conversation. Sometimes neighbouring shopkeepers would join him when their businesses were slow, and together offered themselves the comfort of tedious saws, repetitious observations, well-understood grumblings and declamations, such as friends do, knowing that they are secure in shared beliefs.

Sometimes Ching would grow weary of her many boyfriends and would seek instead the peace of the sweetshop. She lingered in the five-foot way to chat to the old man.

'*Ah Pek*,' she called. 'Have you eaten yet?'

'How's your back, grandfather? Feeling less pain?'

The old man shrugged. He massaged his toes. 'Complain also no use,' he grumbled. 'No wife at home. No one to take care of my back.'

'Why you not married?' he continued. It wasn't right for a pretty girl not to be married, he said.

Ching laughed, 'I can't find Mr Right. Maybe you can look for me?'

From the old man, Ching heard the name of Madame Mao. 'Chiang Ching. Same name,' the old man remarked. 'Means "Green River". Not a common name.'

'My mother says she was blessed in a river. Because she conceived the day she went swimming,' said Ching, laughing.

'She made up the name. She and Chairman Mao. Before that she was known as Lan Ping, "Blue Peace". She was an actress like you.'

'The Chinese people hate her for what she has done, don't they?' Ching asked. 'She is still in prison? Or is she dead?'

'Alive,' said the old man. 'Alive and still going. A tough woman. They didn't dare execute her. I have seen her,' he nodded, 'in the flesh.'

Ching made an exclamation of surprise.

'True. I went to China in support of the Communist Revolution.' The old man shook his head. 'I was stupid,' he said. 'When it began to go to pieces, I ran away. I was one of the lucky ones who managed to survive, and to come back here.'

'Stupid,' he sighed.

Ching could sense a depth of passion and experience in his self-criticism.

The sweetshop was for him a sanctuary. The mouth-watering delights of childhood a safe point of return. The business was set up with the help of a rich relative.

'It is good now,' he scratched his armpit. 'I am an old man. No more crazy ideas.'

Walking away from the sweetshop, Ching counted the pavement stones, her feet taking her lightly past the cracks and fissures, black lines like thread stitching together the grey slabs of concrete. There were ants which hid there, oblivious of large feet menacing their heads. Returning to the troupe, she quickly shrugged off the feeling of unease that had crept into her. She absorbed herself in preparing for rehearsals. But Hui, her director, came to her with a new script in his hand. He cried, 'I have a part for you. A new play.'

Ching studied the title page. 'Madame Mao?' she exclaimed. She was stirred by a sudden current of excitement.

When Ching's mother died, and Ching took up her vocation, she poured a great deal of herself into her training. She learnt her lines rapidly, practised her songs, and spent hours learning how to move on the stage. It was not just those hours upon the stage or the endless rehearsals that turned her into an actress. It was the in-between hours, the hours of plastering thick make-up on her face, the hours of reading the scripts, of training her voice. Sometimes she would touch a note that would hang exquisitely, it was for that moment that she became. More vivid. More in life.

She started to read. Plays, stories, ancient folklore – these constituted her education with the troupe. She absorbed fairytales with ease, learnt of former wars, berated the classics and found the *Analects* pompous. She liked the magic of Taoism, enjoyed oracles and divinations, and while her reading was informal and untutored, she received a kind of education, perhaps better than some received in their classrooms.

When Hui had gone, leaving behind the script, Chiang Ching studied it with a growing curiosity. She reflected that as an actress she lived the life she wanted. No commitment to any relationships. No children. She lived the lives of many and forgot what had been her own. It never was an easy life. But each character she played imbued her with something of its nature. Perhaps that was why she was drawn to strong characters, bold women. When in her more soul-searching moments she asked herself why, she would answer, 'So as to be unlike my mother.'

13

A rumble of voices came from the dressing tents pitched on the grass backstage. A girl's laughter rang out shrilly. Tang hesitated before pulling back the flap and peering into a tent. Whitened faces turned towards him. 'Sorry, sorry ...' he mumbled. 'Is there a girl here – Chiang Ching?'

Someone indicated a far corner. Tang set eyes on the slender figure of the young woman he had watched for the last hour on the stage. Tang, for some reason he does not remember, had come alone to watch a play. Chiang Ching was not billed as the star attraction, but when she came on, he noticed her. She was young, mischievous, playing a minor role. Her costume was frivolous, her manner even more so. She had a strong singing voice, round in its musical intonations. Impulsively, he had gone backstage to look for her.

'Chiang Ching?' he said, and when she looked up, he saw that her eyes too knew how to sing. Tang did not really think of what he could say to her or how he could explain his intrusion. So he introduced himself, 'I'm Tang Na Juan,' and said that he thought she acted marvellously.

She wrinkled her nose, and rubbed energetically at her cheeks to remove the powder, and Tang could feel himself smiling foolishly.

'Er ... would you like to come out, for some supper?' he said. He waited miserably for her to refuse.

'Sure,' she said. She glanced around the tent rather vaguely. 'I suppose they'll be going to supper too, but I'd rather go with you.'

Tang drove to Rasa Singapura. They found a table in the midst of a bustling crowd, and Ching waited while Tang went off to order.

She told him she was on her own. Her parents were dead.

'I've been in the troupe since I was fifteen,' she told him, picking at a slice of cucumber in the *rojak* with a toothpick. 'What do you do?'

'I lecture at a polytechnic,' he replied.

'An academic?' Ching lifted her eyebrows and laughed. 'I'm not one for too much schooling.'

'It's not my fault,' Tang exclaimed. 'Blame my middle-class upbringing.'

Ching slid him a sideways glance. 'I don't mind.'

Tang couldn't help staring at her. After a short laugh to cover his embarrassment, he said, 'Tonight when I watched the opera, I had a strange feeling, as though I was seeing you again. Although we meet for the first time, it is like I have already known you. Perhaps I have dreamt of you.'

He waited for her reaction. She smiled and looked down. She did not say that they had only just met or that she did not like him. She did not discourage him and he took that as his hope.

He liked to say to her now, 'Do you remember that night? What we talked about?'

Serious and interested in quiet pursuits, Tang took Ching into his life, and found in himself a depth of passion that logic could not rule. He could marshal his logical defences and list their differences of values, of thought, of upbringing, of occupation, but it was useless. He had never stopped loving her since that night. In happy times, he believed her to be a blessing.

14

The mirror woman stood outside a red building, her form shaded in the westering light. She was waiting for someone. Students filed out. They carried musical instruments in cases. There was a flurry of movement, something ripped open in the fabric of a universe. A young man lay dead on a patch of grass. His face lay at an angle on the grass. Ants crawled heedlessly around.

People milled around the body in fascination. There were those who told the newspapers, when journalists started to arrive, that before the class ended that morning, many people had heard singing outside the classroom windows. It was a song so plangent it stirred many to think of home, of country, of patriotism. A song? No, they had not been mistaken. They could not recall the words but if they heard the tune again they would know it instantly.

'Who was he?'

'Who shot him? Did you see what happened?'

'It was a young woman who did it. Probably a lover's quarrel. Such a quiet young man too. I was in his class.'

'No. I saw it. It was not a young woman. She was quite elderly. She hid behind the trees over there and shot him.'

'Who was she?'

'I think it must have been someone he knew. Maybe he was in a Triad and the woman was sent to kill him for some reason.'

'Maybe it was the communists.'

'Maybe it was his wife.'

'He must have been involved in criminal activities. Who would have thought of it? Such a quiet man.'

'She was holding a gun. Did anyone see her before then?'

'She was hiding behind the trees. She was there only a minute before the students came out.'

'She was not there. I saw no one. Yes, I was in the garden.'

'There was no woman. No one was shot.'

'You are mistaken, I heard the shot.'

They did not see her again. Those who tried to identify her gave up after several inconsistent descriptions.

And she was gone. The mirror woman disappeared after she shot the young man. I heard a voice say, 'A mistake. Killing him was a mistake. He knew too little.'

'Those more timid will be warned,' a second voice responded. 'These students will know better than to play around. We cannot risk spies.'

Ching

I did not know when I became aware of her presence upon the stage. I was in the midst of a long wail when a shadow moved swiftly across. I caught my breath. The audience waited as silence fell.

'Ma, ma!' the words broke softly from my lips. 'I see this mirror creature.'

A sudden snarl. 'Go now!' I swung quickly to look for the owner of the voice. I could make out two men in the shadows, dressed in bland shirts. They glanced around. They signalled to each other and went their separate ways.

I awakened to the sound of jeers, loud mutters and grumblings. Someone in the wings was waving to me frantically. A fellow actress hurried on stage, and started to sing. I was hustled off. Meanwhile the play continued.

15

Ching

Myth? In my ears I seemed to hear the echo of an earlier time. I fell to musing and I knew, in spite of bad weather, there were vans circling the roads, spreading their dreams.

'Give us our rights, give us our land,' politicians chanted.

And I heard the mirror people chanting, 'Give us our rights. Give us our land.'

And the communists held oranges in their hands, and they wore grey cotton shirts, and talked in 'farting accents'.

★

I cling to the windowsill, waiting patiently. I uncurl my body to dress and prepare to make up my face. Each careful stroke of my pencil shapes my eyes. They grow long and black. I line my lips. I watch my face in the mirror changing and feel at my back a world that is beginning to thin.

As the real world begins to thin, even building and historical sites in the city disappear. The buildings before my eyes look like they have been polished. Someone has come with a scrubbing brush and taken away all the grime. Clean city. Clean and green. But, like a boil erupting, I see more of the mirror creatures at large.

I am in my car on my way to the city when I see a mirror woman. She is waiting thoughtfully, poised at the entrance of a luxury hotel, The Oriental, waiting for her chauffeur-driven car.

She reminds me – of clouds, a cold grey or rain rasping across the grassland. Pattering raindrops on the road.

The monsoonal storms have swollen the water in the canals. The mirror woman's smile is a thin sliver of glass, snaking through mist. Her eyes glint like pieces of metal shining in the sun.

I stop my car at the nearest possible point and dash out. I will speak with her! She gets into her car as I come, half-running. She looks into my face briefly, then vanishes into the car's interior. I watch the car glide away. But I must know, I must know what only she and the mirror people can tell me, who it is I am. We have a connection somewhere in the recesses of my soul. I grow cold standing at the entrance of the hotel.

My mother. Her legacy. Oral stories told of creatures who once lived among us, creatures like and yet unlike us, creatures that we owed a debt to.

She lay in bed, white and thin in her pyjamas. I fed her soft porridge with a spoon. After a while, she pushed my hand away, she lay on her back breathless, staring at a point on the wall. She was afraid but she would not show it. Her only hope was to die peacefully. She had a dream one night. She told me she had dreamt she would come back.

She broke off coughing. Her cheeks flushed.

'My no-good life soon over.'

'What, ma, ma?' I said.

'Your grandmother, she said on day I had my first blood, "Be careful of them. They are there."'

'Who?' I feared she was losing her grip on her mind.

She turned her wasted face towards the pillow.

'Your grandmother.'

Then she said, 'The mirror people are here.'

'Who?'

Mother shook her head. 'The government,' she whispered.

'You mean the legend of the Yellow Emperor and his people?'

But she looked confused. 'The government,' she said, shaking her head. She lifted a hand to her hair. 'Where's the mirror?'

I hesitated then brought her a hand glass. I held it up for her to look at herself. She gazed in silence.

'How beautiful she is,' she said. 'The mirror people are always perfect. We do well to imitate them.'

I placed the hand glass by her side. 'The mirror people imitate us. Not the other way around. We are the ones who are real,' I commented, carefully.

My mother nodded and smiled to herself; her smile was frightening.

A sudden thought arrested me. Had my mother seen her death face in the hand glass? Were the mirror creatures trying to lure her away before her time to go?

Did my mother have a secret knowledge of the mirror creatures? I thought she did. And I wondered at her insistence on their perfection. Did she side with the mirror creatures?

I was still too immature to allow for such knowledge. I could not trust her. Her world belonged to her. I could not cross over, neither could she be in my world.

I date my growing up from that moment, I became more what I was, I grew more into my world. I began to separate from her just before she died.

The hillocks of her cheekbones made deep shadows of her face. Her lips were stained with betel nut, which she sucked for comfort. Over the pillow, her hair lay. I picked up a comb from her bedside table and disentangled the knots that had formed.

16

Roxanne

We in the audience hold our breaths waiting. I see Ching, shadowy, coming forward. She casts herself to the floor and save for a wild sobbing, which fills the air, nothing happens, no one speaks. Tang has been arrested.

Ching

I stand watching the door. They have gone, Tang and the men in white clothes. Ah Mui stands to one side, her red-rimmed eyes look resentful. I recall that I have pinched her for letting them in. I turn aside with a tired gesture.

'Go away,' I say to her. I cannot stand to look into her face. Ah Mui leaves the room. A fresh spasm of tears. I lie on the floor weeping. They have taken away all my hope and support. Without Tang, who am I? How can I withstand their threats?

I collapse upon the stage. 'Tang Na!' I cry, as my tears flow copiously. 'Were you jealous when I stayed out late after my performances? You are a weak man! You are not a man. You cower, you are afraid of me. You fear my hostility. You fear that I will leave you. You fool! Is that a good reason to threaten me like this?'

Roxanne

Chiang Ching weeps on the stage, her hair hanging forwards. The audience is stirred. Some of the women weep with her. Some of the men blow their noses. Few at this moment ask themselves the question: But why does she cry? Who has brought her to this situation? Only she, she herself. No one else can be to blame.

Ching

Tang Na, the advice I gave you, you threw away. Did you think I was only a woman, that I was without shrewdness? In this game we are entangled in, one plays by the rules, or not at all. You played to lose, my husband!

Roxanne

I blow my nose. I think of how far we have come, we, as a people in this city, and how much we have gained and lost. Does it amount to this, after all that our ancestors strove to build?

The stage is dark, the weeping has ceased, the audience applauds. Stage sets are being shifted.

When I take my seat, the stage is once again in darkness, save for a single spotlight and Chiang Ching's head bent over scraps of paper.

Tock, tock, tock … cang!

Ching

Behind the light, a great darkness. My husband is there. I feel his presence. Yesterday or today or tomorrow. Time is immaterial. It drops like water to wear away our resistance. Even memory is a victim.

As I peruse the morning paper in my privileged cell, I wonder at the lack of any real coverage of the city's political situation. They bring me the morning paper when I ask for it.

17

Ching

The newspaper. It becomes a horror to us in the mornings when the delivery-man throws the paper over the gate.

I wait patiently as Tang skims the pages looking for more news on the situation. The front page headlines, then a quick skim through each page, then back to the front page for a thorough perusal, the world news pages, the editorial and commentary page, then the Letters to the Editor page. Often when he comes upon something striking, he will read it aloud.

The amah enters the dining room with a rattle of plates and bowls. Tang coughs as he scans. I hand him the plate of *yew char kuay*, take a pair myself and dip them into my coffee before chewing them.

'Think of all those letters going to the editor,' I remark. 'It's funny but although some people can't even find the time to write to their friends, they will write hundreds of letters to an anonymous editor. They must think their opinions so worthy of being heard.' Many of these letters of course do not see the light of day, sinking into a pile a besieged editor steadily feeds to the garbageman.

In the daily newspaper, without an 's', for, really, all the newspapers belong to one conglomerate, the rest having been closed down for one reason or another by the government, there is a page devoted to Letters to the Editor.

Often one finds, in scanning its columns, enlightening strictures from ordinary citizens against critics of the Chairman's government. Occasionally one may even find argument and logical thinking. Recently, the government ministers decided on behalf of the city that they should raise their own pay. The reason being that if the city's ministers were to quit and work in the private sector, they would be earning top wages. Because any news that had to do with money was bound to annoy the citizens who after all forked out taxes, the Letters to the Editor page was filled with positive feedback.

Dear Newspaper Editor

The government does so much for our country. We should show our appreciation for them. What better way of doing this than to increase their pay? Think of it. If they left the government and worked in a multinational, they would be earning one million a month instead of a year. So let us reward them. All those people who criticise the current ministerial pay increases are not thinking of the good it would do for our country to have satisfied government ministers.

Signed A Loyal Citizen

Aiya, you *kiasu* people! Where else would you find more decent and honest government? I don't understand what all this fuss is about. Pay them more, receive more from them. To attract high calibre people we have to pay them high wages. That's logical.

Signed Disgusted

I don't see what the fuss is about the ministerial pay rise. OK, granted, our Chairman is already being paid US$780,000 and the US President gets US$200,000 and Britain's Prime Minister US$122,000, so that's four times more than the US President's pay, all the figures are according to *The Economist* report on annual salaries of heads of state, but *alamak*, look at the mess in the US and see how efficient and uncorrupted our government is. Also how do you know other governments are not hoarding away their money secretly? At least our government is up-front about the whole business. And it keeps them from wanting more on the sidelines. After all they sacrifice by being our leaders.

Signed One Person's Opinion

Dear One Person's Opinion,

Unfortunately no one asked our opinions. No referendum was conducted before they decided to increase their own pay. How can they say that we of the city were not in the 'best position' to judge? To cite the Chairman on being asked if a referendum would be conducted, 'The people at large ... Are they in a position to judge? Is it within their range of experience?' Does he think we are stupid sheep? And why are the ministers taking all the credit for the city's improved economic position, what about us, the workers? Again another unfavourable policy is being railroaded through parliament. Our opinions are too lowly to be considered. How is it that we were in the best position to judge when we had to decide whether or not we should break away from the union with our big neighbour, which in that particular case, we were kicked out eventually, so we had not much of a choice even then?

Who are the dolts who write such letters to the editor? Does the government employ you and why no proper names? Anyone who criticises has his or her name printed out in full. What's all this about sacrifice? Hah, don't we always get told that we have to be self-sacrificing, society before self, nation above community, etc.? A white paper on Shared Values! Or are these values meant only for us, the lowly citizens? Ministers are not royalty that they need to be fêted with monetary rewards to encourage them to serve.

What is the definition of a leader? Surely someone people can look up to and are willing to follow. It takes commitment and yes, sacrifice. Did Gandhi ask for a pay rise before fighting for India's independence? The idea is ridiculous. And it's not only the Chairman but even cabinet ministers who are benefiting from us, the taxpayers. You know our starting pay for cabinet members is US$419,285 a year, double that of the US President. Satisfied government? I should think so. They don't have much to complain of.

Signed Tang Na Juan

'Some people are feathering their nests quickly,' says Tang, agitated.

'Shhh, I wouldn't speak so loudly.'

But he is shaking the newspaper and upsetting his tea on the tablecloth. 'Look,' he says. Absently, he mops the mess on the table with his handkerchief. He cries, 'I think the government has a department to write such letters for them. Why else are they always covered with a pseudonym? Critics always have their names printed for everyone to see.'

The unseen forces are crowding in. He does not realise it yet but they are watching and waiting. I stare at his familiar face, thin and passionate.

'What do you hope to do?' I say.

18

Ching

Take my words. These black scribbles. My fattening memoir. Words are not harmless marks upon a page.

I stop writing and lean my head on the wall. How long am I to be in this cell? How long do they intend to keep me in? What danger can I pose to the regime? My husband, you are increasingly with me. Is it guilt on my part? Do your eyes look at me with reproach? I recall your movements, steps leading to your arrest that fateful night. Judge me if you will.

Perhaps things might have gone otherwise, but end as they do because of something slight, something like a butterfly's flapping of wings causing an earthquake or hurricane halfway across the globe. Tang would say that the nature of history is such that it is repeated everywhere. No one people has a premium on it. Whose history does a story belong to? It belongs to everyone.

19

Tang is reading when he feels dizzy, so he closes his eyes. Does the room cease to exist? He reflects. *Esse est percipi.* To see is to cause to be. Close to the truth Berkeley may be! *The situation in this city can only change*, Tang muses, *when the perception of the people changes as to its underlying reality.*

'Keng on the phone.'

'He must want me over,' Tang says, getting up.

'What does he want now?' Ching asks. She stands with one hand on her hip.

Tang replies hastily, 'I know you don't think well of him – he is without charm, but a good person.'

'A good friend,' he emphasises.

'I'm not talking about manners,' Ching begins. 'Keng is a strange man. I never know what he's thinking.'

Ching stands by the open window where Tang's bird, a mynah, is hopping in a cage which swings in the breeze. Tang stares at the bird for a long while, then recollects that he has a call to answer.

'I'm going out,' Tang says peeping into the kitchen, where Ching stands instructing the amah. 'I'll be looking over the next issue with Keng. I won't be long.'

Keng has his office near the Cathay cinema, in an old block of decayed office apartments in a rather shady part of town. Tang assists in editing their journal whenever he can spare the time from his duties at the polytechnic.

Keng hands Tang a sheaf of papers, and then turns quietly to the other end of the room, where he prepares two styrofoam cups of tea. Tang perches on a plastic chair. Keng hands him a cup of tea. 'Boiling hot. Lipton's,' he comments as he stirs his own cup.

The room is sparsely furnished and Keng's desk is its main object. Keng tips his chair legs backwards against the wall.

'What do you think?' Keng remarks.

'Good. I think Chong Tian's article should be the lead. The one on childhood joys and pressures. It'll be good to have something in for the parents. But I'm glad I don't have children, sorry, of course, you're a father, but it's no fun being a child nowadays.'

Keng has placed the article Tang handed to him onto a growing pile, which they have marked out to go into the next issue.

Keng scratches his nose and comments gruffly, 'They get them young. Right from the start. In kindergarten. On the radio some children were asked, "What did you do during your holidays?" and they all said, "Study, *lor.*"'

Keng chuckles briefly at his pun. 'Study law.' He swings his chair back to normal with a thump.

Tang has his head bent over another article. He looks up. 'Excellence. Progress. What a life! I remember how I used to *pontank* school and go fishing.'

'It's different now,' Keng says. He takes off his thick glasses, gives Tang a rather odd look from his suddenly diminished eyes.

'Bags under your eyes,' Tang observes. 'Late nights?'

Keng smiles apologetically, 'I was thinking – why don't you make that an article? I could use it in the issue after next.'

'Madness, really,' Tang reflects. 'First, we stream the children at nine years old, then stream again at twelve, then for most schools again at fifteen. Then it's the O levels and A levels, where the chaff will be separated from the grain, and then what's left goes to the university. Some of the private schools stream every year, just to be certain of the grain.'

Keng spits upon his glasses, and reaching into his pocket removes a large handkerchief, and begins to wipe the lens in circular motions.

'I have to warn you,' he says, dryly, replacing his glasses on his nose, 'education is prickly. Very prickly.'

'Right. Everything's a prickly issue.'

Sunlight streaming in through the office window glints off Keng's spectacles. He gathers the papers. 'Are we finished?'

He pulls out a bunch of keys from his pocket, waits for Tang at the door. Out in the corridor, he chooses a key and locks up.

'Sometimes burglars come into the building,' he says. He tests the shut door a couple of times.

'It's quite an old building. It's easy to break into. Do you see that fire escape running outside the building? Once some burglars used that to climb through an open window. I don't think there's much to steal in my office but one has to be careful.'

Tang wonders, *Is Keng afraid of burglars or of someone or something else?*

He does not like to ask. Tang looks at Keng, a square man in thick spectacles, with a mild stubble, and a large head. Very tidy and correct in his dressing even on a Sunday. Tang is himself only in casual Bermudas and a T-shirt.

They walk down a quiet pedestrian lane, with a distant rumble of traffic reaching their ears now and again. Overhead, paper-thin bougainvillea flowers, draped on residential fences, shake like lanterns in the breeze.

Further on they pass what was once a chapel, its Gothic façade, flying buttresses and all, hides a restaurant. The restaurateurs have repainted the once white building, thinking the colour is not attractive to customers: the building is now hued a shade between pink and purple.

'Horrible,' Tang mutters, as is his habit whenever passing the edifice.

They turn up the road and to the left and promenade down the stretch where the library was once. It is a red brick building, ugly but necessary to students, but it now houses the registry of marriages and births. Tang is seized with a sudden impulse to peek inside. A wedding is being conducted.

The bride, an Indian woman, is dressed in lacy tulle and chiffon. Her face is angular and plain and reminds him of a former schoolteacher he had, Miss Ramasamy. He cannot place the groom's face.

A small crowd of relatives and friends stand in a spiral of well-wishing, one of them has a bottle of wine in his hand that he splashes the bride with. The bride waits puzzled and unsmiling through the ceremony. The groom perspires in the close room. Somewhere someone strikes the organ keys and the notes of 'Here Comes the Bride' float out of the building.

Tang recalls those schooldays he spent in search of books, which were impossible to find because no one replaced them in their proper places. The library was like a fishing pond, milling with anglers. Generally, it would take the library assistants three days to locate a book he wanted. By then some other unnecessary book lying in its improper place would have caught him.

Tang wonders if he can approach the bride, Miss Ramasamy … is it? And ask if she remembers him. The woman's face starts to quiver. He puts his hand up to his face, which is wet. Is he crying?

Just then he feels a touch on his elbow. Keng, forgotten, is by his side. 'Let's go, OK?'

Tang is anxious to hide his weakness, covering up with a handkerchief and much blowing of his nose. Keng makes no remark, and if he has seen the momentary tears, appears not to have noticed.

'Think utopia,' Keng continues talking. 'Is it ideal to have a one-party state? We have invested too much power in one party. What makes for good government? Is our government accountable? Who are those who fall by the wayside? Are they taken care of? Many sections of our society are ignored or suppressed. We are a young and independent nation. This should be a time of idealism, but no, what we have is narrow materialism. I think we have a good collection this time. The stuffed shirts are beginning to sit up and take notice. William tells me the Minister … mentioned an article he had written. Apparently at a press conference. William has his contacts.'

They step into a lane. The lane winds down smoothly. The silence is broken by a dog behind a gate barking at them as they pass.

'Look at that dog barking, trying to terrorise us,' Keng gestures with his arms. 'How fat he is! If I had such short legs, I wouldn't pretend to be a dog.'

His euphoric mood is suddenly dissipated. Tang glances at the dog. Keng, walking moodily, turns to Tang, grabs him by the shoulder, and says abruptly, 'Why were you crying?'

The question takes Tang by surprise. He stops. Keng's spectacles sparkle with sweat dripping from his forehead.

'I suppose I've been nervous lately. Maybe it's ill health. Overwork.'

Keng's hand drops to his side. 'Sorry to hear that,' he mutters. He mops his forehead with his hanky. 'I can't take the heat – I'm of northern blood, my grandparents, you know.'

He adds, 'You are a sentimental man!'

'Your articles have vigour,' Keng says, continuing to walk. 'Some will not take kindly to what you have written. It would be very remiss of me not to tell you … you are aware?'

'Yes,' Tang says, though what he is certain of he cannot say.

'Good, good,' Keng replies. 'Some of you academics live in ivory towers.'

His last remark takes Tang by surprise and fills him with some displeasure.

Keng carries on without noticing his expression, 'The government. They are often right. Speaking ironically, of course.'

'There is something disagreeable about living under a government that is always right,' Tang says passionately.

They reach the crossroads. 'I'll be on my way then. Call me if you have any problems.'

They grip hands briefly. Keng takes one road and Tang, the other.

In the sky the light is slowly sinking into evening. It will be a good night, with a few cold stars like pinpricks upon a canvas.

The scholar thinks to stop for a meal. He turns into the Queenstown Hawker Centre, a sprawling enclave of food stalls next to a wet market, inside surrounding blocks of high-rise Housing Development Board flats. He orders a bowl of Hokkien prawn mee. A dollar-fifty.

He counts out the money and passes the coins to the fat hawker. The man wipes his sweat with the back of his hand, smiles pleasantly at Tang and accepts the coins proffered. Tang retreats with his steaming bowl to a table, where he crouches over the yellow wheat noodles, cooked in a broth of boiled king-size prawns, and tucks in hungrily.

As the scholar sits down, he notices that at another table, a young boy, head drooping above his books, is chained by one leg to the table's stem. The boy's parents, who appear to be the owners of a chicken rice stall, rush about busily. A half-eaten bowl of rice and chicken is on the table beside the boy, who apparently was not hungry, and has fallen asleep while studying.

'Eh,' the scholar says uncertainly to his neighbour at the table. 'Look at that.'

The neighbour looks at the boy, looks back at Tang and shrugs.

'They can't have him running off making trouble or getting lost, and they can't be with him at all times, so what else to do? Don't worry, a boy like that is used to it. I see him there quite often.'

Tang feels uneasy. His neighbour has gone back to his own business of eating. The boy's head droops and droops further down till his forehead touches the open page of his book.

This is none of his business, Tang acknowledges. His family is responsible. Tang, although upset, is unwilling to confront the boy's father, so after gazing at the boy for a long moment, turns back to eating. To his right, at the vinyl-covered table he is sharing with a few others, a middle-aged man is bending his head over an appetising bowl of fish-ball noodle soup. The scholar glances at him, and then takes a longer look surreptitiously. To a superficial observer, he looks normal, a man in his fifties, still in work clothes, after overtime at the office, having a meal before going home. But there is something not quite right about his appearance, which the scholar cannot put his finger to. Then it strikes him that the man is shimmering gently in the shadowy light of the street lamps and the light from the stalls.

His skin, which is pale like many office-bound workers, glows with a surreal light that seems all of its own and nothing to do with reflection. Like glow-worms!

'What do you have there?'

'It's a light. It will glow forever and ever.'

The little Malay girl laughed and pushed her cage-shaped brooch at him suddenly.

'Here, take it.'

Siti, the little girl who sat next to him in class, had once invited him and several others to her *kampong*. The Malays in the *kampong* caught the glowing insects in round cages, and then wore them hanging on threads looped around their necks, as ornaments, for part of a night's celebration, before letting them go. A ditty plays in his mind, *Firefly, firefly, where do you go to put out your light?* The scholar opens his mouth to speak, but the man on his left, abruptly interjects into his unspoken thoughts, 'So what did the boss have to say?' Almost as though he was carrying on a previous conversation.

The scholar is startled, but the other man at the table replies, without lifting his head from his food, 'He was not very happy about the whole thing. I can't think why.'

The man on the left chortles, '*Aiya*, what did you expect from such a tyrant?' He continues laughing quietly to himself.

The scholar deduces from the exchange that the two are

colleagues. A third man sitting at the table does not speak or look at the others. He is staring into space and picking his teeth with a toothpick, an empty plate before him. He burps loudly. The scholar whose nerves are strained, jumps in his seat. All three of them turn to stare at him.

Flustered, he says, 'The food here is good, you come here often?'

They continue to stare silently, then the man on his left says, 'Eat up. You won't be getting much to eat later.'

The scholar stammers foolishly, 'Why ... not?' Then recollecting himself, he is dumbfounded.

The man sitting opposite him who has not yet spoken, gently remarks that it is a cold night, may be going to rain.

The scholar interrupts him, 'No, no, look at the cloud cover, it is light and fluffy, it will be without rain.'

As he chooses his statement, the scholar feels an almost ridiculous sense of pride. He emphasises his profound knowledge of the weather with a dig into his noodles with his wooden chopsticks.

The man on his right, remarks with an almost pained look, '*"He sits as quiet as a cat; at springing he is a tiger."*' The last remark completely unnerves the scholar. He finishes his meal quickly, pushes his bowl away, and rises to his feet. He expects them to follow him as he walks away, but he hears no footsteps behind him.

Arriving home, Tang wants to tell Ching of the incident, but it now appears petty and absurd.

I must see the doctor, he thinks. *Crying and then getting intimidated by some people talking. I must really be ill. Maybe I'm coming down with the flu.*

He feels ashamed of his own nervousness. The work pressure must be getting to him.

Ching

I am onstage waiting for instructions. Then it hits me. Why should I wait? What is the power in the director that he should tell me to do this or do that? What makes him the expert, the authority on my art? And those mean eyes of his, black and sharp, watching me above his moustache.

'Do this,' he will say, and expect me like a marionette to jump to his bidding.

'Come here,' and again I go, ass wagging. I am no more than a prostitute to him. I know my art, I know who I am, better than he does. Then the white-hot lights of the stage suddenly flood my eyes. As I blink and hesitate, I hear the director booming, 'Madame Mao, Act Three, Stage Left. Bedroom scene.'

I feel myself move automatically to my place. Somehow someone has made a bed appear. I sit upon it. The sheets are soft and silken. There is a packet of joss sticks at the foot of the bed, on the white silken counterpane.

'Right,' the director shouts. 'You are a woman with desires. You wish to seduce Mao, you two-penny bit actress. You wish to belong to his army. You get to him via his senior officer with whom you will sleep.'

I lean back upon the pillow and let my hand slowly caress my thigh. 'Come here,' I say, swinging long legs idly from the bed. The Red Guard moves besides me. He bends over as I gently run my fingertips round and down his growing mound. I part my legs and draw his mouth downward to my *square inch of paradise*. His tongue nuzzles my inner lips, stirring tender desire, flickering like yearning. I try to resist, reminding myself that it is for a plan. I try to keep in mind the revenge, the revolution, but his tongue probes deeper. He stands up with a decisive movement and divests himself of his clothes and underwear in rough gestures, releasing his dragon.

'You don't need the monk's pill,' I croon. I refer to the

legendary pill the monks are said to have concocted to ensure virility.

He reaches for a packet of joss sticks and lights them with an unsteady hand and puts one in a little holder in the hollow between my breasts, one on the triangular patch of dark hair between my thighs, he makes me hold them in each hand. The flames burn steadily downwards and I begin to feel intense points of heat at strategic places. The heat is so intense I writhe.

My head spins. The Red Guard rides me like a horse leaping over a stream. He sweats, curses, whimpers. I feel the rocking, the shuddering, I am like one dead. I feel him suddenly like a soft hot spot in a warm sea, our two selves have melted, and I am no longer myself, I have nothing solid to hold onto. At the moment of my climax, I imagine the Chairman rocking inside me. I slap him a stinging five-fingered blow on his cheek.

'Stop!' the director shouts.

'Not like that,' he says. 'Not so hard. You want to appear alluring.'

'Do the scene again,' he says.

I brush my hair back from my eyes, lift my face to the spotlights. My audience is in a blinding beyond. My face appears as a pale blob to the unseen ones made up of the backstage crew and technicians who are in the auditorium.

'Try it again,' the director says. He turns to speak to the lighting man about some problems during the rehearsal. I stare at the place beyond the footlights.

I pull out of Tang's arms, my body covered in sweat. 'Was it good?' I murmur. I touch him here and there with a hand like feathers.

'Mmmm,' Tang groans.

The Red Guard holds me in his arms. The director is saying above our heads, 'She was a fantastic lover. One of her string of lovers told this to a journalist. The best one-night stand he had. And she let you know it.'

Her lover said, 'During our one night together she held me,

whispering, "Is this good? Do you like it?" as she arched her body under me. Perhaps it was this that made her not the most lovable, not the one you wanted to be with, though perhaps others would say differently.'

The director shouts. We begin again. The scene goes on.

20

Chiang Ching walks down to Holland Village. The place has changed very much and is dotted with new restaurants offering a variety of cuisine from Japanese to Indian, and the international fast-food chains for those who settle for a quick burger. She walks past these as her stomach revolts against greasy hamburgers and cheap fries, and looks for a coffee shop. Coffee shops have sprung up all over the city. They are clean and posh and offer an extensive range of coffees from all over the world. They have replaced the slowly disappearing *kopi tiams* with their Formica-topped tables and stools, noisy, hot and crowded, but where one could get a good old-fashioned *kopi-O* or *kopi-peng* or *kopi-guni*, and nothing could beat the taste of the coffee beans used, although she concedes that across the border, in Penang, one could get the most fragrant coffee. Because Ching believes that it is only a matter of time before Tang will be freed, she keeps her spirits up.

'Didn't expect to see you here,' Ching cries when she catches sight of Roxanne. 'Come and join me for a coffee.'

'No. I have to run. Lots of errands. Another time,' Roxanne says, and she leaves in the drizzle that has started. Ching waves as she turns. The raindrops blur her form. Roxanne reminds Ching of a furry animal. Warm and natural. Her hair very dark and her skin much tanned from the nature of her occupation. She's also very hairy. Ching, seeing Roxanne's legs, often jokes that she must be an incomplete reincarnation.

Ching

Upon the stage, I walk impatiently. I am angry with Tang. He is so stubborn. I look out the window at an ashen sky. The movement of air is slow and sluggish. A slight drizzle begins. It is not a day for conspiracy, not a day for chanting slogans, yet I seem to hear the patient vans go round, and like an echo, *Merdeka*, can be heard in the air. People gather to listen.

One says, 'Politicians are all liars.'

One says, 'But these are good. The Chairman is good. They are not like the corrupt merchants of freedom you find in many other places. We will be strong. We will be rich. That is what matters. That is how people judge you in this world. We are an example of how a small country can succeed, in spite of so many factors.'

One says, 'You are joking. In thirty years we will lose our freedom. We will have lost our true natures. In thirty years, we will be the clones manufactured by the Chairman. That is his plan. That is the plan of all the politicians. Oh yes, the world will praise him. What a ruler! Yes, he will succeed in bringing down the glass over the city.'

21

Ching

Darkness on the stage. I rush into the wings to change my robes for the next scene.

I think, *The city is changing.*

When the lights come on, we will see in small incipient movements the way a caterpillar moults, crinkling its back, before emerging with flight, this city, the 'I' land. Island. The selfish ego. The consciousness of being alone. Surviving. The faint sounds of the loudspeakers can still be heard, across a heavy sky, the storm lizards are scuttling. At night the small sounds are magnified over and above the hum of the city's traffic.

Silence and a shadow. I see a man walking down a deserted side street off South Bridge Road, in the vicinity of which are small provision shops, now closed for business. He passes a streetlight; under the glare, he could be Tang. He is about the same height. But then, in that brief moment under the light, the features illumined could be those of any man. That narrow face, the eyes cast down. Some ten metres down the street, the man pauses. He sniffs the air, then ducks into the shadowed doorway of a Chinese herbal shop. Another man comes quickly down the street, his shoes softly treading. On cue. He too slips into the shadows. The two men talk in low voices.

'What news?'

'Comrades X and Y are dead. Their car blew up. The bomb went off in the boot.'

The listener swears under his breath. 'What happened?'

'No, not foul play. They think the bomb was faulty. Comrade X made it.'

The second man raps out, 'We can't think about what has gone wrong. These are crucial times. They have arrested someone else today.' He lowers his voice further as he whispers

the new detainee's name. 'He was arrested for a tombstone …
kept it in his garden, the fool!'

'What was wrong?'

'Wrong? Only that it has a saying of Chairman Mao's
inscribed on it, and sings the praises of the man's dead brother,
a revolutionary. He told them his brother's ashes were in an
urn buried in the garden … sole remaining relative … not the
thing to say.'

'Where have they taken him?'

'Whitley Detention Centre,' the second man responds
gloomily.

'Will they charge him?' the first man asks cautiously.

'I think they are accusing him of instigating subversion.'

The first man looks thoughtful. 'Sounds like a sentimental
fool,' he says.

'Well,' says the second man, 'what can we do, but get on with
our work?'

'They are making a mistake. It doesn't do to arouse people's
sympathies.'

'Really!' says the second man, contemptuously. 'You know
very little about the people. You get to know which side your
bread's buttered, and besides there is very little information
you can get from the media.'

'What happens now?' the first man asks.

They begin whispering.

I wonder who these people are who come and go, enter and
exit. Why do I see them? There and there! They walk onto the
stage, they play their parts, and leave. They do not give their
names and their histories. They are floating beings, ghosts
wafting by as air. Are they part of my play? I begin to see them
around the time I first see the mirror woman. I do not know if
they are in league. They are not mirror creatures. They act like
conspirators. They are furtive in the way they look and talk.

They talk like communists. Have they been written into the script? Is this the director's doing?

The scene shifts. A man runs on hastily. His hair is plastered down. He wears a tie. He walks into the Public Entertainment Office in the Ministry of the Arts.

'I want to apply for a permit to hold a public event,' he says.

'For what?' the man behind the counter queries suspiciously. He does not like the looks of the customer. He cannot tell why. Perhaps the customer is a little too correct. His senses are alerted.

'It's for an opening ceremony. New party headquarters.'

'What party?'

'Look, man, what does it matter? I'm only asking for a permit just to be on the safe side, don't even need to.'

'What party?'

The man's belligerence subsides. He seems to shrink. He tells him.

'Sorry, no.'

'What? But we are legal.'

'No.'

'This is discrimination,' the man cries in injured tones.

'Write a letter of complaint,' the man behind the counter says. He looks away. The customer mutters and walks out.

'They're making it harder for us.'

'Every little murmur is taken as dissent,' the second voice sounds disgusted.

'What can we do? They're calling us traitors.'

22

Ching

Traitors. Each of us carries within a small treacherous creature that rebels against all that we would strive for. That is the treachery involved. That is where deceit lies. For all of Tang's good intentions, his beliefs, his values, deep inside himself is his traitor. They know that. They know that inside each of us is someone who wants comfort and security. I think Tang did not realise what he had involved himself in. He was naive. His innocence would lead to his coming to a place few of us want to be, the place where we are tested for our ideals.

This is a story that cannot be written about, they will say. I remember the numerous times I have asked, 'What is this? What happened? Who said it? Why?' And the responses I get are sealed-up faces or, 'There's nothing much to say. It is better not to know.'

These are the nameless things in my world. Like walking down a familiar street and asking, 'What is that tree's name?' And not knowing. Or passing hastily erected flats in a place that was once a mud swamp. Watching your neighbours, all huddled together and never speaking with them. And there, once where only the *pasar malams* presided, are the shopping centres offering Made in Paris, or Italy or Hong Kong. My city has sprung up almost magically. Nothing has remained the same. I have known the transience of what appears solid. Some things are better forgotten, they tell me.

It is like this with those who have lived through the world war. 'Nothing much happened,' they say.

'Nothing?'

'Only grandma died.'

I have often wondered at the amnesiac state of my city's people. Do they forget? Or does the past cease to exist, once it is past?

23

Ching

The walls of my room face each other. Walls. Walls blank and white, without expression, they crowd in aggressively. Why is it that some people can impose their will and make the world conform to them, and some not? Tang? No, he is a weak man. Yet I begin to think there must be something wrong with a place where we are too afraid to think of opposing a government we elected, which is there, meant to serve us. They have no intrinsic authority beyond that which we have invested in them, yet they have outgrown whatever function we gave them, and now they have the ultimate power and we only submit to what they tell us. It is a Frankenstein's monster we have created. A nightmare of the mind. Sometimes we are afraid even to hear ourselves think.

So here I stand at the entrance to the restaurant, enacting my betrayal of Tang, no Judas flower in hand, only a stalk of a lily, its wide white spathe like a signal of the undertaker who comes for the body, too late. It is evening and the stars' cold silence is falling onto deaf streets, where I wait for my cue from the director, obeying his command as though he were God, and I unable to move out of this script.

I play Madame Mao.

He will not let me forget my role. The lives of scholars and artists lie ruined in my hands.

I am no doll, as they will see.

24

The disembodied voice at the other end of the line is hair-raising. The voice sputters like a backfiring car, but Tang can make out the name of the place. The time. He glances at the kitchen clock, which is always a little fast, and decides that if he takes ten minutes to dress, he will be there at the appointed hour. He does not stop to speculate about the owner of the voice. He guesses it will be part of the whole mad conspiracy in which he has entangled himself. It may be the voice of a comrade or a Red Guard. It could be the voice of the director who is prone to screaming.

The restaurant is called The China Den. A strange place, it is rarely opened for business, and all he can see is a dark interior with half-drawn blinds. Perhaps once in a long while there will be light, and tables laid, and he will witness the movement of guests. On this occasion, he peers through the windows at the dressed-up crowd inside. He suspects that they are not ordinary people who have walked in for a meal, but invited guests.

It is just a front, he thinks. This chapel interior turned into a restaurant done up in pink, with aquariums lining the walls, and a long mirror where he sees his own solemn face and the tight smiles of the dinner-jacketed crowd, all shining and polished, in designer wear. The women's faces are well made up in light, discreet and expensive cosmetics, their looks enhanced by money.

Entering, he is ushered by a waiter to his seat at a table for two, given a menu, and left to decide. His eyes flick over the choice. He will have a fish dinner. He closes the menu, stares at his thin face in the mirror, observes the other customers. He counts them under his breath … fifteen in the room, excluding the proprietor, a busy little man in a smart tie, and the numerous waiters.

'What can I get for you, sir?' The waiter has popped up beside his table like a jack-in-the-box.

'Would you like the tea-and-camphor smoked duck, sliced and served between thin bean curd crusts? It's very good. The Yunan honey-glazed ham? Minced pigeon broth steamed in a bamboo tube for starters?'

'Just a fish, I think,' says Tang. 'How about a garoupa, steamed? And white rice.'

The waiter writes it down in his notebook. 'Will that be all, sir?'

'And a wine. I think the house wine would do. Just a glass.'

At least fifteen people in the room who are busy eating or talking and waiting for their meals. Fifteen or so in a smartly dressed crowd, out of which sparkle glistening bracelets, and the shine of polished shoes.

The tables are laid with yellow chrysanthemums in silver vases, with their pervasive sweet death smell, and embroidered tablemats with lace trimmings. Silver cutlery and glass bowls with lighted candles in their maws frame the picture. White ceramic plates with gold edging nestle between fork and knife … for whom are they laid? Can it be a front for criminal activities?

The scholar observes the other customers in the long mirror. He has the feeling that while he watches he is being watched. Possibly by the glassy-eyed garoupas swimming their bored rounds.

He has the feeling that he is in a large fish bowl. A sense of closure. Of a world seen vaguely. The other customers, though each an individual, somehow merge into indistinctness. If he looked at each in turn, their etiolated features seemed to bear a similarity.

The waiter leaves with his order. He takes the menu with him. The chef will catch the dinner fresh from the tank.

Tang watches the origami parrots and porcelain lanterns dangling over his table from iron hooks in the ceiling, swaying crazily in the gust of air conditioning.

Tonight, the lights are blazing in the restaurant and waiters walk swiftly carrying trays of aromatic food and ice buckets to chill wine.

The scholar sips his wine, and wonders why he feels as though a ghost has passed over his grave. There is nothing wrong with these people, only with me, he decides. I am feverish and should see the doctor.

He waits with growing impatience, popping pieces of cucumber pickle into his mouth with his chopsticks. At the next table, a portly man is bent in earnest conversation with a young girl in black. She glances across at Tang, and he is surprised at her look of pale despair. Her mouth is slashed with black. Her three eyes blink at him. With a shock he notices for the first time that she has eyes in her slim hands, which she is using to pick up a wineglass. He looks again. The eyes have vanished. She does not look at Tang again, but smiles at her companion. Uncertainly, he looks beyond her towards the entrance where a new arrival is standing. Chiang Ching is in a fuchsia evening dress, her black hair gleaming, looking softly beautiful. In her left hand she carries a single stalk of an arum lily. She steadies herself and enters the restaurant.

Tang's heart leaps. He is about to get up when she is greeted by the proprietor himself, who recognises her as the woman who plays Madame Mao up on Fort Canning Hill.

The proprietor, who has hurried to her side, welcomes her, 'Table for one?' He leads her to a table where all the other customers may see her, clicks his fingers, signals to a waiter to attend.

'Please don't hesitate to ask for anything special you may wish to order,' he says, graciously. He turns to the waiter who has appeared and yanks his ear towards his mouth, whispering fiercely. Then he bows and returns to his duties. The waiter, rubbing the side of his head, stays to take her order.

The actress places her order and dismisses him without another glance. She, like the scholar before her, looks around the room. No flicker of recognition in her eyes when Tang, half-risen, catches her attention. Tang pauses. Then sits again with a bump. A certain anger passes through him. *Does she ignore me because she is ashamed or afraid, because I am under suspicion all the time, and government spies are everywhere?* He cannot make her out. Their eyes meet, linger and turn away politely. This time the actress has a role, which the director demands from her. She is to be the alluring spy who leads the scholar-husband to his death. As such she is aloof, anonymous, and not the woman whom he loves. He cannot be sure what her feelings are towards him at this stage. He knows only that he is to be sacrificed for the sake of her ambition.

The scholar-husband gingerly cuts into the white flesh of the fish swimming in a stock of spring onions, vegetable oil and light soy sauce. He stabs at it with his chopsticks, picks up a piece and eats. A wave of nausea sweeps over him.

What is it worth? he thinks. *What is the meaning of all my ideals? I am a foolish man who might do better writing an academic thesis on freedom and democracy. And does the one necessarily constitute the other? Is freedom such a necessary good? Is it a good or an evil for such as we humans? What demons do we release?*

He sniffs the air: a smell of pungent incense, which grows steadily stronger. Perhaps it is the scent which has crept into the room which makes him drowsy. He has a sensation of being pulled along by undercurrents like a wooden stick in a river.

The actress looks at him and then away. She seems to be smiling to herself. A beautiful woman should not sit by herself, eating alone. It attracts attention, Tang notes. The other customers are on the alert.

Only last night …

'Wait,' says Ching, hushing him. 'Do you hear?'

A song. As he waits silently, his hand lying on her breast, he too hears the notes as if blown in by the wind.

'Yes,' he says at last.

But Ching places one hand softly over his mouth. 'Listen,' she says.

Those who have heard the song find it hard to repeat. It reminds you, they say, trying to make words adequate. Something of what you once were when you were young and which in some part of you realise you have hidden, sometimes hidden so well it is a loss which you do not know is a loss, until you hear the chords of it sung. And then you ask yourself, 'How have I been living?'

That is what listening to it does to the people who hear. It makes them feel their lives as falsehoods. It draws from them something inexplicable, some picture of what they can be.

The fish on his plate lies helplessly exposed. Its sweet white flesh slowly falls away. Then a flash of light seems to shoot straight towards his brain. Such a blinding colour. It brings darkness upon him. He murmurs, 'Have I died?'

A fat man in white calico and a permanent smile. Tang Na Juan finds himself lying on his back within a wooden coffin. *I am dead.* The horror strikes him as he struggles to sit up. To his surprise he manages.

Looking around he sees that the coffin lies before a large gate with cylindrical tiles atop red lacquered pillars and two large lions guarding the bars. 'This is the gate of thieves,' he murmurs recognising its shape. 'What am I doing here? And am I dead?' he repeats. He steps out of the box and walks over to the gate, which he peers through, but a fog mists his view. 'This is where they hanged the thieves of old,' he mutters to himself and surreptitiously takes a glance around. Nothing but black air and silence. A cricket polishes it wings nearby. He feels the first patter of raindrops.

The scholar finds he is in the wrong script. 'Something's wrong,' mutters the director. In his mind, the director hastily readjusts. The scholar wakes to find himself before the gates of hell. The gatekeeper, a small demon, hastens to his side. 'Greetings,' he says. The scholar is stunned by the change of realities. He recollects himself, stops himself from bowing, and replies, 'Where am I?'

Tang thinks, *There can be no life without death, death without life, they are bound inextricably upon the wheel, which turns eternally. I am taken to a place with bare trees, where the grass is withered, and the wind is a dead silent one. In a clearing stands the Gate of the Demon and my guide, the fat man in white, is the gatekeeper.*

'Hey,' Tang hollers, as the gatekeeper begins to turn away. 'What do you think you are doing with me? Bring me back to the restaurant.'

The gatekeeper pretends to be deaf. He mimes a deaf-mute, raising hands to his ears and turning his small head from side to side in mock bewilderment.

Tang runs to the man. He takes him by the shoulders and shakes him roughly. 'Where am I?' he demands. 'What am I doing here? Under whose instructions?'

The man's head bobs helplessly. He brings his two hands together as if in prayer. He mutters incoherently. Tang takes a step back. He looks around but there is no one else in sight. When the gatekeeper is satisfied that Tang will attempt no more violence, he drops his pose.

In a high-pitched voice, he intones, 'Welcome to the place of your purgatory. Will you change your clothes?' He indicates a pile of white clothes in the coffin which has cushioned the scholar's head, but which he has not observed. Tang hesitates, then boldly strips and puts on the death clothes.

He is travelling through the valleys of death. For seven weeks, the priests are chanting. His wake is being held.

In the restaurant, the actress is telling the proprietor, 'I remember. It was the funeral of my grandfather and everyone was crying or pretending to cry and these big bouquets kept coming in and each time my aunts would get up to look at the prices. There they were comparing the prices, even in death.'

The proprietor bobs his head obsequiously. He always heartily agrees with others. He has found it to be simpler that way, but as to what goes on within his round head, no one can be certain.

'A good funeral,' he says. 'The more wreaths there are, the more it shows how much he was respected in his lifetime.'

Ching responds, 'You have a beautiful place here.' She looks around vaguely.

'Not as good a place as your grandfather may have in his after-life,' murmurs the proprietor politely. He signals unobtrusively to a waiter to fill her glass.

'That is so,' says Ching. 'In his death he is well looked after. We burnt him wads of "other-world" money. As he lay in his coffin, he had a thousand-dollar bill wrapped over his mouth, a paper fan in his left hand, a willow twig in his right – he had the means to buy the goodwill of demons, the instruments to ward them off. We burnt him a beautiful mansion to live in, his favourite cars, all furniture and utensils that he may need. When his soul arrives at its abode, he will dwell in complete luxury.'

Tang has paid the gatekeeper a small fee. The gatekeeper unlocks the gate and indicates that he should walk by himself through it and beyond. He is in a passageway. On the walls of the enclosed high corridor are carvings of entwined fish. The motif continues all the way. The tail of one fish is held in the mouth of the other. Together they form a Möbius strip, twisting in endless motion, without beginning or end, never reaching the other side.

'Death,' says the gatekeeper, who has suddenly appeared by his side, his round face smiling, 'and life are what appear like two sides of a coin, parallel worlds. But they are not. You walk only on one side all through eternity. It is not for you, an ordinary man, to see to the other side.'

Tang feels bemused, 'Who then? The immortals?'

'Only when you are no longer whirling upon the wheel. But come, you will meet your judges.'

'You are absurd,' he says, to cover his anxiety. 'There is no other side. There are three spheres: earth, heaven and hell. Some say seven. Are you talking of alternative universes?'

But his round figure keeps moving swiftly on. Tang follows him, muttering.

Their footsteps resound all the way down that corridor, paved with terracotta bricks, most of which are chipped or broken. Occasionally his foot catches in them and they cause him to stumble. He curses the small round man behind his back.

They reach a large wooden door set into a stone wall. Upon it the gatekeeper raps. *Tock, tock, tock … tock, tock.* It sounds like a code. The door swings open. A strange man who resembles a bird from the waist down stands at the entrance. Behind him Tang glimpses a room with inhabitants, the nature of which he cannot quite see. The bird, upon seeing him, twitters, 'Oh … here he is.'

He does a small two-step back on thin feathered legs. The noise that issued from the room when the door opened has died away. Tang enters and then realises the gatekeeper has noiselessly gone from his side, no doubt to return to his gate.

The room's occupants, he sees with shock, are a succulent pig lying on a sofa and a polished snake with hooded eyes, in the process of uncoiling itself on a cushion. For the next few minutes each creature takes in the presence of the other. He is aware only that if he should speak his voice would reflect his fear.

Skin crackling, the pig moves abruptly, breaking the stillness. It moves to continue eating. Its snout is buried in a bowl of what looks like hot porridge, judging from the amount of rising steam. On a silver fork, which the creature holds cleverly in its front trotter, is a piece of pickled ginger which smells strongly, skewered with a black jellied slice of century-old egg. By the pig's side is a red lacquer tray with a small china pot and a small teacup edged in gold, from which he now and then bends to sip.

After the first few minutes, the pig pays Tang scant attention. Its grotesquely fat body quivers as it swallows.

On the other hand, the snake seems a little too interested in him, Tang thinks. Its wicked eyes are like holes in its sharp triangular face. *I wonder if it can read my thoughts*, Tang wonders with a gasp, as the creature fixes its eyes on him. The bird does a little hop and skip, and prancing back and forwards, is the only creature that seems delighted to see him.

In self-absorbed bliss, the bird salutes Tang, saying, 'You must be pleased.'

'By what?' Tang spits out, rudely he fears.

'By your death.'

'I am not dead,' he gasps.

The pig lifts its snout from the bowl and remarks, 'I hate humans. Nothing good comes out of their lives. They always think that what they do is important. Huh! Nothing matters.' It shakes its great head.

The snake, having studied Tang to his distraction, turns to look at the pig, which has once again become absorbed in its feeding, and says distinctly, 'You are a fat slob.'

That venomous remark goes unnoticed. Tang is startled.

'Do I frighten you?' the snake addresses Tang suddenly, with a quick turn of its head.

'Not at all,' Tang lies.

The bird jabbers to itself.

I do not care, thinks Tang, *if it knows I have lied. I wish only to leave this place.*

They begin to quarrel among themselves. It begins idly with the bird ending its fidgeting with a tantrum, stamping its feet and glaring at the snake, who has apparently offended it in some way. Then the pig joins in.

They do not seem able to settle the matter. Tang is beginning to look for an escape when the bird says, 'Let's take him to the next room.'

The next room, as Tang discovers, is covered with mirrors from floor to ceiling. The bird shuts him in with a mocking admonishment, 'Look at yourself.' When the door of the room has closed, he does not attempt to open it. Instead he gazes in wonder at his many reflections.

The light in the room is very clear, like light at dawn. Soon he sees his reflection begin to take on increasingly repulsive aspects. In one he sees himself as a serpent with a forked tongue sticking out. In another, he is a bull with two heads. Up in the ceiling mirror he is a pig with enormous nostrils flaring and then in another instant he is a raven with tearing claws.

The room has a hundred reflections, a hundred mirrors, and in each of them he sees his self in a different aspect. Yet some part of the reflection remains recognisably his – his eyes buried in the fat blubber of a pig's head, or his smile on a cat, or his fingers instead of a bird's talons, his body joined to a tiger's head. Feeling faint with gazing, he sits upon the floor, his head spinning from the many reflections.

From the room of mirrors he finds he has mysteriously travelled to another, this time a room which is in darkness. As he stands trembling from the gust of cold air that hits him, a list of his possible punishments is read aloud by voices that boom inside his head.

The wild voice intones: Twelve hundred years ago, *The Book of Ancient Mirrors* recorded that a man's soul must travel through seven courts of justice. He must stand accused of all possible crimes.

'Crimes?' Tang cries aloud. 'What have I done?'

Voice of a Red Guard: Do you, Tang Na Juan, believe you are fit to escape the punishments?

'But first …' says Tang. 'Let me know what I have done.'

The voice continues: Have you broken promises?

Have you tortured animals?

Cheated a friend?

Murdered someone?

Lied to someone?

Stolen?

Blasphemed against the Chairman?

'Wait,' says Tang. 'You do not give me time ...'

The Red Guards all together chorus: Eaten too much?

Gossiped maliciously?

Have you been rude to your elders?

Rebelled without a cause?

Were you cruel to those more unfortunate than yourself?

Are you a traitor?

'Who can be innocent?' Tang cries out, exhausted.

As each possible crime is read, he feels a jab in his ribs with what feels like a bamboo spike. Upon finishing, his body is bruised and aching. He is in no mood to answer any more questions. He is then forced by invisible hands to kneel on a platform of iron nails. A rope winds around his wrists, which are pulled to his back. An iron screw is applied to his feet. Someone turns it.

He screams, 'I have confessed to nothing. I am innocent.'

His left then his right cheek are slapped. A knife is held to his lips, the sharpness of it stings as it is drawn tenderly downwards, his lips are split apart. They pull him to his feet when his knees are a bleeding pulp. They haul him to a mechanism across which he is laid and bound. It is a wheel. Before he blacks out, he feels the wheel begin to turn.

In his nauseated state, he is aware of a face bending over him. A light has been turned on, though he cannot be sure if he is dreaming. It is the face of the man whom he will come to recognise later as the Captain of the Red Guards. One of those bit-too-nice faces that may come with being handsome. He could almost be Mr Nice Guy, he could almost look innocent, if not for that bit of suaveness, of knowing his own charm. His skin glistens in the light like fish scales. It shines. His eyes are hooded, heavy. He licks his lips in a reptilian movement.

'Do you know how I maintain discipline in my home?' the Captain says suddenly. 'Do you? I feed the children spoonfuls of my saliva. Say what you like, it keeps them obedient to my will. None of them has ever answered me back. Hmm? Children should try to please their parents, to win their approval and love, don't you think? That's what's wrong with the world today, that's why there is such a rise in juvenile crime. We are too lax.'

The Chairman's right-hand man seems to bear a grudge against the idiocy of the rest of humankind. He is certain he is right, that he is brilliant and that everyone else is too stupid to realise it. From his wife at home, subdued under the load of children and housework, he expects respect. He keeps her in order.

'When a hen begins to crow at dawn, it means disaster upon the nation,' he fondly quotes to her. 'Women are ignorant creatures,' he says.

He is lord and master as far as his narrow sphere of influence goes. Beyond that, he hesitates to move, just in case it should be otherwise. He dislikes loud women. He cannot understand the Chairman's taste for a certain such woman.

Tang in his confusion is certain he is the most evil man he has ever set eyes upon. He feels his fear of the man as something irrational, which he cannot quite explain. He struggles to reach a more conscious state, as though restrained by a dream. In this state he hears the voice of the director seeming to say something.

'The bill, sir,' says a voice.

Tang looks up unsteadily. He becomes aware of the waiter standing attentively to one side. He looks at the bill, neat in a leather folder. The amount registers in his mind. Reaching into his pocket for his wallet, Tang automatically counts out the relevant notes.

He looks up again at the waiter, but the face reveals just a young man doing a job. Tang drops the money onto the bill.

'Thank you, sir. I'll bring you the change.'

The next few minutes of waiting do nothing for Tang's befuddled state of mind. When the waiter returns, he removes the notes but leaves the coins as a tip. He pockets the bill without looking at it again. The waiter wishes him goodnight. Stepping out of the glass doors, he suddenly realises that he has not seen Ching at her table. She is no longer in the restaurant.

The taxi rolls up and as he sinks gratefully into the back seat, the thought that was hovering in the back of his mind comes to him, *The waiter returned me twenty-two dollars and eighty cents, which is two-fifty short. Cheat!*

He remembers the director, *I wonder what he was trying to say?*

25

Ching

Before every entrance is a back door, as everyone in the city knows. The back door possesses a strange feature. It will only open with the presentation of a red packet. With money inside. Furthermore, at this back door stands a doorkeeper, a short fat man dressed in a green jacket with gold buttons, sleepy-eyed and suspicious. If anyone tries to slip in, he is quick to stop the impecunious intruder. Just a short fat man with the rounded belly of a Buddha and the beatific look of one.

Such a man seems to say to bystanders, 'All are welcome,' but this is deceptive, as I am to find out when I approach.

'Good morning.' I smile in my most charming manner. 'I would like to see the Captain of the Red Guards on urgent business.'

The fat man looks me up and down, dismissively. 'I'm sorry, madam, but he's not in.' Meaning that he is not in for me. I certainly saw him enter the front doors of the building not long ago. Snapping open the clasps of my black handbag, I withdraw a red packet of money. Silently, I hand it over. The doorkeeper takes it with both hands.

'Thank you,' he says politely, 'but he is still not in.'

My face shows consternation. I swear under my breath. The bastard. Surely with the red packet in hand … what else am I to say and do?

While I muse, a group of people has clustered behind me. I turn as I sense their presence.

The man I wish to see keeps a Dobermann. Prejudice, certainly, but Tang has long held the view that people who owned Dobermanns must have natures very much like theirs. An ugly, unfriendly dog that is apt to bite even its owner. The Captain keeps the dog on a leash for most of the day, releasing it only at night to roam the garden. The dog has bitten several would-be assassins and burglars.

As with his dog, so his method with his children, whom he keeps under his control, though they are now grown. When babies, they were fed with spoonfuls of his saliva, along with their mother's milk. He believed that taking his saliva like medicine instilled obedience – to him. He discriminated between his female and male babies, according the male babies special treatment, such as stripping them naked and posing them with a bottle of champagne and a lighted cigar for snapshots.

He has little respect for females. His wife is secondary, serving him in the background. His first wife became hysterical and ran away from him to her family home. He brought her back, claiming to her family that she was unpredictable. Her family was intimidated by his wealth and position and furthermore, did not place much value on girls, so they let her return, telling her it was her duty. A month later, he had her sent to a mental institution, divorced her, and took his young secretary as his present wife. Such is the man I hope to see.

'Well-wishes to you. We want to see the man who is in charge of this place. The Captain. We will make it worth your while.'

The tall lady speaking behind me has a grating voice. I shiver.

I feel certain: they are mirror people. The woman is surely the one in my dream, who stepped from the chauffeur-driven Mercedes-Benz. Her bearing denotes a dignity far above the ordinary.

This time she is dressed simply in a white halter-neck. Like yet unlike any model I have ever seen in the pages of a magazine. She is too beautiful to be a model, lacking the mechanical proportions and shallow confident beauty. Instead her beauty seems to soar from her soul, enveloping her in a radiance and cold glory.

The mirror woman places a slim hand on the arm of the doorkeeper.

'If I do not see the Captain I will kill you,' she announces calmly. The unexpected threat does not perturb the doorkeeper. He has heard such threats before.

'Lady,' he says, 'do you think me helpless? I have eaten more bitterness than you.' His hand slides to his revolver at his side.

She stops him with a slight gesture of contempt. The doorkeeper turns pale. Staring at her like he has seen something unpleasant, he falls to the ground in a cringing mess. He wails, 'I did not know.'

The mirror people carry the obstinate doorkeeper by his armpits. He struggles feebly between them like a giant fish they have hooked. They take him to where the sluggish river flows and there they drop him in.

They do not wait to see if he floats or sinks, but return at once to the door of the building, which houses the office of the Captain.

The leader of the group, the mirror woman, sweeps into the building with her entourage. Before they enter the lift, the receptionist at the front counter catches sight of them. Some strange mistrust or dislike must have gripped her for she calls out to them.

'Eh,' the receptionist says brusquely. 'Who you want to see?'

The mirror woman glances at her, shrugs and continues into the lift. The receptionist picks up the phone and calls the security guard to stop the party. Unfortunately, the man is nowhere to be found. So she gives up and decides to wait for their return, when she can give them a piece of her mind. Strangely enough, in the next few minutes, she forgets them.

I walk in the wake of the mirror people. What do the mirror people want from the Captain? Standing in the glass-vaulted lobby, I feel somewhat lost. Sunlight drenches the room. The people walking in and out busily have a sense of purpose, while I am astray like a fish out of water. I do not know on which floor or which room the Captain is in.

I approach the reception desk where a young woman sits

reading a magazine and running her fingers through her hair. She looks up at me. 'Do you have an appointment?'

'No, but I am on urgent business.'

'That's what you all think.' Then, suddenly recalling, adds, 'A group went up, and though I have rung up the Captain's secretary, there is no reply. You can't go up there as well, you'll have to make an appointment.'

I feel flustered from my morning's effort. I have been brushed aside as of no consequence, while the mirror woman has pushed her way through.

I turn away, then decide to take the fire escape stairs up to the fifth floor. The fifth? Who is it that has told me the floor the Captain is on? Surely not the receptionist. How then do I know? Yet irresistibly, I am pulled up the stairs.

The door to the Captain's office is ajar. I hear strange sounds as I near. I enter cautiously. On the floor, I see the mirror woman squatting by the Captain's fallen body. She raises her sleek head, I clutch the door handle, the light sways.

The Captain, working hard on papers at his desk, looks up as she intrudes. 'What …? I'm sorry, do we have an appointment?'

His hand goes to the telephone. The mirror woman smiles at him in what he imagines is a seductive manner. The Captain thinks wistfully, *All women appreciate me, except my wife.*

She steps up close. 'No one is ever ready to meet us,' she says, simply.

He takes a harder look at her, then stands. His 180-centimetre height and broad chest are intimidating. He makes a movement towards her.

In one rapid twist of her hand, she reaches to his shirt front and has driven her slim hand inwards through the weave of the fabric, under his beating skin. When she swiftly withdraws her hand, a gaping hole appears. The Captain crumples. In her hand is a slimy mass of bloody organs. Blood drips from the chunk in her hand and stains the carpet at her feet.

Through the high glass windows of the Captain's office the mirror woman can see the sky, she can see the little people scuttling at the feet of buildings paying homage to the great god, urbanisation.

The man who has fallen against her, sliding to rest at her feet, is still warm. She licks her lips with a delicate tongue.

The mirror woman gazes at me. I am unable to remove my hand from the rattling handle. With some effort I let it go.

There is an electric stillness in our mutual gaze. A slight wind runs up and down my arm. The mirror woman turns to her victim coldly and swallows what is dangling from her lips. She makes a sucking sound. The Captain's mutilated body lies on the carpet.

Saliva collects in my mouth, I am too ill to swallow. The mirror people smack their lips. One of them bares his teeth, for one moment his sharp teeth look like little picks. My heart leaps. I imagine a strange desire in their eyes as they look at me.

But I am mistaken. My presence does not perturb them. Finishing her feast, the mirror woman rises. She wipes her mouth on a handkerchief, which she takes from her dress pocket. I see her dabbing her lips with that square of fabric and the gesture passes as ordinary. They all go outside, leaving me alone with the body. As they pass, I catch a whiff of something like decaying fish. The stench! I breathe deeply and fight off nausea. Left alone with the body before me making a statement, I shut my eyes, back out of the room and hang onto the wall. Then I make a dash down the corridor. The echoes bounce off the walls.

In the newspapers the next morning the Captain's death is detailed. Upon examining the corpse, the police medic noted the loss of internal organs.

The phone rings but I let it go on ringing. I stay in bed and put my head under the quilt. The room is cold as it rains outside.

The rain makes sharp sounds as it hammers at the windowpane. My fingers cramp. I rub them together. My thoughts circle around the thought that during the Chinese Communist Revolution, peasants roamed the countryside killing feudal landlords and eating their entrails. First destroy, then create a new world. No construction without destruction.

When the phone rings again, I get out of bed, stepping on the newspapers.

'Roxanne?'

'Ching? I didn't know if you'd be home. How are you feeling today? I'm just checking that you're all right. No news of Tang? You would have heard, I suppose, about the Captain's death?'

'He deserves his death,' I croak. 'Revenge is sweet. The First Emperor, Chin Shih Huang Ti, ate his murdered enemies, I suppose you know that? The Captain's dead and that can only be good for Tang and the rest.'

'Ah, yes. Yes, oh, OK,' Roxanne speaks soothingly. 'But what are you doing the rest of the day?'

'I don't know.'

'I wish I could come over, but I'm bogged down with work. No rest for the wicked. We'll find a time to meet, OK?'

We finish the conversation and I replace the receiver. *Well*, I think, *so much for the Captain. I will have to find some other means to get to Tang.*

I go back to bed. I must have fallen asleep. For all at once the dead come to me. They whirl about my bed, their bodies so pale they seem transparent. I can see their dangling innards, the bloodless veins. Hollow and rapacious, these ghosts seem intent on surrounding me as though to suck out my life for their want.

Their eyes seem enormous.

When I open my eyes, the sky at my window looks bleached – a strange pale colour. There are slight slimy traces on the bedsheets. Perhaps a scrap of snake skin.

I peer into my mirror, touching my face anxiously. I pat my hair. I dress my face with powder and lipstick till I calm down and recognise it for a dream. I stare at my face in the mirror until it seems a stranger's.

With the Captain of the Red Guards' death, a series of strange killings blossoms: people murdered with their internal organs ripped out. In one reported case, a man was chopped to pieces, cooked in a curry, then dumped in plastic bags into a garbage bin. The dull stink of death fills the city streets.

Death. Death. Death.

Each day brings more and more reports of the dead. Who is dying? Who is killing whom? It is hard to say. More than one battle is fought in the city. Buildings are burned to the ground. The MRT is jammed at many stations. Bus drivers curse at passengers, fist fights follow insults. Many do not turn up for work, many are fired from their jobs. People wander in a daze, not knowing where they are going. Gangs form.

At a Sixth Avenue block of condominiums, Encik Ali, finds himself at the centre of a brawl. A group of thuggish youths have tried to push their way in. They say they want an actress.

'No actress here, *ai*!'

'This is how you will be treated, old man, if you stand in our way.'

'No actress. Go. Go.'

Their laughing faces surround him.

Never very strong, Encik Ali's heart gives a last leap of life, and prematurely expires.

The youths take to their heels.

Down the brown river, shaped like a *kris*, the former doorkeeper floats, his rounded body ever more bloated. He goes downstream like a grotesque statue of Buddha.

Meanwhile the scholar-husband is being interrogated. He is in a cell, his hands holding his head.

'I have told you,' Tang says. 'I know nothing. Nothing. I have never joined any communist organisation. I started the journal out of my own beliefs about what should be done, what needs reforming here. In this country.' His voice is weak, he almost mutters, 'Bloody country,' but stops himself. 'I have never met those people in my life. Most certainly I am not in any organisation with them.'

I am in my living room one day after my futile attempt to meet with the Captain of the Red Guards when the doorbell rings. Crossing the terrazzo floor, I jerk open the front door, and see a young man in the corridor.

'Who is it?' I ask, not recognising him. 'Who do you want?'

'Are you Chiang Ching?' he says. He has a pleasant manner, a lilting voice.

'Yes,' I say, and let down the chain. The door opens a few inches wider. The young man makes no move to enter, he says instead, 'I am here with a message. Will you let me in?'

Bemused, I allow him to enter, as his face is open and amenable. I lead him to a chair and seat myself on my Made in Italy sofa. I lean back upon a cushion and let one slipper dangle from my foot. The young man does not turn his eyes away from mine.

'I come from the Emperor,' he says.

All at once I am filled with a sense of unease. The placid outlines of the room break up, the walls turn wavery. The name of the Emperor recalls to me some deep forgotten memory that I had not realised I possessed. I shake my head impatiently.

'An envoy,' I say, 'from the Emperor! What does the Emperor want?'

'Only to let you know that he is aware of your attempts to reach the Captain of the Red Guards and that he knows of your husband's arrest.'

'What conversation can I have with the Emperor? Why should he bother about my petty affairs? There has been no dialogue between our peoples for a long long time,' I remark, aware that as I speak, I seem to speak with a knowledge of long-ago things.

'We know that,' he says quietly. I glance at his smooth young face. An envoy! A dark young man in an army-green windbreaker, with only his metallic-coloured eyes to give him away and the slight halo of light which gives his head a cucumber shape.

'But what am I to him?' I continue in an agitated voice.

He smiles for the first time, his teeth showing pearly white, though the light in his eyes mocks me. 'You are, as you know, the former lover of the Chairman.'

I am not surprised to hear it from his lips, the words fall naturally as if they had to be said.

'But,' I say, 'if I had any influence with him, surely you know, I would have used it on my husband's behalf – the Emperor mistakes me.'

'The Emperor realises that it was a long time ago. But the past does not disappear as if it were nothing, though human minds barely keep records. He will know you again with our help. You will be helping your husband and yourself.'

'And the Emperor – how does he benefit?'

'He needs you to start the revolution, so the people will turn against the Chairman, and the mirror people will emerge. Then will come the end of the oppression. As for yourself, you will be honoured for your role, through you the city will have its saviour. All the arts will ring with your praises. Plays, stories, poems, novels will be written, speaking of you.'

'You will have the power to free us, to free your husband, and the city. The people labour now under the whip of a relentless man. Justice, have you not thought of justice?'

His words mesmerise me. His eyes, softly glowing, look into mine and see their reflection. Have I not heard their voices? The thin light hesitant notes of a fragile song upon the wind. The opera. The lament of the chorus. In my hands now lies a solution.

I laugh aloud. 'Who are you?'

The envoy says, 'We came when the Chairman called us at

the time of clashes with the colonialists. He appeared to believe in us, then. He spoke our tongue. He wooed us out from the glass. We came. Uncertain. Exultant. We thought our time had come, once again. But the Chairman, he could not be trusted! We were uneasy with him. He baffled us. Somehow we could not enter his mind. He led us but he did not trust us.'

'Can your people be trusted?'

The envoy smiles, 'Perhaps he was wise. Wiser than us, for when he had used us for his purposes, which was to get independence for the city, he drove us back to our world where we have been waiting since. But now, a shift has taken place. The city becomes easier for us to penetrate.'

I think over what he has said. 'So you propose to me – if I take it, I free my husband … how?'

'We will see that he is free, that he is not detained overly long. We will speak with him, persuade him,' the young man says gently.

The idea of rekindling the Chairman's love entrances me. I have no thought for the implications.

'We want,' he says, 'someone who will put the Chairman in a vulnerable position.'

A pause.

I speak boldly, 'I am the best person, you would say.'

'Yes,' he replies, his eyebrows curving upwards in admiration, I feel. I observe how handsome he is, in spite of or perhaps because of those eyes.

I lower my eyelids. 'That is all very well, but what access do I have to the Chairman? And why will he want to see me? I am no spring chicken – I am, how do you say – not as attractive. My worries have given me wrinkles on my brow,' I say, reluctantly.

The young man replies, 'That can be arranged. Also the time and day. There won't be problems.'

I slant my eyes to look at him sideways. 'And if I agree, what will you do for me?'

I manage to emphasise the *you* so it sounds almost personal.

The envoy manages a thin smile. 'We will find ways of persuading the Red Guards to release your husband.'

'Yes, yes, I know,' I say quickly. 'But how can I be sure of this? How can I know that your plans will succeed? Of course I do not doubt your capabilities, but even so …'

The young man shrugs, 'It is up to you.'

I continue to argue, 'But what good will it do me or you and your people for me to seduce him?'

'You will gain access to his confidence,' he says simply. 'You will help to launch the revolution.' He looks at me almost as though he is seeing something beyond or inside of me, something the naked eye cannot see.

I reply archly, glancing at the halo of light above his head, 'You are persuasive. This revolution you speak of, has it anything to do with …'

I pause, and almost add, 'the legend.'

He reads my mind. 'Yes,' he says. 'It will be the time. As you once noted. The breaking of the glass. The recovery of what was once lost to us.'

He adds, after a little pause, 'And to you and the people of the city.'

'If they should want it or wish it back,' I agree.

It seems as if another force is directing my actions. 'Yes,' I say to the envoy, a little amazed at hearing my own voice and words. I wonder why I agree so easily. Almost imperceptibly, my voice takes on the richer operatic tones of an actress. As if in a dream I watch my body shift slightly, subtly, on the sofa.

'Yes,' says the woman playing Madame Mao. 'I will return to the Chairman.'

We look at each other with understanding. The woman feels a strong pull inside herself towards the mirror man. She is excited by his plans.

He is young and attractive. Before more minutes pass, I find my body lying quite still lengthwise, as the mirror man kneels between my thighs. Gasping, I hold him. There arises in me a strange sense of power, the sort of power the Empress Wu Tsetien (AD 684–705) would have felt. What she, at the time the emperor's favourite consort, must have felt when the young crown prince, later Emperor Kao Tsung, pressed against her intimately, the time he emerged from his bath and saw her! What anticipation of future glory!

Gently the envoy prises my legs apart. I run my fingers down his warm muscled back, touching the smooth skin lightly. I contemplate my future.

After he has left, I look at my face in the mirror and scarcely recognise myself. The face of Madame Mao looks back at me, exultantly. My cheeks are flushed with sex. I look young and beautiful. It is as if I have stepped back into my past. Excited by the beauty of my face, more beautiful than I remember it to be, I think triumphantly of my future conquest. *There is no way he will be able to resist me*, I think. A slight tremor of … is it anticipation of revenge?

I am alone with my dreams. I pull on one of my favourite dresses, a midnight blue halter-neck silk that slides to my ankles, smooth the soft folds with my palms, swing my heavy sheath of hair over one shoulder. Then I tire of this game. I go to the window and look out. The evening light has burnt the sky to crimson, the trees and the rooftops burn, the road is illuminated with that peculiar light of the sun before it disappears. Night approaches.

In the night the suns retreat to a watery underworld of the dead, to travel through it till at last they awaken amidst the branches of the fu-sang tree. Like birds, they shake themselves. Their mother, Hsi-ho, tends them, washing their faces, harnessing their fire-eating dragons to the sun-chariot parked atop the mulberry tree of life.

Within the Yellow Springs, which run in the underworld, the light is always clear and bright, luminous, and light and water cannot be easily distinguished. When the ten suns/sons are ready, she packs them into the chariot. From the east they will rise slowly.

'Time,' she calls, 'time.'

And time begins to move, so the sand trickles through the narrow stem of circumstance, and life on earth begins again. The sun-chariot lifts off and the city lights begin to blink as the chariot makes its way to the ruo tree in the west. They fly slowly in the initial stage, then rapidly as they near the apex of heaven. The city people looking up see them as ravens crossing a brilliant sky.

'The sun-ravens are crossing,' the old men in their rattan chairs waiting along corridors to greet the morning will say.

There is a third tree, the jian tree, that connects heaven to earth. Down its trunk the spirits descend to the city, as Jack the Giant-killer clambers down in the fairytale after stealing gold. Down this tree Hsi-ho comes. Leaving her sons to fly onwards without her.

She finds me waiting.

All last night I have lain in bed filled with a sense of foreboding. It is as if a path has been laid for me.

'I have only to tread it,' I whisper to myself, 'so courage.'

This afternoon, with the sun at its brightest outside my window, I hear the voice of the sun-mother. My body thrills with the sweetness of the light that is shed. My despair vanishes.

'I will go with you,' I say, 'to learn to be a warrior woman. Like Hua Mu Lan,' I add in a whisper, for the amazing feats of this legendary woman who had to ride into battle disguised as a man continues to inspire generations.

'And then ...' I continue slowly, 'the next step.'

I do not speak of the next step, neither does the sun-mother, who looks upon me with great kindness. But in my heart I whisper the deeds of empresses and mother dowagers, and of the one empress in the long Chinese history who actually ascended the male-dominated throne, the Empress Wu Tsetien. There were other women who have ruled, but as the figures behind the thrones whereupon sat their weakling sons. These were the dowager-mothers. The real powers.

But Empress Wu Tse-tien sat herself upon the dragon throne, accepted the mandate of heaven, founded the interregnum Chou Dynasty in the span of the Tang, and ruled for twenty-one years.

Women have little common sense, was what they said of her years later.

A promiscuous demon.

What will they say of me?

Hsi-ho, my benefactress, touches my being with a scintillating glow. I feel the power of the sun flood my entire body to the tips of my fingers. I feel my hair stand on end. I am incandescent. Even individual strands of hair dazzle.

With the sun in me, I feel capable of facing the coming events. This is power ...

I was Helen of Troy. That was the first role I played on the stage. Later on it would be Nora, Nora in Ibsen's *A Doll's House*, the one who stirred women to walk out of the door. I played her part.

But, when I was younger, I had the role of Helen thrust upon me. Helen, the object of men's lust and a pawn in their power struggle. Helen, the victim. I was Helen of Troy in a school play at a time when I was gawky and ugly.

I did not play her role by my choice or the director's choosing. I was only a stagehand, but the beautiful actress playing Helen had taken sick with appendicitis at the last moment, and there was no one else available to change into her costume and appear on the stage, so I was grabbed and shoved on.

It was my first role on stage. A disaster. I was to appear on a sort of rolling platform that was to take me slowly across the length of the stage with Faustus declaiming his lines towards me. But at his first sight of me, the famous lines in his mouth became a mockery.

'Was this the face that launched a thousand ships?' he roared.

The audience tittered, then openly laughed, as he continued his litany. When the rolling platform reached the other end, I jumped off and fled, to the accompaniment of hilarity.

I would face no one for the rest of the day. I refused to return to the set. However, instead of putting me off acting, the incident served to spur me on. I would be an actress and it would be my revenge on all of them. In particular, I resented the director of the play who had allowed me to play the silent part, and allowed the audience to laugh at me. I would constantly be at odds with all my directors, all who sought to manipulate me and tell me what I should do.

They and others like them, these are the fat cats, sitting on their haunches, purring in plump contentment; stroke their backs, yes, down to their tails, see how they arch their spines, how they love this attention, oh yes! That's why they won't give up their places by the burning fireside, that's why they sit on all others, except for those who stroke them nicely and whisper sweet words into their fur-lined ears, oh, you clever puss!

They are the fat cats with money in their pockets and Gucci shoes on their feet, and surely I smell not the stink of felinity but of overpowering *Magic Noir*. They smell of power, those stinking bastards. Of course they have the hand of the Minister of the Arts; they are his pets.

They pretend to rebel. Naughty, naughty puss! Shaking a finger in mock anger, winking an eye. The Minister is a clever man, he knows that he has to keep up appearances – see how we let the arts flourish here! Look, there! See that rebel, how he jeers at me, at the establishment (but oh, no, never mention politics – dirty word, much worse that anything distinctly sexual – we can let them have sex, but keep off the topics that concern us). No politics! Are you qualified to give an opinion?

Ah, you see. Why do you complain?

But politics is the substance of life of every person, whether they are aware of it or not. It is what shapes us, there go I because of what this god decrees.

But what can I do?

The Emperor? The mirror city. A childhood fantasy. A dream dimly heard upon the lips of the old. Their alphabet traverses the parallel lines the city imposes, the strict constructs of a building plan, a road over there, a waterway. And the city is growing. Up and up, the buildings rise.

In the watery underworld, the mirror creatures watch and bide their time. Their words travel vertically instead of horizontally. The eye is led up and down the page, from right to left. They begin where others end; they work backwards, so they face the past.

Inside their language are large gaps, spaces within lines, sometimes a dot hangs in suspended air. Yet one dot, one line, one empty space has individual significance.

The mirror people are not easy to comprehend. Their thinking is different. They think in spaces. In their past a philosopher once remarked upon the significance of emptiness. It was something the mirror people could understand. It was said the hub in a wheel, which contains nothingness, is the essence of the wheel. Without the hub, the wheel is useless. Without the emptiness in the wall there would be no window. Upon emptiness therefore, upon stillness, the centre, the spaces, the mirror people built their world.

It is a world where it is not so easy to recognise power: power is bending in the wind like a reed, like a t'ai chi movement, softness not aggression; power lies in the feminine. This is not to say that the mirror people do not have a grasp of worldly power, or that they lack ambition. Those who have observed them know otherwise. Now, too, with years of imprisonment, they have hardened. They change as we in the city have changed. In their eyes I have seen the changes. Their eyes are cool and indifferent. They clamour for their freedom.

26

Ching

'What can you do for me?' I ask the Emperor.
'It is not for a woman to make history,' replies the ruler of the mirror city.
'In other words, you are telling me to stay home, do nothing?'
'That would be wiser. Where are your children?'
'They died.'
'Indeed?'
'They were aborted.'

I squat on the banks of the river. The tides wash up the great stage, darkly lapping at the edge of the light. I ask myself what it is that I seek. Kapila? What oracle can I hope to find when around me the signs of construction have erased the presences? Somewhere, is there a gate to the mirror world?

Am I to live with my regrets? If I can see the dead, what questions I shall ask them! Do our loved ones remain with us? Is there forgiveness from the dead?

The patient waves run hissing, in eternal acrimony with the stone, the fluid ablation with time. Washed upon the shore, the brown husks of coconuts, thick tangled skeins like a woman's pubic hair, which the seafarers, lifting muscular brown arms to pick up large knives, hack open. The tops fly off. Inside, the translucent liquid glistens.

Drink deeply. Taste the land. Bite the thick flesh.

This is where all stories germinate, inside woman's genitals. The land heaves in labour. Let the cycle begin again.

The blood is pulled back and forth by the moon-goddess.

Remember the Empress Chang-Er, who drinks the potion of immortality, flies to the moon, saving her people from the everlasting reign of a tyrant. Who says a woman cannot sit on the dragon throne? Who says there are no heroines?

'I wish to know about the Emperor,' I say aloud to the whispering waters.

Then upon the wind comes her voice: the storyteller!

In the Dream Water Calendar of Time the world ends when the last god dies. Gods are dying all the time because of the formalism of ritual which accompanies their worship. Sincerity of heart and intent is missing. The temple is a hollow place. To keep the gods alive requires a great deal of sacrifice on the part of the adherents. The faithful have to offer incense daily and pray many times. So the gods will die because no one is willing to devote so much time to them.

In the mirror city, the Emperor cares nothing for gods because he is semi-divine himself and possesses supernatural powers. He has no use for gods, dismissing them as ancient superstition. The Emperor keeps a Pekinese.

In my mind I hear echoes of greatness of an imperial time. Long live the Emperor! Long live! The ruler of the mirror city.

The ruler of the mirror city is a creature small in stature, strangely deformed. He appears at once grotesquely ugly and startlingly beautiful. His eyes are eyes of no known living creature, their colour is that of a kaleidoscope, shifting in its lights and intensities. It is near to impossible to stare down the Emperor, if anyone dares try. His people cast their eyes down before him. They bend with their head to the ground, knocking it three times. His appetite for power is boundless. He believes completely in himself, he is the ruler, and the city exists only for him. He is glorious.

On the night after the envoy's visit, I open my eyes to find myself within the mirror city and confronting a huge pair of stone lions at the entrance to a garden. I did not need to be told where I was. The mirror city is like a forgotten memory. Without invitation, I walk through. The earth is soft. A wet burst of dew brushes my cheeks upon the wind, carrying with it the fragrance of roses and jasmine.

I am startled out of my meditation to see a serving maid in soft embroidered robes bent over a small fallen figure. The maid, a young woman, is in the act of covering the figure with a thin blanket. She looks up at my approach. She has limpid eyes. Her innocence and youth touch me strangely. Such a girl I must have been once! She does not seem afraid.

'He fell down here,' she says in a soft sweet voice. 'I went to my room and got the blanket.'

I peer at the figure's face and recognise … the Emperor! The maid speaks without a trace of servility in her voice. She seems to regard me as her equal.

I catch a whiff of brandy on the breath of the fallen Emperor.

'I came to meet him,' I say, sharply.

The maid says, 'You can wait inside. I will ask the gardener to bring the Emperor in. Can you wait?'

'I will wait.'

The maid gets off her knees and leads me into the Emperor's palace.

I can hear the maid's voice. 'In the garden. Maybe it was too strong. Drinking … collapsed.'

The gardener walks into the palace bearing the unconscious Emperor in his arms. The Emperor looks ridiculously small in the man's brawny arms. The Emperor's personal attendant appears and hurries to help.

There is some commotion in the palace as maids run to and fro. I laugh quietly. A drunken emperor. Is this the all-powerful figure of legend?

I amuse myself with watching those around. Where I sit is an ante-room to the inner chambers. The walls and columns seem to be made of yellowed agate. I have a feeling of being under the sea from a porousness in the environment, the way the light seeps in from nowhere. The vaulted ceiling is high, arching upwards into shadows, too high for my eyes to see. I turn my head quickly as a young woman walks past, her bare feet padding softly, a young woman with a strange face bearing a resemblance to a fox. The woman glances back and shows long teeth in a smile.

'You may see the Emperor now,' says a guard to me. The fox woman disappears down the corridor. I pat my hair and apply fresh make-up. The guard stands by patiently.

Upon entering the room the Emperor uses to see his guests, I am surprised by the frugality of its decor. The only touch of colour is in a great embroidered piece of cloth, hanging as a backdrop on the wall, telling the story of a Mughal emperor and his favourite consort, his serving maid. The red and blue colours are strong and the stitching exquisite. The story is told in sewn panels.

The Emperor, I see, is now lounging, with open eyes, in a comfortable chair. He studies me for a long moment. His elongated face is a little pale. His eyes are a curious colour, and shaped like pods. When his eyelids fall to cover his keen stare, it is like the dropping of tea leaves. Seeing my interest in the piece of wall embroidery, he remarks, 'It is an interesting tale. Sit.'

His words are softly spoken. He coughs and waves to a serving maid to pour out cups of tea. I sink obediently into a chair and continue to observe his face. He looks up at me. He has a great dome of a forehead. 'The girl,' he begins, without preamble, 'was his lower serving maid, young and beautiful, but he did not notice her. How could he when he had so many young and beautiful girls and women around him? The emperor kept a pair of pigeons, white ones. He had them looked after with great care and assigned them special diets. It was said they were a present to him from a great queen of a faraway country. He named one of the pigeons Baber and the other Akbar.'

'One morning he took them out of their cages and went for a walk. As he was tiring, he saw the young maid and calling her over, instructed her to hold them for him until he returned.

The girl knew, as all the palace did, that should anything happen to the pigeons while they were in her care, the penalty would surely be death. She closed her slim hands around them.'

'When the emperor returned to her, he found her standing where he had left her, but only one pigeon remained. "Where is the other pigeon?" he cried. "Where is little Baber? What have you done?" The girl replied simply, and fearlessly, "It flew away." "And how?" the emperor shouted. "Like this," she said, and opening the hand holding the remaining bird, released it.'

'It was that one simple gesture, so outrageous, that made the emperor fall in love with her.'

I have been listening intently. 'A beautiful story,' I breathe out at last. I take a sip of Dragon Well tea from a little porcelain cup. The taste bites my tongue.

'Yes,' continues the Emperor. 'You see, here she is shown with her hand on his shoulder, standing by his side. Have more tea. And now, will you tell me how you came upon me?'

'I was in the garden,' I say. 'I do not know how. I wanted to see you. To speak with you and then I was in the palace garden. You were lying on the ground. Your serving maid was covering you with her own blanket.'

'Ah,' says the Emperor. 'Yes.'

'A lovely girl,' I say. 'The gardener carried you in. You were … incapacitated.'

The Emperor touches a little silver bell, and a guard appears.

'Have my personal attendant whipped for failing in his duties. Where was he?'

The guard bows and turns to go. The Emperor stops him with a gesture, 'And have the maid and gardener put to death for daring to touch my person.'

The stony-faced guard bows again.

'Oh!'

'Yes,' says the Emperor turning to me politely. 'You are about to speak.'

'Surely …' I exclaim.

144

'They knew the law.'

His eyes meet mine squarely.

'It is inhuman.'

The Emperor says, with a short laugh, 'Humanity cannot be a part of law. The law is all. This is the Emperor's creed.'

When I later tell Roxanne about the Emperor, I add, 'Think of it, how different are the bureaucrats in our city when it comes to regulations? Put someone in a bureaucratic job and you remove every scrap of individual humanity from that person, all you get is a shell, and a lazy stickler for the rules. Who objects then?'

Roxanne looks bemused. 'He is only a legend!'

Her teaspoon clinks against the saucer as she lays it down. I wait for her to take a sip of her tea, which she does after a pause.

I peel a red layer from the slice of *kueh lapis* on my plate, and eat it.

'A legend, certainly,' I scoff. 'What have I learnt from him?'

On 1 October 1949, Mao Tse-tung stood on the balcony of Tian An Men, the Gate of Heavenly Peace, in Peking, the palace from which emperors had ruled China, and announced the birth of a new dynasty: the People's Republic of China.

'Mao not only saw himself as the new emperor, he thought he was greater than the First Emperor of China. A worse tyrant,' Tang had said some time ago, watching me rehearse my part at home.

'History,' cried Tang, 'is in our souls, for better or worse.'

27

The mirror creatures. What do we know about them? Among readers in the city, a book circulates: *The Water Essays*. Written by an ancient traveller from the city to the mirror world. In libraries, this book is classified under Mythology, instead of Travel. The author died shortly after writing the book. In the book he records observations he made on the mirror creatures.

The brush-strokes, watery lines make up the soft, secret writing of the mirror creatures. The mirror creatures' written language goes from back to front, which you read from right to left, and up, down, up, down, instead of across; in every respect, the opposite of alphabetical language. Furthermore, it is in ideograms. The images conceal sense.

Each dot, stroke, gap, alters the meaning of the picture created, for example, 水 means water; 人 means person; 大 means big; 太 is an emphasis on the word which follows, for example 太大 too big or 太太 is madam; 天 means sky.

The mirror is used to define identity, to define *I*, but who superimposes definition upon the other, the mirror creature or I? The mirror creature or my alter ego?

Their organisation is a strictly hierarchical structure. The mirror world has its own strata. At the lowest level, the creatures are almost insentient: they resemble the flatfish that lie in the mud, almost indistinguishable from it, their eyes are on the left sides of their heads, which are flatish. They eat by opening their mouths and letting whatever passes drift in. They are not creatures of much discrimination or choice. But they are valued as they would not be valued in another world. They are valued because every creature in the hierarchy of the mirror world is considered of value to its stratum of being.

What would the mirror world be without its stratification and categories? Each stratum is rigidly defined and each creature stays where it is. Unless they are of the flying fish variety who, for short spurts, believe they are of a higher level, but they are soon brought down by their lack of real character or talent. These vagrant wanderers are tolerated because they soon return to their own defined sphere of existence and the hierarchy is not violently disturbed.

At the next level, the one higher up, you get the common guppies or creatures of their sort, because, of course, the mirror world is not composed solely of the fish creatures but also tigers, dragons and turtles, to name a few. But to keep things easy … we come to the next level. Here we have the killers, the predators of the deep, sharks, etc. At the highest level are the fully sentient beings. These are hard and beautiful creatures that look like humans, but are not.

Here are the four broad categories of mirror creatures. The mirror world, however, is so structured that it has one hundred and six levels of being. I have come across mirror men with gills behind their ears, or sharp claws instead of human nails. Some carry the eyes of a fish with its unblinking sight, some see well in the dark. You would not know them sometimes, if you do not observe them with care. They would pass as humans.

28

These are the streets of the city with the starling flocks of Filipina maids on their days off, cramming pavements. Cold towering concrete. Glassy shop fronts. Neon lights. Clean green wayside trees. Fines for littering ... a virtual parkland, a mini-Disneyland often thronging with harassed pedestrians. Under rain, the city lies glistening. It is like a luminous pearl in an oyster with a hard scalloped shell to prise open. White light bounces from it into the clouds, as though from a giant mirror. The rain is cold and grey. It could be anyone's city. It has no past, no roots, so that one can say, 'This is mine, it belongs to me.'

No one has a memory of the land, at least no one from the current age. Perhaps such remembrances are stored in the land's great chthonic memory. No human creature, except perhaps the Chairman, dares to rewrite its records. Perhaps only the human arrogance of the Chairman surpasses understanding. Yet it is understandable: the need to take possession, to be able to say, 'This is mine.'

Back in the city's past, when the city was not yet a republic, the colonialists governed. Clashes over who owned the land became a movement.

In a city left disordered by the world war, a dispirited populace, many with faces ugly with worry, saw the mirror people as something beautiful and rare. They gave people a glimpse of a magic world, a *fata Morgana* to desert-stricken souls. These were powers that went beyond the rule of all politicians, who fiddled only with the material surfaces of things.

The Chairman was young then and a revolutionary fighting for independence. Day after day, his men drove about in much-weathered vans, blaring their independence messages through portable loudspeakers.

'Give us independence now!'

Small crowds gathered to listen. The people were on the whole apathetic. It did not matter all that much. The people preferred to consult the temple mediums regarding their future. They knew there were potentialities more powerful than any politician. These were the forces to pacify. They are the creatures that exist with us, our mirror selves. The creatures from the watery underworld. The creatures living in the Yellow Springs. Some call them death creatures.

Ching has heard from temple mediums that when the spring at the foot of the fu-sang tree, the entrance to the underworld, is once more bubbling hotly with steam breaking through its surface, it would signal the beginning of the mirror creatures' coming.

People have begun to see them on the streets. They are recognisable because of their extreme natures: some are dazzlingly beautiful, while others cannot be looked upon by pregnant women.

Those who have seen them declare they look just as humans do; others, more percipient, note the glimmering scales on their skins under sunlight, the gills behind the ears, and a whisper of a sabre-toothed tiger in the way they walk.

People begin to dream again. It is a time when ordinary people see visions. Their nights are filled with colour and activities. It is considered good fortune to see one of these creatures.

The Chairman, in his fight for the city's independence from foreign powers, in a time long ago, was sent a dream of victory. The Chairman dreamt of a battleship which was sinking. Men rushed about shouting. A man stumbled to his knees and began the Lord's Prayer. The ship wore the names of his enemies. He saw it go down. He thought, *It is a signal of an end and the beginning of a new era.*

And he awoke refreshed and emboldened. His dream of creating a world would not happen all at once, but it did take place. And because he had the backing of the mirror world, the city prospered and became something to marvel at. All this happened in record time.

But the Chairman thrust aside his memory of the mirror

creatures. 'People forget,' the mirror creatures say. 'But the land does not shake off its past as easily as men do.'

29

Ching

I walk by the river listening to the woeful descant of the tide. I am the river woman, the dragon-mother commanding the little fish to surface. They rise upon their tails, twirling on the water. They pay me my dues. In the river the gleam of the whites of their eyes. The catfish slithers past, its whiskers grinning like the Cheshire Cat. The wash of music is attended by a scuttling hermit crab in search of a hiding place.

The stage swims in the dark. Ripples and lines. I cross the stage with my robe trailing. I am unable to rest. I am tired of thinking, of staying at home being afraid, and of watching my acquaintances slowly drop off.

'Darlin', this is not the way it should be done,' I say sarcastically to a woebegone actress. 'Higher. Higher. Lift your voice.'

I take out my frustrations on the inexperienced ones, make snide remarks to the stars, run rings around Hui, the director, who has been sympathetic, not least because he is attracted to me.

But even to him, I am cutting and quick. 'Why make Madame Mao such a whore? Do you imply that women have no other weight in politics than the sexual cards they play? This is better,' I say, pushing the lines of the rewritten script into his reluctant hands. 'Will you make the changes? Are you afraid? Are you a man?'

I see in his eyes that he begins to feel, with the rest of the cast, like killing me.

As soon as my back is turned, I know the amah talks on the phone, for hours, to her friends. Complaining about me, most likely, I think.

The mirror people have not been idle. A series of strange happenings has occurred. Buildings disappearing. Whole streets vanishing. There are new people, new voices, new faces in the city. There is a new greed. A new hunger.

I brush past a throng of people. Then I pause. A *samfoo*-clad old woman is squatting solitary by her little business: a square cardboard box on which she has spread her diagrams and magic.

'*Ah Po*, I want my palms read,' I say, abruptly sitting down on the stool in front of the palmist. The old woman's wrinkled face is like blueprint for a new world. She looks at me with eyes sharp and bright. She takes my proffered hand and turns it within her own coarse stained one. She strokes the palm she is beginning to read.

I am dimly aware of passing feet on the concrete pavement. Not far off, a crowd gathers where a snake charmer has spread his blanket. The strains of his music reach my ears.

Held by the palmist's bony fingers, I am unable to escape the memory tide which pulls at me, a dream I had the night before of a dead landscape. An upheaval of rock and sand. A dragon's tail flicking through the earth. Red soil parting. A green-gold tail. The scales incandescent as mirrors. I caught a glimpse of my face, multiplied. For one moment. Then the tail swept over the land shattering all buildings in its path.

'Death?' I cry sharply to the fortune-teller. 'Whose?'

The old woman's rheumy eyes blink rapidly. 'Look,' she whispers, 'go over there, stand at that corner. See that broken-down house with the tree growing out of the roof. Go there. You will see. Go, go.' She gives my hand a little push.

I take out my purse and pay the old woman her ten dollars' worth of prescience. I rise to my feet, looking back once at her, but her head is bent over her diagrams. I walk quickly to the corner of the dilapidated three-storeyed Chinatown shophouse she has pointed out.

I stand there, self-consciously, as the passers-by give me curious looks. Some of the men look then look again, wondering if I am for sale, then deciding I am too well dressed. I push my hair from my face and think of leaving.

His voice rings out from the top of a red-tiled roof clearly, in obscenities.

As his body comes flying down.

30

Roxanne

The lights in the auditorium come up. The audience applauds vigorously. The actors take their bows. The curtain closes. The audience begins to disperse and I go backstage to look for Chiang Ching.

'Ching?'

The actors shake their heads. Then one of them says, 'I think I saw her onstage.'

I enter the stage through the wings. Chiang Ching stands facing the almost empty auditorium. The curtains have been drawn aside by stagehands, so that props can be easily moved. From my angle, she looks innocent – there is something childlike in her figure. She must have looked like this on the night of her debut, limpid-eyed like an expectant girl who faces life without qualms and thinks the world her oyster. Then she sees me.

'Roxanne,' she says, approaching. 'Did you enjoy yourself?'

The young girl spell is gone. Her dark eyes stare at me from behind a whitened mask.

'Shall we go for supper?' I say, when I have finished my congratulations.

She replies, 'Some of the cast will be having drinks, but wait for me in the foyer. I'll join you.'

Ching

When Roxanne has left me, I remain on the stage, thinking. Someone has jumped. Whose body did I find smashed on the concrete? My thoughts have been too much with Tang and my anxieties. I stoop and touch my palms to the wood.

Voices laughing. Someone calls out a name. A high current of excitement as is usual after a performance, which won't fizzle out till the energy is worked out in drinking or dancing the rest of the night.

No one seems to notice that I am still on the stage. The stagehands have cleared the props. All around me is empty space, under my feet the stage. I feel entrapped as though I am in a glass jar and invisible to the rest. I trace characters on the stage with my finger. I have scribbled over two hundred pages of my memoir by now. I begin each morning, an hour before breakfast, after I brush my teeth. After the morning meal, which usually consists of porridge and salted fish or pickles, I slip the pages out, and continue. Sometimes I pause to remember. Sometimes I fall into a dream and do not write anything for hours, then days.

A sound startles me. It is my guard with my meal. He sees me sitting on my narrow bed, staring into space. He does not speak to me. Now and then I run out of paper and have to bargain with him to bring me more. He generally does so. They wish to keep me occupied, I believe.

Once he shouted at me, 'Do you eat paper?'

I did not reply, for my body was bulky with the wrapping of the pages. But he brought me more as I had requested. He looked at me curiously as he did.

'Wait here,' I said. 'Let me show you where I keep them.'

I began to pull up my shirt. 'Here,' I said. He rushed at me and knocked me down with his palm open.

I stared up at him, as his face grew red. He cursed me under his breath, and left. I breathe in painfully. I pick myself up, my head throbbing.

I look around me, bewildered. Hui, the director is waving to me, 'Come join us.' I shake my head. Roxanne waits for me in the foyer.

31

Ching

The mirror creatures are among us. As I walk to the foyer, I think I see them lurking in the shadows. When I look into the mirror now, I do not know my face. What strange creature am I? In some way I feel the mirror people hold the key, which I would wrest from them. Without it, I am lost. The days increase and there is no one, nothing for me to hold to. Can I hold onto Tang? He sinks!

One night, I am given a dream.

I dream of a white chapel in the Gothic style. Flying buttresses and steeples. The chapel of my dream resembles the chapel of the convent school I attended as a child. In my dream this chapel is as huge as a cathedral and soft like a cake. Pink and silver balls of sugar dot its main steeple. Inside the chapel people eat and drink as if in a restaurant. They are oblivious to the nature of the building they are in, either as a cake or a chapel. Mirrors on the ceiling show the people in distorted gaiety. The light bounces across sparkling wine bottles and the glittering jewellery around the necks of specious women. A sort of perspective is created whereby I can watch them while they are unaware of me, though I stand in their midst.

They are such beautiful people. The men wear large gold watches. The women have hair that shines and glistens like black sheets, a waterfall of night. Their confidence says Christian Dior or Yves Saint Laurent or Versace.

Before my eyes the image of a city opens up, like a ripple of water in a large pool. It is a city, a glass and steel concoction. Buildings which tower like mountains stacked high with concrete lives, people piled on top of each other, so little space to live in they hang their washing on bamboo poles stuck outside their windows, dripping wetly onto the neighbour's washing one floor down. Their washed linen waves in the humid wind like so many flags.

When the image vanishes, I am again in the chapel. Its sacred walls are draped in cakes of many colours and shapes. I recognise the chapel. It is the St Stephen's with the stained glass windows that the congregation can look through and see heaven. St Stephen's flanked by Victoria Street in front, and North Bridge Road, Stamford Road and Bras Basah Road on the other three sides, emptied now of faithful worshippers. Awaiting demolition. The building, which was built in the last century, languishes as it waits. Funny how buildings draw their lives from the presence of people.

I am lonely in the dream, wandering by myself, wandering outside to catch a breath of fresh air. A chauffeur-driven car draws up to the entrance and a lady steps out. I see at once that it is one of the mirror people. Her skin is glossy, almost luminous. It would be hard to place a name on its colour. Her eyes shine. Her curved lips hint at a smile.

She passes me, brushing against me as if I am of little consequence, and then she has disappeared inside. Her scent hangs in the air. I can still feel the soft silky sensation of her, her light green slip of a dress that flowed about her like water.

The chauffeur stares at me haughtily. I wonder that he can see me.

'Why don't you go?' he sneers. 'You don't belong here.' He turns away before I can reply and climbs into the silver-grey Mercedes-Benz. The car pulls away. I am alone again in the darkness of the night. A few stars make the sky a little less threatening. I think I can make out Osiris's belt. I think I can make out the weaving girl's star.

The city bursts into pneumatic vision in a crack of lightning and a distant rumble across a flat land. The sound comes slithering over the tin roofs in the neighbourhood and sets the palm trees shaking. In the air the filemot residue of a day passes away, a hushed calm suggests a storm. In one of the poverty-stricken shophouses, from an upper-storey casement, a little girl watches as the sky changes colour. As the storm gathers force, the figure of an old woman can be seen carrying a broomstick. Enter Feng Po Po, riding a tiger-shaped cloud, pushing along the hesitating winds. The little girl looking up at the sight bursts out laughing.

Behind the old woman, figures of a more threatening nature can be seen clustering. They mutter. They grumble. Their faces lour. Their voices are coarse. They wear the aspect of a muted conspiracy.

The girl shivers as the first cold winds hit her through the open window. She hastens to close the shutters and presses against the catch to fasten it. The little girl has a wistful face. Outside the patter of fast drops of rain can be heard.

Then I see a cabal of mirror people. They all face in one direction, towards a recess in a rock where a strange being can be seen. A bright sweetish light emanates from the being. The people lift their arms up in the air. They shout in song. An orange appears in each right hand. They lift up the oranges to cover their right eyes. The song continues. A voice booms, 'Stand to the left, all traitors.'

A few people begin to tremble. A man catches sight of me, grips me by my shoulder with his bony fingers. He presses hard.

'Traitor,' he hisses, bringing his pockmarked face close to mine. 'Conspirator and fool!' He drags me with him to the light. The chanting stops. The people as one stare at me. Panic grips me and I start to push people aside. The voices shout. Hands lunge out at me. Laughter breaks out.

'Do you really think you can get away?' a voice nearby says.

I ignore the cold flat voice and carry on running. I am screaming. Then I see a woman, her padded sides like a box, all jutting edges and square figure. She smiles at me in a curiously empty way.

I struggle with her, as she holds me in a tight grip. I kick wildly at her nothingness and start running down a corridor.

And then a room and dolls. Dolls. Dolls clinging to the drapes, hanging on with arms and legs. A doll with straw-coloured plaits dangling by the sides of a flat painted face.

The room is very small, like a doll's house. I am suddenly aware that the people all live in such tiny rooms, like cubicles.

At the passage's end, I find myself in the toilet, balancing over the squatting bowl. I am trying to shit. My shit stays stuck fast to my arse.

There is more screaming outside. I am safe in the toilet, but I am afraid they might break down the door and see me.

I am afraid that the door might vanish and I will be left to the scrutiny of all passing. A desperate sense of the precariousness of my position assails me. I pinch my nostrils. I fart loudly.

'Comrades,' the revolutionary addresses the assembly of the people. 'To deceive the enemy you will have to act as the enemy. Much as we hate these farting dogs who lick the shoes of foreigners, preferring to speak in their language.' Here he pauses and makes a series of sounds which resemble very much the sounds of farting. 'They speak like farting,' he shouts to jeers and whistles. 'Yes, we too have to imitate them. When walking on the streets, carry the English-language newspaper. Speak only as they speak. Comrades A and B, step forward. Demonstrate to your colleagues.'

The hall has a full-blown portrait of Mao Tse-tung looking benevolently down at the assembly. Comrade A, a thin young man with a smooth pale face comes forward. In one hand he is carrying an orange, in the other a copy of *The Straits Times*. He steps onto the platform and takes a seat. He looks into the distance, shakes open his newspaper, after carefully placing the orange beside him. He pretends to read.

'Comrade A is sitting on a park bench,' the relentless voice continues.

Comrade B ascends the platform a few seconds later. He is in a dull grey shirt with a Biro sticking out of its left breast pocket. He approaches Comrade A.

'Excuse me,' he says politely, in as close to farting accents as he can manage. 'Do you have the time?'

'Twenty to twelve,' Comrade A replies. They glance around. 'What is your number?' Comrade A says softly.

'Number thirty-seven,' Comrade B answers.

'Very good,' the first one responds. He pulls out of his pocket the torn half of a bus ticket on which small scribbles make it decidedly a conspirator's note. Comrade B pockets it silently. In his turn he presents the first man with the matching half of the bus ticket. He moves away quickly. After a few moments, with a look around, Comrade A gets up and walks slowly away.

There is loud applause when the two finish their little act. The comrades stamp on the floor. They shout, 'Bravo!' and other farting words. The presenter glides to the front of the platform.

'Good. Very good. Now dear comrades, let us put into practice what we have seen today. But do not be mistaken in the nature of your tasks. You may be asked to perform small tasks but still be careful. Be cautious. Watch for suspicious-looking men slouching about, who could be plain-clothes spies. Today's lesson is over. Please leave.'

The comrades rise as one and bow, chorusing a loud, 'Thank you, teacher.' They file out of the room with clattering feet and silent tongues. They will go on to the next class where they will be taught out of a little red book.

32

Ching

'Ching!' Hui calls and waves as I am heading backstage. He is standing by the stage, giving last minute instructions to the lighting man.

I stop. I do not know what to say to him. We have been more enemies than friends of late. Perhaps he wants to tell me of the party later in the evening. Tonight's our last performance for the season.

'OK, OK, got it. Go break a leg!' the lighting man says, good-humouredly. He adds the last part for my benefit, and gives me a grin.

'Quit flirting, *buaya!*' Hui says to the man's retreating back. He peers at me in a concerned manner. He looks me up and down.

'Why do you look so worried?' I say.

'You OK?' he asks. 'You look kind of strange.'

'I don't know what you mean and does it matter?'

'No, no.' He pats my arm. He is kind and sweating under his armpits. He can't help sweating. It's because he's fat.

'We'll be celebrating. Stay back after the show.'

He breaks into a sudden sweet smile under his moustache. 'We'll drink tea under the moon. How about that? And champagne. We'll all be glad of the break.'

'I'll be glad,' I say.

'Hey, now that it'll soon be over for this year … look, let's shake hands over the past. I really like you, you know that.'

'OK.'

I kiss his cheek, which is shaven and smells of cologne. He goes away looking relieved.

I muse on the different men in my life.

A tea ceremony under the moon. The hill slopes away in darkness, but we spread our rugs close to a lamp-post. There is sufficient light from lamp-posts scattered about Fort Canning Hill for late-night wanderers and lovebirds.

The actors giggle as scandals are unfolded, tea prepared, and champagne made available. Someone strums a guitar. The softly flowing tranquillity of the night ... and the shared values of a nation.

There are five factors to drinking tea:

1. A tranquil setting.
2. The company of two or three persons.
3. High-quality tea: green, oolong, black.
4. Very pure water.
5. Beautiful utensils.

Some would add in a sixth factor: mindfulness.

Someone says, 'Have you heard that new jingle on TV? *This is my country. This is my home.*'

'*Aiya*, all that patriotic stuff.'

'Be glad you live here. No war. No one starving. No army dictatorship.'

Someone begins singing the song with declamations inserted. Some giggle, then subside. I listen along with the others.

A scrap of moonlight
a whiffler of dust
a playground where the ghosts of swings hang crazily
and rising in a monolith: the ten, twenty-storeyed flats
this is 620 square kilometres of land
the size of the city-state.
2.7 million residents
we live like an enormous Dagwood sandwich
with the ingredients piled one on top of the other
and we share the filling
ten floors, twenty of sameness

We watch our neighbours ... Number 41 has a new hi-fi, bloody loud he plays it. Number 27 is always gadding about (it's dark in the flat), and opposite, that window there, that young Ah Mui is always dressing up, latest fashion. There they are sitting, shitting, farting, fucking, talking, walking, eating, watching television, wailing, screaming. Why don't they draw their curtains? How do we meet their eyes in the lift in the mornings? We squint hard, concentrating upon the orange light shifting button to button, up, down, up, down, floor to floor.

Watch that button of light.

We have nothing to say. In the lift's corner someone has piddled. We hold our breaths and tongues till the door opens at ground level, and a gust of fresh air greets us.

Shall we share our lives, our wives or husbands, hear our children yelling, what an aroma of cooking from next door!

'Hey (banging on the wall) can you turn down your bloody hi-fi? Hey! I got my exams coming up.'

'Bloody shitter, can you make less thunder in the bowl, hah?'

'Eh, line the water with toilet paper before you start, then the water won't splash up to your bums when you shit, and I won't hear the plop-plop, OK?'

'Kiss, kiss, so loudly. Do you want everyone to know you're some kind of a slut, miss?'

'Stop crying!'

'Shut up. Shut up!'

'I'll hit you if you talk to me like that!'

'Ouch! Police! Help!'

'I'll kill you!'

'Why don't you turn off the TV set when I tell you to? I'll throw it out!'

'Let's junk it.'

Out goes the television, the kitchen chairs, iron pipes, ironing board, cupboards, dumbbells, bicycle wheels, potted plants, bamboo poles … might as well chuck this … never liked it … my jade statue of Kwan Yin! What need do we have for material possessions?

Out, out … and down … twenty floors below
they may land crooked upon the five-foot way
or on the heads of passers-by
a dog or cat
an old grandmother
a baby's pram …
it was depression
too much television
exam stress
marital problems
careless fingers
temporary insanity

And down the chutes for the garbageman to discover in the mornings: dead babies, mostly female. The babies have taken the long ride down the chute together with the garbage. Down, down, one floor, the next, with the garbage bags of leftovers, empty tins, bottle jars, oh down and down, who knows whose garbage it is? Who knows from which floor the baby comes hurtling down? In a block of anonymous flats all alike, neighbours crammed together, unwilling to listen, to see, there is too much noise, too much vision, it is better to tune out and watch television.

… yes, let's drink to all that
in a little pavilion seated by a lakeful of water lilies
a scrap of moon
a bird's wing
we will talk of pleasant things
of the natural relaxing, spontaneous joy of drinking tea
among friends
Where is death?
It is only in a shadow
the slip of a figure
as thin as light

a whisper in the wind
of those gone from us
we share their pain
sorrowfully

The actors have their eyes closed, and are swaying. For a moment, we feel together. We are a community.

Sometime after the arrests and detention of twenty-two persons by the Internal Security Department, a White Paper is put forward to parliament. It concerned Shared Values.

'Let me tell it to you,' I say, leaning forward, into the charmed circle of tea-drinkers, drunk with song and moonlight.

1. The Chairman before the nation and the nation above the individual.

2. The Party as the fundamental unit of society.

3. Protection and concern for the individual.

4. Agreement instead of rebellion.

5. Full support for the Chairman who is semi-divine.

Any queries? Any complaints?

'I have no complaint,' murmurs an actress, 'only a little question.' She lowers her voice, 'But the Chairman ... is he not already god?'

Tang? I feel your presence with me. I can hear you speak. I see you writing at your desk. I look over your shoulder, and I read. *We tend to see tyranny in the form of an army with guns, but in reality it is more subtle, it begins in the minds of its victims, sometimes even the law makes it right.*

The Chairman is not the popular demagogue I have fleetingly accused him of being, he has not that sort of appeal to the masses. He talks incessantly about rationality and order. He is effective. Such efficiency is ruthless.

He is dangerous.

And right.

No question at all.

The director hums. In the great dome of his mind, he reflects, *If you believe in something enough, you may be sure it will appear in the landscape, at least of your mind.*

The director acknowledges that the city is a child-product of the Chairman's mind. Is it any wonder then that there should be conspirators abounding? *Brother will betray brother to death, and a father his child.* For what cause do they fight? As many as there are. For as many as do exist, there are as many grievances.

It is promised … *a man's enemies will be the members of his own household.*

33

Ching

Out of a nearby pong-pong tree hanging with green fruit, the paradisiacal bird of understanding flutters towards me and over my head. It gives a cry before it vanishes into the blue. I am startled from my reverie. It is a message from the dead. After all, this is August, the month of the dead, the month when the hungry ghosts are released from purgatory to roam the streets of the city in search of home and food. 'Feed me, feed me,' their gaping mouths cry. 'Only when I'm fed will I be content to rest in the grave.'

The old women of the street will be lighting joss sticks under the spreading branches of trees. The women squat and feed cut red paper into a fire, while suffocating ash flies madly.

The air swirls with black smoke. The gates of hell open. The dead walk.

'Nothing to fear,' my mother once said. 'But don't touch them. Don't let them walk through you.'

'What happens then?' I asked. In my mother's eyes, I saw a legion of demons possessing the house of the body.

The dead tramp the streets with steps that are uniform. Their eyes turn neither right nor left and they walk only in straight lines. A peculiar habit, perhaps because they cannot swivel their eyes or necks around. Mother told me that once as a girl she had been followed by a hungry ghost that seemed to think she was a long-lost descendant of his.

'I kept walking, kept looking back, he was coming closer.' She tried walking faster but the ghost kept right behind her, so she ducked around a corner of a building, and the ghost went on straight ahead looking for her in vain.

'They are blind but they know what is ahead.'

'How did you know he was a ghost?'

'See the deadness of their sight. Look at their skins, like chalk. You'll know it's a ghost,' she said.

The dead are dressed as they were when they died. Many of them are those who have died in inauspicious circumstances. They have been drowned at sea or have had a terrible accident or were murdered.

The murdered ghosts are the hardest to appease because they will always want revenge. Their mortal bodies have been abandoned in the roadside bushes or dumped into drains or hidden under the earth – put in makeshift graves without proper burial rites – so they walk in everlasting torment. 'Take me home, take me home,' is that other cry that arises from the ghosts – they want to return to the family burial plot, to ensure proper burial rites, to ensure ancestor worship. Those who find that their families have forgotten about them, moved away and neglected the burial plots, are doomed to roam forever as dissatisfied ghosts. My mother would be such a dissatisfied ghost, I believe, for when she died, and I moved to the city, the villagers paid little heed to the grave's upkeep. My father's side of the family had long disowned her.

I am struck by a sense of oppression. The buildings bow low in obsequious closeness, even the trees seem not to let in the wind. By the roadside, I recognise the ordeal tree with its bark of poison. I let my hand run down its bark. Make a potion, drink it and if you die you are guilty. The tree comes from Africa. If you want to abort a fetus, there are ways of doing so with bits of bark from the roots, so the wisewoman told me.

'Drink.' But the black medicine destroyed my womb forever. 'They were twins,' she said later. Her eyes filled with dark mischief as she stooped and held my swollen belly. I tossed in perspiration and pain as the medicine did its work.

'There, there,' she crooned, her skeletal fingers embracing my flesh.

I threw up violently. As the yellow vomit spilled from my

mouth, I felt like my life right up to that moment was somehow being wiped out.

I would become a new woman after that, for the old one writhing would be gone. Maybe that is why I can think of the self the Chairman once loved as another self, another woman. She was just so much yellowish vomit lying on the blackened wood of the old woman's floor.

My skin prickles with sweat as I wait for the dead to come up the street. I stand safely to the side, holding onto the ordeal tree for safety.

Witches float if they are guilty. 'I am innocent!' Her ghost's eyes are wide, black-lined and swivelling. Her robes flap in the wind. Out of her mouth a screech. I am from a different world, yet our lives are yoked together.

I have always wanted to see the dead and now I am being given the gift to do so. I am on a narrow street on my way to a mansion in Queen Astrid Park. I am going to meet the conspirators. I have been told that they are about to gather under the pretext of having a party. The late afternoon is still sunny, the sky just the right shade of blue, with the clouds taking away most of the heat but not the light. A good day. By the roadside an iguana darts out from the hibiscus bush across the road. It has a fierce little head. I stop. Then it is gone and only a sudden silence replaces the previous tenderness of the road. A worm-eaten silence. A silence that knows secrets. I feel called upon to wait for the next occurrence, which is not long in coming.

Each ghost comes now to me like a faint remembrance of people I have known in the past. The ghosts waft past me like a momentary smell. Sour like rice vinegar. I feel sweat trickle down my brow. I close my eyes.

Onwards. The road signs flash at me as witchlike I fly. The road dips like a thread of light reaching backwards and forwards upon a street that curves and dips and never ends. The milk-white frangipanis throw themselves down from the overhanging branches. I am aware of an increasing sense of unfamiliarity.

These houses suddenly take on an aspect indistinct to my remembrance … a disjunction is created.

The house in Queen Astrid Park sprawls before my eyes. I walk slowly up the driveway. Amidst windmilling palm trees and Christmas firs standing pointedly, there are people in the garden. There can be only one name for them: conspirators. I feel as though time has stopped, for I see my ghosts before me. The drifting in and out people. The nameless ones.

I move up onto the porch, edging past wrought-iron chairs filled with laughing guests. More conspirators are clustered in the living room when I enter. They mill around like softly flowing water, holding sticks of carrots or celery in their hands or glasses of wine or soft drink. They look mild and meek.

My host has a sheep's face and longish hair. Round-rimmed glasses complete his portrait. 'Ahhh,' he says, 'you are Chiang Ching. Yes, let me introduce you to …'

Soon I find myself steered to the buffet table, my hand clutching a plate.

'Help yourself,' says my host, nodding amiably.

I pick up a pair of ice-tongs to heap on my plate the *bee hoon* from an enormous crock standing in the middle of the table.

They look most unlike any rioters or villains. In fact my host looks unexceptionally clerical. He is softly-spoken and his manner unassuming. As the party continues, with balloons being thrown into the air, I begin to feel like I have walked into the wrong room. Such bland and mild faces no one would suspect of harbouring revolutionary fervour. Then I am introduced by the host to a man who, he whispers to me, is the chief conspirator. His name: Chin Peng. He has a childish round face upon which a guileless smile would suit most admirably.

'He is a man to be feared,' remarks my amiable host in my ear, after the introductions, and when the man has turned his attention to the rest of the room.

'Indeed,' I reply, out of my depth.

'A remarkable man. Say what you like,' my host continues,

'but everything is right for the cause. If I have to kill, I will. Whatever is for the cause is good.'

I jump because he has laid a soft hand in the furrow of my back. 'Do you kill many people?'

'Me, personally? No,' he says. 'Many of our recruits are sent to shoot at someone. If they are raw and new, you let them pick any target they prefer, usually a passer-by or an old woman at a vegetable stall. Only the senior recruits will have the chance to shoot at someone important.'

'Forty dollars,' he says, still buzzing at my ear. 'You get forty dollars for going out to shoot someone. Sixty dollars if he or she dies.'

'E … easy money,' I stammer. 'And the Party provides the weapons?'

He affirms with a nod. 'Look,' he says, pulling at my arm, 'do you see that woman standing there? The one in the red halter-neck. She is a fearsome killer, quite a senior cadet.'

'Who has she killed?' I ask curiously, staring at the sharp-featured woman, who was laughing into some man's face, rather coyly.

'Oh, let me see –' he rattles off names I do not know.

'Is it difficult?' I exclaim. 'Is it difficult to do what you do?'

'You don't ask questions,' the man replies. 'You do what they tell you to. You know that anything they ask in the name of the cause is right.'

There is a mild commotion in the room. In a totally self-absorbed manner, the red-dressed woman has suddenly flung her legs around the waist of the man with whom she has been speaking, and mounting him, places her hands upon his shoulders. In this position, she goads him to move.

The man begins to walk in a somewhat stilted manner with her upon his back, his arms by his sides. He bends forwards as if his burden is a heavy one. Some of the party begin to jeer and point. She ignores them and he continues on his penitentiary round. The woman jumps up and down as much as she is able on his back, shouting incoherently. With her hands, she strains forwards to move him along. The man bears it all patiently.

'Why does he not tell her to get off?' I cry, pitying him.

Many men are now gathered around the moving pair, whistling, and making comments.

My host shakes his head in an agitated manner. 'She is close to the chief,' he remarks.

I feel a sense of outrage. Did that entitle her to humiliate this man? Someone should stop her. I make a move forward, but he clutches my arm and hastily drags me to an adjoining room.

'Be careful,' he whispers in my ear. 'You do not know what you do.'

I recall my purpose in coming to the party, and decide it will be better for me not to make a conspicuous move as yet. I silently agree and meekly allow my host to lead me to an armchair.

I sit down. From my position, I still see the activities of the room beyond with the party guests making merry. But the woman seems to have tired of riding the man. She is using one hand freely to slap him and pull his hair. Finally she slides down, her dishevelled dress revealing her pale thighs. She wears no stockings underneath her dress.

Mopping his forehead with a handkerchief, my host smiles at me benignly.

'Tell me,' I say, in a daring moment, 'what is this cause you are fighting for?'

He hesitates before replying. 'To do away with oppression,' he declares. 'Have you not read your Confucian ethics? We are entitled to do away with a ruler who wrongs the people.'

'We are patient, very patient people,' he says, while his opaque eyes watch my face, which I hasten to adjust into a sympathetic one. 'Up to a point, up to a limit, but there is a line, which once we are pushed past, we lose control. A bad ruler should be overthrown by the people by force, if needs be.'

'Don't you think so?' he asks me suddenly.

'Oh yes,' I agree, 'yet my husband was arrested for doing

nothing more than writing a few critical articles. He was no conspirator.' My heart is heavy when I think of Tang.

'A foolish man,' I say.

'Very foolish,' agrees my host, critically, 'he should have come to us, we would have helped him.'

I do not wish to ask him how. I speak slowly, unsure of how to lay down my cards. 'I would like him to be freed.'

He says, reassuringly, 'We realise that.'

'Is there anything you can do for him?'

He considers, then touching me lightly on the elbow, says abruptly, 'Does he fight for the cause?'

'The cause,' I say. 'No one seems to be very clear what the cause embraces. The Chairman has accused the Catholics. He sees communists under the bed. Everyone fears the mirror creatures. The English-educated fear the Chinese-educated and vice versa. The different races fear each other. Who is it that we are against? Is it the Chairman?'

'Hush,' says the host, caressingly. 'We do not speak his name here. There are spies.'

'Spies, here?' I exclaim. 'Yes, even you may be one,' I say, recklessly.

His face turns pale, his eyes narrow, his narrow pleasant face undergoes a change. He looks at me in a manner somewhat hostile.

'If it comes to that,' he comments smoothly, 'so might you. Who are you? You walk into this party, you wish us to free your husband who is under arrest by the Internal Security Department, by what means you do not specify. You lead us to think you mean violence.'

'Is that not so?' he hisses.

I am suddenly afraid.

'Please,' I say. 'You mistake me. I think it may be a good idea if we go back to the room where the others are. They may wonder what we are doing.'

His face accommodates the suggestion, and he is once again sheeplike and smiling.

'Come then,' he says. I allow him to escort me back to the party. Taking rapid leave of him, I head to the buffet, and with slightly shaking hands, pile up a plate with food. I find a seat beside two men engrossed in conversation, and picking up a fork begin to eat. I feel a melancholy longing for the safety of home. I am feeling suddenly troubled by the atmosphere of the party, which is in full swing. I feel oppressed by the polished floor, the shining cabinets with delicate and expensive ornaments, the soft lustre of celadon vases, the paintings on the wall framed in gold, the expensive stalks of pussy willows bursting out in white cat's fur.

Scraps of my neighbours' conversation come to me.

'On Tuesday ... no. I think not. Perhaps someone informed ... the chief.'

I am intrigued. Someone has been killed. A young man in a harmonica society. He was shot as he exited his class with the others. One of the conspirators. Someone has shot him. Apparently the young man was an informer for the Chairman.

'But who killed him?' one man says.

The other man does not seem certain. 'The activities of the conspirators are not made known to all members. The chief often has his own agenda,' he complains.

The two men seem unsure if the killer or killers are of their party.

'Perhaps he wasn't a traitor. If that is the case, then it is a challenge to us from a rival group.'

'Why would they kill him? He was only a junior recruit, one of our newest members.'

'Maybe he learnt something and was about to let the chief know of it.'

The man next to me lowers his voice, 'Has anyone been in contact with his family?'

'Yes,' says the other man. 'They said he wasn't behaving any differently.'

'Families are rarely observant. He's just another piece of furniture!' They laugh.

Just then someone puts on pop music. As a sugary voice croons about love, the chief disappears to an adjoining room followed by about ten people. They are the members of the central committee. I wonder if I should go with them or wait till the host comes for me. I do not wait long, for soon the host is by my side. I get up and go with him.

The door closes on the sounds of the music, and the now subdued voices of the other partygoers. I find myself in the room with the chief and the central committee. The meeting lasts perhaps an hour. When it is my time to speak, I make some attempt at keeping the anxiety out of my voice. My proposal is heard, debated, and unexpectedly, dropped.

'He is not one of us,' protests a thin weedy-looking man. 'Why shall we risk anything for one who may be a spy?'

To my outrage, the others agree. The chief does not raise his head throughout the discussion. He does not look in my direction. The effect is intimidating. Even when he addresses a number of questions to me, his eyes do not look into mine. He is looking at a point beside me or at the papers before him. Finally I stop speaking because the wind in my throat has constricted my larynx. I begin to shake. The long silence which follows unnerves me so much, I find myself forgetting all courtesy and dashing out of the room. I pass quickly through the living room where the guests are still standing around in conversation and the music is playing. A few couples are dancing. I fling open the front door, stumble down the stairs and out to the dark road. I am lucky, there is a taxi cruising. I wave frantically and it stops. I climb in and give the driver my address.

As the taxi backs into the driveway and turns, taking me away from the house, I imagine the council still discussing my conduct. Only now I begin to realise that I may have done something foolish in running away. Will they look for me? They surely think me a spy. They will fear identification. Perhaps I should have said to them before leaving, 'I will tell no one. No one will believe me. I am a suspect because my husband has been arrested. Surely you know no one would listen to me.'

But it is too late now. I wonder how it is that they should have welcomed me there, that I should have so easily obtained the address of the meeting place. Perhaps the very manner in which I received information of their meeting was suspicious.

It was last Sunday. There came the ring of the doorbell. I approached the peephole and peering through it, I saw a young man in a blue shirt outside.

'Yes?' I shouted.

He asked if I would let him in. He wanted to see a woman called Chiang Ching.

I opened the door rather crossly. 'Yes,' I repeated.

He handed me a note, then turned and left quickly. I noticed that he walked with a slight limp. As his back receded down the shadowy stairwell, I closed my door. I went to the sofa and opened the note.

'Chiang Ching, the conspirators will be meeting on the 24th at 7 p.m. at Number — Queen Astrid Park. They may be able to help you regarding your husband.'

It was signed in an illegible hand.

I thought hard and long before deciding to go. Queen Astrid Park was an area where wealthy people congregated. An upper-class area, where every house was a mansion with a pool in the garden.

The taxi comes to a halt before my block of apartments. I pay the fare and dart inside as if the demons are after me.

I bolt the door. I think, *What will happen now? What can I do?*

The kitchen clock proclaims 11 p.m.

I decide to go to bed.

PART TWO

34

The scholar stares morbidly through a square pane of glass that serves as a window to the room. Waiting. Always waiting. Because at the water margin they will take him. He waits because there is nothing else he can do and because the days stretch out wearily from the rising of one sun to the next, and because there is a sort of hopeless dread inside him that he refuses to acknowledge. Sometimes it's better not to think too much, otherwise life would seem pretty hopeless. He wonders idly if the postman has been. It is a kind of dull expectation of letters that do not come, but it is at least something he can cling to daily.

In the Botanic Gardens, a yellow-vented bulbul, beloved of emperors, sings quietly. Then comes the silence of approaching evening when a man is seen slipping inconspicuously through the trees. The shadows are drawing over the Gardens.

The fading light is rubicund where a sun-raven perches on the branch of a rubber tree. 'Mad' Ridley planted rubber seedlings from South America in the Gardens in the nineteenth century, leading to a huge rubber industry in the region, and rubber plantations like the ones once owned by the scholar's father. It is in one of these trees that the sun-raven now sits, preening its scarlet feathers, drawing to a close the light of day. Soon the bird will join its fellows in the ruo tree in the west. It cocks its eye over the scene before it.

The man checks his wristwatch and, exclaiming, hurries on. He reaches a pond where a woman is waiting, her rounded back turned to him, seated upon one of the park benches, staring idly towards the water and floating lilies. The man slows down his steps. He sits at the other end of the green bench.

'Nice day,' he says conversationally.

The woman nods and without taking her eyes off the pond, says, 'Do you have the time?'

The man replies quickly, 'It's five past six.'

Passwords completed, the two relax and exchange quick glances. The woman is quite attractive, the man notes dispassionately.

'It will be the National Monument in the Gardens,' he whispers.

'Ah,' exclaims she. 'And by what means?'

'Explosives.' The man gives a rapid look around the vicinity.

The woman draws in a satisfied breath. Her eyes swivel around in a quick check and then her gaze returns to the pond. 'Good. It will be a devastation.'

'There will be four of us to do it, two to plant the dynamite, and one to keep watch, and one to keep the car engine running,' says the man, a little coldly, piqued by her indifference towards him.

She murmurs, 'And it will be us two, and perhaps Comrades X and Z?'

'Yes,' the man replies. Then, after a pause, because of a certain affinity he feels towards her in the darkening light, 'Do you think it will be any different?' he says. 'You know what they say, you carry the burden of yourself with you wherever you go. I mean, if the problem was only external, but it might be in me, the grass is greener and all that …' He hesitates.

'What do you mean?' The woman is openly staring.

'I mean,' he stutters, 'oh, nothing, of course.'

She frowns briefly, then turns upon him with a suddenness that takes him aback, 'You too?' Then, quietly, 'Do you know you are under watch?'

Before the man can reply a motion behind the trees startles both of them. The sun-raven takes off from its branch with a flutter of wings. The woman slides off the bench and nonchalantly strolls away, without another word or look. The man draws in his breath and waits. A dog bounds out into the open, followed by an English couple with a baby pram. The man remains seated, thinking of her words, 'You too?', wondering what she meant, staring out at nothing.

The sea rolls in. A litter of broken seashells and corals lies abandoned on the wet beach. The wind blows in from the north.

In the small back room of a *kopi tiam* on Beach Road, the middle-aged proprietor peers out from his slatted window. He is waiting. A young man comes cycling up to the shop. He jumps off his bike and approaches the wooden door. The proprietor quickly goes to open it, before the young man even begins to knock. A parcel is passed to him.

'The same,' says the young man, with a somewhat intense stare.

The proprietor makes propitiatory gestures as the young man sits down. 'A mistake the last time. Please send my apologies to the … to the chief. The letterboxes look alike, you know how it is in the *kampongs*, some of them don't write their numbers on the boxes clearly. It won't happen again.'

The young man replies stiffly, 'He took the pamphlets to the police. They will be on the alert. The chief thinks it may be better if you take another route.' Painstakingly, he begins to trace a route onto the back of the parcel with the Biro he keeps in his breast pocket. The proprietor watches and nods, scratching his greying chin. Satisfied, the young man takes his leave, after cautioning the other to be careful.

'Act naturally, don't draw attention to yourself. Cut your hair, it's a bit long.'

Then he is gone and the proprietor is left with the parcel of pamphlets, and the blue-black tracing of his new delivery route.

The road tilts upwards towards the end of the sky. Rows of squat red-roofed white-walled houses with large slatted windows like so many eyelids blinking. The small figure of the proprietor can be seen outlined against the fading sun, pedalling up and round the curve of the road. As he passes, he catches sight of a slogan pasted on a tree.

Citizens, why should our lives be in the hands of others? Fight for your freedom. The sign of the Chairman's party was on the poster.

35

Ching

'You were dragged in?'

'I walked. My hands were not tied. I wore pyjamas.'

I see Tang standing bewildered. He seems not to notice me. He fixes his eyes on the face of a man before him. The interrogator. How white Tang's face is!

A room so characterless, it strikes him like a blow. Day after day he is taken to this room until his pain and his fear paint the walls and ceiling. In them, he sees his own frightened fate. The room is made whiter still by a bright overhead light. The face of his interrogator flickers. He is dragged to an armchair under the light.

I do not think Tang tries to run away. For one, it would be impossible to get out of there. Furthermore, his legs do not have the will. Tang tells me how he feels his bottom sinking into that chair. It is so soft. The softness holds him.

He looks across at his interrogator and becomes dimly aware of his fear.

The interrogator speaks. 'Tang Na Juan,' he says softly.

Tang's world has begun to constrict into that face. Then his brain snaps to attention.

Tang tells me why he is paralysed with fear. The bastard sits on a chair an inch or two higher than his own. His interrogator sits upon a hard swivel chair.

Tang says to me, 'I felt like a cobra in a cage faced with a mongoose in the opposite corner.'

On another occasion the interrogators stand him in the centre of a room under a brilliant glare while they hide their faces in darkness. He sees only a pasty greyness flowering as the row of faces blur. He cannot distinguish who is speaking to him. Standing there, half-naked, a blast of cold air pours downwards upon him. His teeth chatter. He hugs himself to keep warm.

182

Their voices stab him from out of the darkness. Each word punctuates the space.

'I thought of you,' Tang says. 'I wondered if you had ever felt as I did, in front of an audience, playing a role. I doubt it. Your parts are different. And you would go off-stage and leave your part behind.'

Tang continues, 'Someone shouts, "Are you listening? Do you want to sleep? You will sleep when we are done with you." Someone rises and approaches. He brings a fist up close to my eyes. "Speak. Admit you are a traitor like that Japanese arse-licker, Wang Ching Wei, who sought to be president and ruler under the Japanese invaders! Or Chang Kuo Tao who betrayed the cause numerous times. Admit. Confess. Tell us who you are."'

Tang muses, 'I once thought that if I could plan my life completely, I would be in control of it.'

Tang thought that being the man he would be the strong one only to discover that he is a being precariously held together. He says, 'Can you understand that?'

He would seek from me understanding. I will give him words, but words he will listen to, and demand that I give again.

36

The Chairman sits in his pavilion letting the wind play in his hair, he smiles to himself. Such power as he has may have overwhelmed a lesser mortal. Before him lies his empire.

A guard enters. Bows.

'A woman. An appointment,' he murmurs, 'the actress, Chiang Ching, is here to see you.' His eyes flicker a glance at the Chairman's still face.

The Chairman gestures for him to bring her in. He shows little surprise but he has trained his face to look impassive. He is waiting. He wonders how she will look now. It has been some time since they last met, when they had been lovers. He remembers his ardour.

Ching

'Power is everything,' I said, when I heard the story of the yellow canary and the Chairman from Roxanne. 'You think that people want to live; that is a big mistake. There comes a time when you begin to realise that they prefer nothing more than to experience life on the surface. All their loves, hates and passions go no further.'

'Only the great crave power. Most people are content to let their lives go by while they sit in their armchairs drinking tea. That's what life is for most people, you find they don't want to be heroic, they don't want to dream, they don't desire a life lived intensely, the superficial is what counts. That's when you begin to realise you are alone. That what you want is more than what the world can give you. That there is no outlet. That life is a flickering television screen, that magic is sold to you like pills over the counter, that there is no *other*.'

I enter, face veiled, my steps soft and slight. Then I remove the veil and we look at each other. It seems an eternity.

'You are as beautiful as when we first met, even more so,'

says the Chairman, gently, as he takes my hand and we sit facing each other on two cushioned chairs.

'Beauty,' I reply, with a coy look, 'is ephemeral. Power is everything.'

The Chairman laughs. His face transforms, it becomes gentle. 'Indeed! You are the same woman I knew, that I have always known and loved.'

37

The old woman hesitates. She waits on the kerb as the cars roar up a din. She hears a sound, *thrum-thrum,* like a great heart beating. *Thrum-thrum.* It reverberates through her bones. It forces her heart to beat in rhythm. Rhythm as thudding as waves crashing on a rock. The heat, the noise, the crowd combine to create in her a sense of vertigo. Unseeing, she stands there while passers-by push their way forward. A few people turn to glance at her curiously. Their eyes take in a tiny woman whose blue *samfoo* is faded from years in the sun. Her skin is deeply burnt. On her feet she wears a pair of red clogs. She raises one foot tentatively to cross. But on the road, a white Mercedes-Benz cuts across the path of a red BMW, their horns tooting madly till their race is brought to a halt at the red light. The noise causes her to gasp and to press her fingers to her chest. Thrumming. Thrumming. She shrinks back. Now what does it remind her of? Glass windows of tall buildings close blind eyes to her agitation. The old Indian man flipping *roti pratas* is gone. In place of his stall is a shiny glass-fronted shop. The name of the shop is scrawled in gold letters. It is Dior, Armani, Chanel, Versace, Kenzo or one of the newer Hong Kong boutiques.

The old woman's heart is thumping and she presses the tips of her fingers firmly to her chest to ease the pain. She has to rest. Breathe slowly.

She sits down on a wooden bench on the pedestrian walkway, in full view of Takashimaya, the towering twin blocks. Chocolate brown. Their insides filled with beautiful luxury goods.

She feels that she is past the age for desire: of luxuries, beauty, wealth. Everywhere she looks there are construction sites, digging going on, sinking of foundations, the rising of new buildings. Hokkoda. Large red letters. The telephone number of the firm. A large board at a nearby site announces itself as part of the new Mass Rapid Transport System.

Demolition. Reconstruction. The buildings fall and rise anew, money-gleaming phoenixes of a modern world. There is no room for the old.

When the commotion begins she turns her head. People screaming. They are running, panic on their faces. Out of a nearby construction site, a shape rises. Like a shadow. A Black Hand of Death. Its heartbeat roars in her ears. She stumbles to her feet. She must get away. The crowd sweeps her along like a fish caught in a wave. She is tossed, sweating, and falling over her feet.

A woman cannot be allowed into the underground Mass Rapid Transport System, the Japanese site engineers say, or the tunnel will collapse. Because of that the woman journalist on the transport beat has stayed outside, while her male photographer crawls in for his shots.

But this is something else, the old woman thinks. It cannot be a woman's doing. They cannot blame women for it. She remembers the tale. Four dragons: one in each direction, their heads at one end, their tails meeting at the centre. Four of them under the earth. Bad luck to dig. Bad. Bad.

The dragons preserve fortune, wealth, heritage. In digging the engineers may cut any one of them in half. If you killed one, it would bring bad luck to the city.

The old woman sinks down to the ground as people rush ahead like a hungry shoal of fish, leaving her behind. Where do old storytellers go to die? She is certain she will die. Her heart is beating at an unnatural rate. Someone struggles to pull her up.

'*Po Po*, are you all right?'

Breathing deeply and staggering against her rescuer, the old woman screams, 'Ah, dragon.'

The man pauses. He looks behind her as if he expects to see some weird shape. The old woman clutches his arm, staggers murmuring, 'Too late,' and falls to the ground.

38

Tang is home.

It is telecast over the news that night: short excerpts. A full-length version of Tang's confession will show an hour later on two channels in four languages (three of them translations). Ching watches his face but keeps her thoughts to herself. She brings him a mug of tea. She carries on with chores that do not need doing, she pretends she is not waiting as he is for his turn on the glassy screen, his turn to confess to his interrogator, his turn to simper and be fulsome and grateful, licking the bastard's hand.

A hot night, a man escapes into the dark streets under noctilucent clouds. He boards a bus and lets himself down when he thinks he has gone far enough. The provision shops are locked up. Green canvas covers wooden trestles. On the five-foot way, under bamboo poles of strung washing leaning out of high-rise flats, are cane baskets filled with drying prawn crackers and shellfish. A fetid smell rises of the salt sea. A smell of stinking betrayal.

Desperately, Tang calls from the nearest phone booth, 'Have they broadcast the retraction?'

'Where are you? Shall I come?' Ching asks.

'No,' Tang says sharply. 'I'm all right. I'll ... be home shortly.'

His voice frightens her. She pauses. 'OK. Come home when you're ready.'

He swallows. He knows he cannot recover the self she has loved. He cannot be the same man.

'See you later,' he says and adds, 'don't wait up for me.' He replaces the phone into its cradle. Rock-a-bye baby. And steps into the airless night. *Just a short walk*, he says to himself. He knows he has cut his own road short. His mind shirks the memory. He hails a taxi.

Tang finds himself in Esplanade Park. He cuts across to the

Queen Elizabeth Walk, which looks over the river. It will be a long night.

There is a man walking down a dark road, his face is lit by the moon, and at intervals, the streetlights. In the shadow his face is terrible to look at. It is the night of the lantern festival. Children are milling upon the suburban streets and holding in their hands their lanterns of red cellophane. For them the world is a safe place. The night is calm, a sense of peace steals through. A little girl stands holding a goldfish lantern in her hand, she waits patiently as her elder brother does up her shoelaces, which have come undone.

As Tang walks down the suburban streets, he wonders about the occupants of each lighted house he passes. Sometimes he catches glimpses of them through the windows: watching television, setting the table, having a family meal. In some upstairs windows, he glimpses young faces bent in study over spread books. He feels lost and alone separated from them by the darkness and his solitude, by his very captivity though he walks a freed man, by the thoughts surging painfully through his mind, and by the metallic moon judging his actions. He does not seek recourse. He makes no appeal for company or to be taken back into the fold. It is too late for that now. Those whom he has thought of as his fellow countrymen have been traitors to him, caring nothing or little for his efforts. He knows it has all come to nothing, a fool remains a fool in this city. There is no pardon. He turns down Sixth Avenue. He may as well return home.

But the voice of the Captain follows him. 'Oh, come on,' says the Captain (with the voice of the inner demon who whispers to us, 'You're guilty!'), 'surely you can do better than that? We know everything.'

The scholar suddenly shivers. As he passes the guardhouse, he sees an old man, the new security man replacing Encik Ali, sitting abstractedly over a small radio. The old man comes to, becomes instantly cheerful, gives him a wave. Tang almost breaks his stride. He feels tempted to ask, 'Have you heard me on the radio? Will you watch me on the news?'

But the moment passes. He gives the old man a nod.

Some days later, unable to bear the loneliness of his burden, he places a call to an old friend. Their conversation is brief.

'Hey,' says his friend, 'how are you?'

A short laboured conversation takes place.

'Why don't we meet for lunch?'

The scholar understands. The man is afraid that their conversation may be tapped. As a former detainee, it is likely that they keep some form of a watch over him.

'OK, meet you at Newton Hawker Centre tomorrow. Noon.'

As Tang replaces the receiver, he imagines how it will be: awkward, with his friend attempting to be kind, to be brave, but worrying all the time whether he is compromising his family, his job, his own safety.

'There's a place where you can get good fried pork chops,' his friend will say, gently steering him with one hand.

Tang will allow himself to be led. In a short while they will be seated amidst the crowd with plates of white rice and a large dish of fried pork chops in tomato sauce and sliced cucumbers between them. And a large gap into which they will fall. Only trite remarks and fear remain.

39

Bras Basah Road is no longer as it used to be. Gone are the old shops smelling of second-hand books, dim interiors and equally dim old men plying their wares, be they books, tatty comics, esoteric textbooks, mechanical tools and gadgets or sports trophies. A sense of desolation occupies the empty and half-demolished shophouses. In this city, you can't walk away and return to find things the same as they were. What then of the city's inhabitants who have to live with so much inconstancy in their landscape? Is there a foundation for a stable identity?

For Ching, crossing the road on her way to the MRT station, the idea of a stable identity is an elusive one.

The passengers are stepping off the east and west bound trains at the MRT station, its façade brand-new with paint. Inside the building the air is tight with tension.

In the afternoon, the postman arrives. Roxanne receives a letter. She stands in the merciless noon light, and frowns down at the disturbingly familiar handwriting.

The train tracks are starting to show their lines across Chiang Ching's forehead and in the corners of her eyes. The rattling of trains, her heel tripping her up, steel benches, and then the cold wait for his arrival. She is patient in a dress bought at a recently opened Hong Kong boutique, her face carefully painted, her smile at the ready.

But she has a sudden sensation of emptiness. Perhaps it is the white vastness of the underground train station or the mass of unfamiliar passengers, so much excess humanity.

He slips through the crowd like a quick eel among clinging weeds. A Red Guard. His eyes quicksilver, little wrinkles widening, rippling outwards like tiny worms in a clear stream, his hands like hieroglyphs making lively insinuations. She blushes.

'Hello.'

Their words are somehow empty. She has expected more, but they talk like old friends. Seeing him come out of the crowd of train passengers, in casual batik shirt and dark jeans, a Parker pen sticking out of his breast pocket, a folded *Straits Times* under his sweating armpit, she experiences a sense of incongruity and thinks, *We are like conspirators.*

'You are coming,' he says when they meet near the Tube Information Centre. His head is wagging from side to side, repeatedly. She replies that she will see him at the appointed place. She says, 'I have to go.'

'Remember,' he says. She promises. He is satisfied, takes a quick look around, and leaves.

On her journey. Taking the Mass Rapid Transport to Central. The insides of the tunnel walls are lined with gigantic posters. Big smiling faces or not so smiling. The lettering is luminous. To be read even in the dark.

Ching sits folded tightly into herself staring out of the window.

Strive for Excellence. Smile. Be Courteous. Don't Litter. If you do, pay a fine of $1000. Don't Spit in Public Places. Flush the Toilet after Use. Don't Take More Than You Can Eat (this is on a poster for buffets and shows a man struggling with a heaped plate). *Have More Children* (a large poster of a family, a man and woman with three children – a bit late for some that had heeded an earlier slogan to *Stop At Two*).

Ching looks down the tunnel. Proverbs and words of wisdom provide train passengers with food for thought. She considers the words of wisdom passed to her from Confucius, Mencius, Sun Tze and a host of others. *Know Your Enemy.* The art of war is … knowing how to be subtle. How to hide your hand. How to mask. Looking down, Ching finds she is holding a message in her hand. On the thin scrap of paper, Ching reads: *A journey of a thousand miles begins with a single step.* She crumples the paper automatically. She thinks, *Our credo. Their credo.*

And then this afternoon William's note. His handwriting is tight and scrawled, 'You are my last hope.'

Roxanne looks around the room rapidly as if she expects William to be there. She reads the words and weighs their import.

It is Saturday. Today, she is not on the weekend roster, and so has not gone into the office. Her husband has gone to his half-day work at the office as usual, and will not be back till late.

'I'll be at Island Country Club, dear. Kevin wants me to meet a couple of businessmen. Might be back late. Say six. Depends. How's your day been?'

'I stayed home. Did a bit of exercise. I'll let the amah know you won't be eating home. Have a nice time,' she replied, her tones carefully pleasant.

He murmured an affectionate farewell and then the phone line went dead.

Roxanne wonders why Jeff's deep warm voice still has the power to evoke pain. Her hand folds over the notepaper, which looks like it has been crumpled then smoothed out. She stands, her head tilted to the open window.

She listens to the sound of car tyres sliding coldly down the wet road. There is the gentle, hesitant patter of rain, falling off the eaves of the roof. Last night there was a storm. She stood as now, by the window staring out at the darkness, and watching the swaying trees flash as lightning cracked across the sky. The wind blew her cheeks cold before she thought to move away and shut the panes.

The broken fronds of the coconut palm lie on the driveway. She thinks, *I must tell Ahmed to clear them away.*

Bits of scented rose petals lie under the bush. A few flower heads lie broken by the wind. The morning glory flowers, wet-laden, droop their plum-coloured heads. The rain is sadder, quiet and subdued like herself. Roxanne thinks of William, of his clown face with his thick spectacles perched high on his nose, and his lop-sided sweet smile, of his passion.

'Not for me,' she recalls with a smile. 'For his ideas.'

Outside, an iron-dark cloud stealthily parts to allow light to break through as her memory goes further back.

'If,' she mutters, '… but then again. Why does he write?'

And she laughs to shake off her unease. She sometimes talked aloud to herself when thinking through something. William is someone to hold on to. It is almost love, she thinks with sudden panic. Why the thought should frighten her, she does not know. Perhaps she has grown comfortable with her place – she is used to thinking of herself in terms of Jeff.

'Perhaps it is love,' Roxanne says aloud. But a love for home, details that shape us, attitudes. With William she felt she had no need to explain herself – he seemed to understand instinctively. They speak the same language.

Roxanne sighs. She and Jeff have little empathy. She had married Jeff in a whirl of romance. 'You never can tell whether it will work or not,' a colleague advised her. 'What are you waiting for? He's nice-looking. And rich. I might wait a hundred lifetimes and not have someone like him.'

When Roxanne first met Jeff, she was struck by his height and shoulders which were well built. His high cheek bones lent a sculptural elegance to his face, and he had beautiful ears with long lobes. To finish the impression, he was wearing a white silk shirt and a Gucci tie.

Jeff's clothes are all sartorial elegance. Later she discovers he will only wear brand names. Later he will put on weight from excessive entertaining of clients.

Roxanne slid into marriage because she had fallen in love and only later woke up to realise Jeff did not love her as she did him. Perhaps it was understandable, she tried to excuse him, he was a lot older than she, and he had been married before. With men, the time of youth is their time of love and passion. In their later years they grow reasonable and cynical. She is uncertain now if she still loves him. Even when she tries to do so, events and his attitude towards her conspire to drive it out of her heart.

After marriage, he made it a point to keep telling her, 'Live your own life and leave me to live mine. Don't interfere.'

It took her a while to realise he meant it.

When they are together, going out to parties, he embarrasses her. He is always grabbing other women closely when he dances with them. She pretends to look the other way. He always talks to these other women in an animated fashion. He is always charming. But she is the wife. She has a different treatment from him. Sometimes she wonders if the other women whisper behind her back, saying they pity her, or mock her for not being able to keep her husband satisfied. At other times it does not matter what he does or what others think.

Roxanne realises that Jeff is totally obsessed with the idea of the Chairman, that he thinks of him as a demi-god. Every word spoken is ideology. Every instruction a certain command. *Jeff fits in*, she thinks suddenly. But Roxanne, too, is no longer the girl she was. The convent girl who thought vaguely and romantically about being a nun. She has grown used to wealth. Jeff owns the row of shoe, clothes and bookshops down a stretch of Katong Road. His family accrued wealth by dint of uncanny business acumen, and he is the eldest son: as a child, he had only to point to a toy in a shop window and he would have it. Roxanne is used to a swimming pool in the garden, expensive dresses and restaurants. Holidays around the world in first-class hotels.

Years ago she opted for a career in journalism. But even there she feels the presence of Jeff. It was inevitable that she was hired. The public relations manager at *The Straits Times* is a friend of Jeff's family. She and her husband are like two strangers living together, clinging to a shipwreck from some loneliness deep inside both of them. Sometimes she longs for a responsive chord in Jeff, some real tenderness, not lust, and then she stops hoping.

Through a square of window Roxanne sees the sun burst

out from within the clouds in a dazzle of light. It blinds her. She feels her hands go damp and her heart constrict with quick pain. She clutches the note tightly. Suddenly, she decides. She will go.

It is 2.30 p.m. with muggy steam rising from the asphalt, bouncing off brick walls. Cream-coloured frangipanis bend low over the pavement to leer at passers-by walking under the sickly fragrant trees. Walking down a heat-hazed street, the woman playing Madame Mao is sweating. She feels her palms breaking into a sweat, her hair clings to her forehead in wisps, her soles pad damply in her shoes.

'They are coming here,' she whispers to herself. The absurd figures. Caught in an endless round of recrimination. The Punch and Judy show. And the sweat running down her hot thighs triggers the memory of his hand, the Red Guard's caresses. She feels her hot sweaty thigh against the palm of his equally hot sweaty hand. A tremor passes between them. The very air smells of sex.

She thinks, *I should have taken my time, maybe. Thought about it. Written it down in my journal. Pasted it up on a Post-it. But there wasn't the time and anyway, I had to see for myself.*

Ching waits along a row of ramshackle three-storeyed Chinatown shophouses, empty, roofs broken through by the outgrowths of tree trunks, targeted for rebuilding, and there he is, the man on the roof, shouting that he will jump, shouting obscenities, 'Your mother is a pigwoman! Your father conceived you in a dungheap!'

The director leans forward in his leather chair. 'Now I will make him jump.' The man jumps. There is a sickening thud as human body smashes against hard asphalt. Ching watches him flying down like an angel, while she is still some distance away from the building.

'I had a dream,' Ching whispers, 'of evolution. There was a line, which began with a fish and another and another. The fish, each one bigger than the last, and at the tail end of the biggest fish, a very small dog, then another and another, and each bigger than the last, and at the tail end of the biggest dog, I was. I was sitting on a chair and the chain of being ended with me.'

On absurdities. Jeff once told Roxanne a story when they were courting.

He said, 'As a kid, I kept guppies. Then I took them out of the tank and put them in a bowl of water and froze them in the fridge. They all died.'

'What did you do that for?' she asked, a little stunned.

'Wanted to see what would happen,' he smiled absently.

She did not know what to think and risked a cautious smile.

('I wanted to see what would happen if he took a dive off the building. Maybe it would take him to that someplace else he was always dreaming of,' explains the director.)

'This is it, you hear me. We're stuck, understand.'

Tang is screaming at her.

'Do you think they will let us go?' Ching says, her face impassive. 'They have spies everywhere.'

Tang thinks, *We are all trying to leave, some more desperately than others. Other people come in looking for work in the city, but we try to go. Not all, but enough. Enough for them to mark us as traitors.*

When Roxanne sees that the man who had jumped from the roof is dead, dead as the road upon which his body lies broken, his eyes forever open with the life driven out of them, his arms splayed, she turns on her heels and walks away. Quickly. As if the further she goes, the less of him she will remember.

She wonders if he had known he would jump when he sent her that note. That note! 'You meant me to see this?' She stops to retch. Her stomach aches as it clenches and she shuts her eyes. She opens her eyes a moment later and sees the drain filled with her vomit. Just beyond the drain about five metres away is the open door of a bakery. The freshly baked scent of bread hits her nostrils. Leaning against some railings, she presses her hand to her mouth. 'William,' she whispers. Her palm is damp. She continues on her way. The sour remnants of a romantic dream hang on her like sweat on her shirt or bile in her mouth. The sun simmers the air into a haze.

Roxanne is standing, blankly looking at the man she has married. The sun has set. Their faces are lit by overhead electric glare. Their luxurious and modern living room, fashionably designed, is suddenly a prison.

'So you saw him,' Jeff's voice is low. His face looks hollow. He drops onto the sofa. 'He was a traitor.'

'How?' Sudden fury catches Roxanne by surprise. Jeff looks alarmed.

'He was. You know that Catholic journal. The one the government shut down. He was writing for them. I told them all I knew about him,' Jeff starts to stammer.

He stops and coughs. He turns his head so as to avoid looking at her. Roxanne's heart is beating quickly yet she feels calm. She takes in the fact that he is frightened. She does not remember when she has last seen him so hesitant, so vulnerable. He speaks quickly, his cheeks flushing. Roxanne sees that he has forgotten to put Brylcreem on his hair as he normally does, and his hair is sticking out at odd angles. She gazes at the bits of grey in his hair dispassionately. Jeff's shoulders shake with suppressed emotion.

'I had to tell them. I … I had been involved with the communists before. They would have enough evidence to arrest me. I had to tell them.'

'Yes,' she says, as the seconds wash past, 'I see. He is dead. I was there.'

Jeff shivers, 'You remember, do you? I remember he was sweet on you. He was always hanging around, but he gave up when I got into the picture. No match, eh?'

The walls begin to shatter under the weight of her pain. Jeff is blabbering to her that he had been a communist sympathiser who had renounced his ways. She feels a wormlike recognition crawl up her spine. This wall he has hidden himself behind, this mask behind which she has never been able to peer, is gone, and she wishes to turn her eyes away from what she sees.

Her husband begins to pour out of himself all the dredged-up dirt in his soul. It comes out of him like a wave. She feels its onslaught and shivers. He feels he has to control her, wrestle her into agreeing with him. He needs her to absolve him. She has to say, 'You had no choice!' and then he will feel the ebb of guilt, then he can recover his composure.

The softness of night outside the window, its innocence – what a contrast to the man before her! It is where she prefers to keep her eyes but she forces herself to pay attention; she waits and waits for him to stop, for the moment to come, and when it does, it is like lightning, all she can do is flinch.

'Jeff,' she says in a confused way when he has finished and is quaking in his misery, 'I don't have anything to say.'

This is not what he has expected from her. He averts his eyes. He is alone with his information. There can be no absolution.

'I had to,' he whispers, running pudgy fingers through his hair, the gold wedding band catching the light. 'Don't you see?'

Roxanne watches Ching for some reaction to her story. Her thumb and second finger twist her wedding band. She feels like she is only beginning to feel sunshine again. She has been in bed with flu for a week. 'He made me sit with him till two or was it three in the morning. He kept on telling me. And then he would wait. Wait. For me to tell him everything was all right.'

Roxanne's voice is subdued, 'I can't even find it in me to hate him. I look at him and I just feel like everything has died.'

Ching sits unresponsively behind her sunglasses. Lately, a feeling of glass surrounds her. She begins to think of herself as being apart from the world and the concerns of other heads on human shoulders. What went on inside those heads appeared a tangle of old hatreds, prejudices and emotions. When she walked through the subway brushing past thousands of these heads, she felt like an automaton. Where the signs indicated, she went.

'He's dead,' Roxanne repeats. She knocks over her glass of *kopi-O* with a sudden move and jumps from her seat as the brown liquid runs swiftly off the table.

'Here, take this,' Ching pulls a wad of tissues out of her handbag. Roxanne crumples down on another seat.

'How could he?' she mutters. Perhaps Roxanne refers to her friend who has killed himself. Perhaps to her husband who has played informer.

Coffee steam melts into the air. A woman from the coffee stall comes to mop up the spill.

'Dreams,' Ching murmurs. 'You dream that you are alive. Your life is a dream. His death, your death, my death. All fragments of a common dream.'

Roxanne frowns, lightly tapping her fingers against the laminex top of the table. 'I don't get you,' she says. She leans her head on a hand.

'I saw him die too. I know he's dead. He's dead, Roxanne. What do you want me to do?' Ching hesitates. 'I'm sorry.' She trails off.

After a moment, 'So, how is Tang?' Roxanne mutters.

'The same,' Ching replies. 'Tell me whether anyone in the press sympathises? Is there any chance of getting his story out?'

Roxanne hesitates. 'I don't know,' she mumbles. She lifts her hand to order another glass of coffee. Ching knows she lies. The old man sitting at the next table eats his *ham chin peng* with gusto. Ching catches his eye and he stares back phlegmatically. He pours his coffee from cup to saucer.

Ching turns to look at Roxanne, but carefully conceals her feelings.

'They are asking me to interview the Chairman,' says Roxanne.

'Really?'

'Next week,' she says.

'What will you say to him?'

'Any questions you may like to suggest?' Roxanne murmurs.

'No. Nothing.'

Ching looks at the old man draining his saucer. The traffic kicks up dust. So much noise. So many people. The cars whizz past. Roxanne is swallowed up by the immensity of one man's dreaming.

Merdeka!

'I have brought this city to where it is today,' the Chairman says.

The Chairman is much in the minds of the people of the city. To some he is a god. In physical appearance, he leaves one with an impression of a great size. His features are squashed in a ruddy face, his forehead overwhelmingly predominant like a rock about to fall from a cliff. His ruddy complexion, women remark, indicates a virile nature, yet in personal behaviour he is austere, his vitality going into his intellect. His hair gently recedes, and is springy and black. The Chairman knows there are those who hate him, who wish to see him gone, but he will not go.

'Even when I am in the grave I will rise, kicking,' he announces. 'How many men have a chance of immortality?'

'Give the people what I want for them, fill their stomachs, their pockets, tell them that without me they will not survive. They will believe it is the truth. Let them destroy who amongst themselves is not in line. Those who wish to rise will do so on my terms.'

And their souls will shrivel; they will forget what it means to be a poet. They will forget the Li Pos, the Rabindranath Tagores. What means the murmur of water? The catching of fireflies? The lights in a lantern procession? I am afraid of beauty. I am afraid of what is not here. When I have built this city, its soul will be commerce, its language that of the businessman, its heart will beat with mine. I will not allow unchecked the weeds, the unwieldy, those that are not in order.

'Chairman, would you stand before the rest and proclaim yourself a visionary?' Roxanne is thinking, *How frightened I am to sit before such a man to question him!*

Roxanne recalls hearing a rumour about the Chairman's behaviour as a boy. A story most likely untrue. The story is that he once wanted to possess a canary, which belonged to an uncle, and his uncle refused to let him have it. Later they found the bird plucked clean of its bright yellow feathers. It was cold and dead at the bottom of its painted cage, its beady eyes wide open in agony.

'Did you do this?' hollered his uncle, dragging the boy to the cage and confronting him with the evidence.

The boy did not flinch. 'Yes,' he said. 'If I cannot have it, then no one else shall.'

'That,' said Roxanne's informant, 'is about the beginnings of megalomania.'

'It is a lie,' says the man himself. The Chairman paces the length of his room, his step reminding Roxanne of a caged tiger, intense, impatient. *Oh, oh,* Roxanne thinks. *What am I then?*

She wonders why she should suddenly see him in this light. In the Chairman's study, a magnificent stuffed eagle stands upon a wooden pedestal. Its yellow and black feathers, sprayed with a lacquerlike gloss, are poised stiffly in imminent flight. With its tearing beak turned to one side, its stern profile and one cold eye may be seen.

'My pet,' the Chairman says in caressing tones.

In that effigy he sees his dream of power. The bird is encased in a glass box so no dirty fingers may touch it, no accidental straying hands break its immobility. Roxanne thinks he keeps it caged for fear it may fly away. To her the bird is death held in check. In looking at it, he can believe in forever.

It is the sole outstanding ornament in the room.

The books facing her, she learns, are of a practical nature: on government, politicians, history, economics. There are no novels. Roxanne listens to the Chairman and looks at the stuffed eagle. She falls to musing. His voice continues booming. The bird. The Chairman. The Chairman. The bird.

'Do you not think so, Roxanne?' demands the Chairman.

The Chairman proclaims, 'I am not a democrat in that I do not believe we are all born equal. Some of us are born to rule, most are born to follow. There are few minds able enough to decide for the good of the rest. If one were to listen to everyone, nothing would get done. In one small city like ours, there must not be too many rulers.'

'There must only be one thought, one mind. When the people speak, it is with one voice.'

Scribbling away in her notebook, with her compact tape recorder turned on as backup, Roxanne thinks: *How absurd that in freedom there has to be one who is free to do as he likes at the expense of another. So the balance stays: one is free and one is imprisoned by the other's liberty. Perhaps the people of the city do not much care whose freedom it is – they know, as ordinary people know, that it is easier to leave the decisions of fate to someone else.*

She asks about the conspirators and he dismisses them. 'They are fools,' he says. 'Without conviction. Put them in a cell and they fall apart. Not one of them has any backbone, so to speak. But they can be used by others made of sterner stuff.'

The Chairman's detractors say he is afraid of death. Roxanne puts the question to him, 'Do you believe in a religion?'

'Live a good life,' he replies, 'and you will have no fear of what happens after. In my time we were taught right from wrong, good from evil.'

It is said the mirror people play upon the Chairman's fear of dying. They torment him with thoughts that his master plan will fail, that other forces will crush his city. He is driven, so common wisdom goes, by the quest for immortality.

Ruthlessly he fights the mirror people. He has the upper hand but secretly he is afraid. They have an advantage. They hold his soul in their cold and callous hands.

40

The Chairman says to Roxanne, 'Before World War II started, I was about to set out to England for my university studies. With the outbreak of war, it became impossible. This taught me something about life: it is unexpected. It is also unfair. You learn that sometime in the course of living. Why is it that we all expect that life should be fair? We think to ourselves, I am a good person, I treat you right, I expect you to treat me right, but that is not the way it is, that is not the way life works. Perhaps if we were to start out with the assumption that life is unfair but we do what we can nevertheless, perhaps then we can be happy. You look surprised? You think I am not the person to speak of happiness? But I value happiness.'

'What do we need? First the basic things: food, clothes, a roof over our heads when we sleep. When that is satisfied we think of luxuries and education and then the search for the meaning of life.'

'But first things first. Life is a war. Life is not meant to be easy. Nothing in life is ours for free. I had to learn that during the war. You ask me why I chose independence? Because no one, no one is going to look after your interests for you. That was what the war showed others and me living here.'

'Let me tell you something. When the Japanese cycled down the Malay Peninsula to invade our island city, all the colonial guns were pointing seaward. They did not expect a land attack. After midnight, the Japanese crossed the Strait of Johor in motor and rubber boats to enter the city blithely. The two British battleships posted to guard the city were sunk on 10 December 1941, two days after Pearl Harbour was attacked.'

'When the Japanese started dropping bombs from the air, all the city lights were on to show them their targets. The key to the city's main generators lay in the governor's pocket and he was at the cinema.'

'We are not born with silver spoons in our mouths. I tell

you, no one gives a damn about anyone else. You want to survive? You work, you obey the laws, you get smart. You get to know your enemies.'

Roxanne thinks, *The Chairman faces me now, his body turned slightly away as though to guard some inviolable space, but his eyes meet mine frankly.*

The Chairman says, 'Do you think the city was always as it is now? This place was a slum! You are starting to take what I do for granted.'

'What were the options? Death, sickness and madness. It was mayhem.'

'Once a Japanese soldier called out to me, but I pretended to be deaf. I was on my bicycle: I cycled round and round, I did not run away. I put on an idiot's expression. The soldier came up to me and yanked me off my bike, "Get in!"'

'I crawled into the truck he pointed at, but when his back was turned, I jumped out. I ran as fast as I could. I heard them shouting. They shot someone else, who had followed my example. Then the truck took off.'

'I hid in an air-raid shelter, cramped next to the wall and an old dying man stinking of tuberculosis, who had crept in.'

'Now and then he coughed and spat, then a man got up, one of those still healthy men left, and pushed him out.'

'The old man swore and wept, but he did not return.'

'Then a woman started wailing and her neighbour picked up a towel and covered her head with it because she was afraid of the sound, and the woman's body shook, and now and then a muffled moan emerged from underneath, then the shaking stopped and I knew she must be dead.'

'I knew then that all who held our destinies in their hands were false. Their promises were empty. We can rely on no one except ourselves. This is our destiny. We are on our own.'

'Men were called up to travel in trucks, homes were raided.

Men were taken away and shot. First they had to dig a pit, then the soldiers began shooting them so they fell into the pit piled on one another.'

'It happened that an uncle of mine dived in before the gun shot, so he was alive. He lay on top of dead bodies and on his back many more corpses dropped.'

'He thought, This is a worse way to die, and cursed his own cowardice and survival instinct. His mouth was filled with his own vomit that he could not hold back. The soldiers filled in the pit with loose sand. After some moments, my uncle began to dig his way out. He could not stand the heat, the suffocating lack of air, the proximity and stench any longer. His head broke through the surface of the pit, he hauled his body out, he thought, *I am alive.*'

'Then he found himself staring at a Japanese soldier still sitting by the pit's side. The soldier stared, then raised his gun. My uncle jumped on him, grabbed the gun and shot him and started running. He ran and ran as though his lungs would burst, till he reached his part of town and found his wife, his sister, his daughters, in various positions of death inside and out of their little house.'

'There was so much hate involved. Hate has to be used wisely, like all energy forces. Look at the city. It is clean, green and peaceful. It is prosperous.'

Roxanne slips in her last questions, 'But, Chairman, why do the people perceive that they may not criticise the government?'

The Chairman winces mildly. He says politely, 'They are entitled to criticise, as long as what they say is reasonable and legitimate.'

'So what is …?'

The Chairman cuts in. 'Look at the fruits of the tree, as a Christian may say. By that you see. Does it bear good fruit or is it barren? Look at my harvest. I have selected the best for my government. We know what is good for the people.'

He looks at the clock.

Roxanne takes the hint. She gathers her things, 'Thank you very much for your time.'

41

They are walking up the road. Two figures. Small now. Concentrated like the juice at the bottom of the glass that the director stirs. Lifts it up for a final swallow before replacing it carefully on the wrought-iron table. He purses his thick lips, wriggles his moustache and pulls thoughtfully at his double chin. He is fat like a pig. They respect him. They know that he holds much power. He watches them. He thinks they will be coming closer. Absently he brushes a piece of white thread from his pyjama trousers. He feels the power surging up in him from his toes which need their nails cut, from the small of his back. He feels it pour down the open chakra at the top of his balding head. He will be the great director. The one they depend on for how to say their lines, for their movements and interpretation of actions. What is your psychological motivation here? Why do you say this? What do you think the playwright intends? What do you think the character is thinking of at this stage? He holds the reins. He knows when to let them go, to let them think they are free agents, to let them believe that their actions are of their own deciding; he knows when to hold them in the tight grip of his palms so they know like the Monkey God that they cannot leap beyond the five pillar-fingers of the Buddha's hand. It is not only the power which intoxicates him; it is the charm of seeing them resist. Stupid fools. They did not understand that everything in their lives was contrived at a higher level. Dimly, they struggle with this and that, with policies and politics, like small fish gasping. If they only knew that whatever they did or thought or said made absolutely no difference!

In the philosophy of the *Tao Te Ching*, the way to rule a nation is like frying fish: to do it lightly so the people do not know they are being ruled. He, the director, knows this, and with his clever mind manipulates what truth is for the good of ruler and ruled in accordance to a Machiavellian scheme of personal power.

*

How to run a totalitarian state, as described by an ancient Chinese writer.

Han Fei-tzu (c. 280–233 BC), the principal theoretician and one of the greatest minds of China's Legalist school of thinking, whose ideas influenced the First Emperor to commit his infamous burning of books and murder of scholars, commented in an essay entitled *The Five Vermin:*

> The wise sovereign does not tolerate the existence of the briefest of writings: in his state, the Law constitutes the one and only doctrine; there is no further question of preserving the teaching of former sovereigns; the state cadres will be the people's only masters of thought …

42

Tang tries to escape. He goes up the path of the neighbourhood post office, a glass and chrome building, standing squatly like a sentinel. He imagines how it sucks into its maw and spits out mail, page after page of scrawled information – *Ah Sek is going into hospital for an operation, Ah Ma is impossible, I'll be off to Tioman on a holiday soon* – only he wouldn't be adding to it, he is going in to buy stamps.

There is a queue. Tang stands at the back of the line until it is his turn at the counter and then he asks for enough stamps to get himself posted off as a parcel. The postal clerk, weighing parcels, declares he is too bulky and the stamps insufficient.

'Most of us are too bulky,' Tang replies, biting his lip. 'With the weight of our worries. What are you going to do about it?'

But the clerk, who has pretty eyes and is dressed in a white *tudong*, is not prepared to take on any further after-hours jobs; surely there is no need for her to go beyond the call of duty!

'See, I don't know. I don't care. *Tiadapa*. You crazy?'

'Are you sure you don't have the stamps?' Tang asks.

She purses her full lips. Too many hysterics in the city nowadays, people who can't keep up with the modern rush. The other day a man sent her a letter saying he would jump off a building from the twenty-fifth floor if she did not marry him.

Well, she thinks scornfully, *that would work for naive young girls in the past, which was how girls got trapped into bad marriages.* Not her. She is modern, she will have her period of freedom before settling down, preferably with a more stable kind.

'Are you sure?' Tang repeats.

But she has turned her head away to the next customer, who is fat and full of self-importance, and wishes to have his turn.

It is one of their methods, Tang reflects, as he trots along the pavement, as the cars on their way to the city whizz past. To keep us. 'Have you eaten yet? Have you eaten to the full?'

It is the food, he decides. The food which goes into a stomach shapes a person, controls not only his bowels but also his emotions. Tang hurries, his head absorbed with thinking. He barely glances at the glass-fronted shop windows along Orchard Road exhibiting brand goods, but inside one, a bespectacled man examining many shades of Yves Saint Laurent ties swiftly replaces the hangers and slips out. He almost bumps into Tang, then slides quietly into a trot behind.

Tang mutters, 'You would think, that as we progress, there would be more humanity, but we are less, much less so.' And pays little attention to the man following him. The bespectacled man is a government agent.

You meet him in the Botanic Gardens. He sits with you on a bench.

'Life is elsewhere,' he declares. You remember it is a title from a Milan Kundera novel. It sounds proverbial. You say, 'You are a plant. A government spy. You are trying to catch me out.'

But of course, you don't mention this aloud. You agree with him amiably. He tells you that their agents have approached him.

'They say, "Spy for us. You are a Catholic. You go to church. You know these people. Tell us what they are doing." They browbeat me with my National Service record and my medal for excellence. Serve your country.'

You ask, 'When was this? Where was this?'

'In a hotel room,' he says, refusing to be more specific. 'It was arranged.'

You think, *Maybe he is testing me.*

You pretend little interest, but he raises his voice suddenly, 'I told them, "No. No. No."'

He drops his voice, '"No," I say.'

He looks uncertain.

You are thinking rapidly, *Ah.*

The expression of his face darkens slightly. He tells you that he has tried to escape.

He goes into a diatribe, 'Once you have said no to them, life is difficult. You know little things won't be repaired. You find yourself stuck in a rut. No pay increases. No promotions. Slowly your responsibilities diminish. Maybe you find yourself on the way down and then out of work. It is better to leave now. I know of too many chaps who hung on, believing that things would get better, having faith. Surely they can't do this to me, I am a loyal citizen. I only said one word too many. When they have lost all they have, they say, "We should have tried to go." But the place. It holds them, you know. They are afraid. Afraid of leaving. Because you see they can't. It's like a man who has given away his soul. Without your soul you are nothing. Without his soul, no man can be a hero and try to leave.'

You think to yourself, desperately, *He is plumbing my thoughts. Can I trust myself to speak with him? You know you have been trying to leave. You know that it is hopeless.*

You exclaim, 'Are you trying to leave?'

He says, 'You know they will watch for you when you apply to emigrate. They will note your name and if you do not manage to go, they will know who you are.'

'It is a chance I have to take,' he adds, squirming. 'They already know who I am. I have nothing to lose.'

'True. True,' you say and hesitate. You decide your method is to agree but not to say anything that would commit you.

He leans towards you, 'Young people are saying this place is a temporary one. They don't see their permanent future in it. It's just a place to make money and leave. How daring. So much courage,' he sneers. The change of his attitude makes you speechless. You are instantly wary.

'You should know,' you say, and look at your watch. He instantly reverts to normal.

'You have to go now? Perhaps we can meet for a drink sometime.'

You watch him sharply but his face is blank.

In the city there are people leaving. The emigration officers are at their wit's end, swamped by persistent demands. The newspapers highlight the situation calling it a BRAIN DRAIN. All those who wish to emigrate are traitors. This slows the drain a little. At least those who have something to lose should their application fail, think again before applying.

Those who cannot subscribe to the state, but yet cannot pledge allegiance to other states because of timidity or a lack of confidence in the order of the world, dither.

Tang starts keeping a collection of bonsais in the living room. He likes pruning and shaping them. Tang's favourite is the bonsai gulmohur. The plant's buds are little unripened potentialities that strain along the plant's stems, hairlike roots disclosed to the air. The tiny plant, clinging insecurely to an ornamental rock, sprouts buds that do not flower.

'My life exactly,' Tang murmurs, and touches the plant on his way in.

'I went to the post office today,' he informs Ching, who has entered the room. 'I asked the postal clerk for enough stamps to get me posted out of this city.'

Ching gives him a blank stare. 'Where can you go?'

Tang replies, '"Anywhere but here," I told the girl. And she replied, "It would cost you more than you have," and called for the manager. She thought I was dangerous. She thought I would do something desperate, pull out a gun maybe, threaten her.'

'I have been dreaming,' he declares, after a pause.

'Yes. I hear you,' Ching replies, brusquely. 'Late in the night, crying out. Why don't you see a doctor? You'll feel better.'

'I don't feel like it. I'm quite well.'

But she persists in that strange flat way of speaking she has recently acquired, 'You'd better go. You look pale and you have dark circles under your eyes.'

'I dream,' Tang interjects.

What dreams haunt him, he cannot say: falling from a high building, missing a plane, being chased by strange people.

Perhaps he can scarcely remember himself. Only vague shapes threaten. The dark is a good time for ghosts to travel.

He thinks of his anxieties as something elusive that he is unable to pin down, which makes it worse than if he can put his finger to it and say, 'There, I have it.'

The fears lie in wait in the shape of ordinary things: the objects in the flat, the shifting weight of the curtains, even the little roots of the fragile bonsais arouse in him a sense of menace.

Technically, he is a free man as long as he does not involve himself in political comments or organisations or anything high-profile in nature. In other words, he is a free man if he will lie low. Like the tapeworm.

Tang is free. He has confessed. He is free. He is a coward, and, furthermore, a public coward!

'I have lost my good name!' he mutters. 'When a man dies, he leaves his name. How does the Malay proverb go? *Harimau mati meninggalkan belangnya, gajah mati meninggalkan tulangnya, manusia mati meninggalkan nama.*' (When a tiger dies, he leaves his stripes; when an elephant dies, he leaves his bones; when a man dies, he leaves his name.)

'What am I then?' Tang whispers. 'A mouse? An insect?'

The blow has left him feeling particularly vulnerable because in all his life he has acted in full faith that the world had only goodwill toward him.

Ching

I am on my way out when Tang asks, 'Where do you go?' He puts his hand over mine. I waver. He notices the slight movement my fingers give of withdrawing then stopping. But I allow his caress.

'I am helping the cause,' I tell him, a little sharply. 'Surely –'

'Whose?' he interjects, puzzled. 'I am free now. Well –' He pauses to reflect on his gained freedom.

I am confused. 'Mine,' I say, simply.

'Well, all I can say is be careful, Ching,' he warns. 'Don't play games. You don't understand these people.'

'And you,' I say, a touch of hysteria creeping into my voice, withdrawing my hand, 'have you shown any understanding?'

I am sorry once the words are out, for he is a crushed man after his detention, and fighting with him is like pulling the hair on a baby's scalp.

I speak more quietly, 'I do only what I am told. I follow the script. I obey the director, as you know.'

Then I laugh, 'You are free indeed. Free as any one of us who is able to walk upon this stage.'

Tang stares intently into my face, I turn away. I bite my lower lip.

As a little boy, Tang had peered through a paling fence into a lalang-covered field beyond, and on a makeshift stage, he watched, as labour-worn singlet-clad men in the field did, the infamous Rose Chan performing a strip tease.

'Is that her panties?' he asked, awed. 'That black thing between her legs.'

'No, silly,' his elder brother hooted. 'It's what women keep between their legs. It's like a black cat.'

He lowered his voice, and said to Tang with a patronising air, 'They like you to stroke it.'

Reminded of this exchange, Tang has a sudden image of Ching as a strip-tease performer, slowly divesting herself of her layers of clothing till only nakedness remains.

Ching

The clouds are fat and sodden. The sky seems doused with water, still dismal and dripping at the ragged edge, and there is little light creeping through. The temperature is below twenty-three degrees Celsius on the thermometer.

Down the road and across the junction a cinema is playing old re-runs. I come here when I am depressed.

The bridge. Up the twenty-two steps and across the wooden planks with the dangling lanterns of bougainvillea running along its rails, and down another twenty-two steps to the cinema with the bold lettering across its façade, The Imperial.

At the end of the bridge, the creepers form a high hedge, over the tops of which one can see the thatched roofs of *attap* houses in the midst of a clearing adjacent to the back of the cinema. In the early morning, the courtyard of the cinema pulsates with the noise of hawkers. Fresh fruits, vegetables and flowers, still dripping with cold water, lie upon straw mats. The early risers congregate.

Inside The Imperial is a cavern, lit only by small lamps. The usher says, 'Ticket?' And tears it before handing it back. With this ticket, I enter the dark underworld of silver heroines and heroes, exorbitant deeds, and careless affairs, languid stares and tight lips, high-kicking legs and flying-in-the-air stunts.

I push aside the ruched mouse-eaten velvet red curtains at the entrance and stumble in. In the cinema are rows of soft plush chairs. I sink into one of them, while I hear the crackle of plastic packets of dried cuttlefish and chilli olives being opened.

It is a womblike world that holds, nestles and soothes me.

From this world I have suckled my early milk. The old movies bewitch me with a little charm, a little romance, a little happy-ever-after. I wrap my arms around my body. In the dark, tears are easy to hide.

Outside, a further storm is incipient, but meanwhile the air is dank. The humidity renders the air unbreathable. Passers-by yawn and trudge, keeping to the dry paths, keeping off the grass because of warning signs which are there to enable the grass to grow so that the city may look green.

44

At sunset when the shadows are drawing over the Botanic Gardens, a man can be seen strolling past the bronze *Girl In The Swing* sculpture. His walk is purposeful but pretends not to be. Now and then he glances around. He reaches a pond where another man appears to be waiting, seated on a green park bench, staring idly at the water. The first man slows down his steps, and takes a seat on the same bench.

'Ducks,' he says, abruptly. 'They used to have ducks here. Fed them as a kid.' He jerks his head in the direction of the water.

The second man grunts. 'You're late,' he says.

'I was held up,' the first man explains. 'It's only five past.'

'It'll be the statue,' the second man says, without looking at him.

'Ahh,' says the first, letting out his breath.

'Comrade X has made a bomb for the occasion,' the second man remarks gloomily.

'Wonderful,' remarks the first man, eager to please.

'You will accompany her,' says the second man.

'I will drive the car,' volunteers the first.

The second man affirms this, then says, 'You are under watch. Be careful.'

The first man looks startled, then guilty. 'I have been careful,' he protests.

'Not enough. People are talking. Your colleagues at work. Your neighbours.'

The first man jumps slightly. He has long suspected that he is being watched. He wonders how the comrades manage to obtain their information. They must have spies watching those who watch him.

The second man consults his watch, 'Make contact with X. She will tell you the details.'

A dog bounds out into the open suddenly, followed by a strolling couple with a baby pram. The second man gets up.

When they have gone, the first man is still seated, staring thoughtfully at nothing.

The water lilies bob. A conversation begins in his head:

What are you doing?

I want to destroy this city, I want to tear down the walls, I want to escape.

There is no escape. You will carry your prison with you wherever you go.

That is not true. When I have left this behind, I will be at peace.

No one can be at peace before they are dead.

45

Tang pauses at the oak door entrance to the Writers' Club. The last time he was here, he and Keng were discussing plans for the next issue of the journal. During his absence, there have been changes. A new room has been constructed on the veranda for those who wish to drink tea and stare at the garden, an extension of the restaurant inside. Tang moves stiffly in. The bodies passing him he does not recognise, and for a moment, wonders if a period of absence can render a place unfamiliar.

The Writers' Club is a colonial-style bungalow, with a wide veranda and white railing, facing a large expanse of garden, which is run around by a bright yellow palisade. A large flame of the forest spreads its branches from the garden towards the veranda where the restaurant diners like to sit and admire the scarlet flowers. The Club consists of a comfortable smoking lounge, which is often filled with a white haze, a reading room with its stacks of old magazines and newspapers and soft plush armchairs, a small library connected to this room, a bar for those inclined to imbibe and a respectable restaurant with food at reasonable prices, a couple of small conference rooms for those who wish to hold readings, get-togethers or their annual general meetings.

There are several new faces, young ones in their twenties or thirties, in jeans and sloganed T-shirts, pleased with themselves and their world. They laugh loudly, order more food, and manage to convey that as writers, they are somehow one notch above others. These are the Writers' Club members whose white badges bear their names and titles: author, poet, scriptwriter, playwright, biographer, journalist, critic.

Tang sees a skinny man with a badge that states his occupation: Freelance Autobiographer. The man passes him on his way to the bar. He does not look up. Tang laughs, aloud.

'Sir? Do you have your identification?' Tang is interrupted in his laughter by the voice of the receptionist.

'No … I am here to meet someone.'

'You will take a seat here and wait while we call your host.'

Surprised, he sits down. 'Does a given status confer a spirit?' The receptionist ignores him. Dismissed, he settles uncomfortably in an armchair, then suddenly Keng is by his shoulder.

'Hello, hello,' Keng says. He has a wide smile on his face.

Keng points to a wrought-iron table on the far side of the sunlit veranda. 'Over there,' he says.

Tang claps his back. He claps Tang's. They pause to eye each other.

Tang says, 'I was blinded coming from the bright sunlight into the dim interior of this lounge. I couldn't see anyone.'

Keng looks like a deserted house that ghosts may like to move into.

The thought strikes Tang, *We are both much thinner, but even to the casual observer, our resemblance will be more than superficial. We appear as St Stephen's did after the building was slated for demolition, and the congregation had been moved to other churches, and meanwhile the church stood on Victoria Street, empty and silent. It was then that passers-by commented that the building looked suddenly aged.*

Keng looks as if his façade has dropped. The glimpse of the soul beneath is not a pleasant one. Tang wonders if he may well look the same.

A waiter springs forward with menus, as they seat themselves.

'Hainanese chicken rice for me. Thanks, waiter. What will you have?' Keng snaps his menu shut.

'Give me the curry *laksa*.'

'Right, sir. Any drinks?' says the waiter.

'Bring two Anchor beers,' Keng orders. The waiter takes it down and leaves.

Keng clears his throat, 'It's crowded. It's a weekday but it's full of people.'

It is all he seems capable of saying for the moment. Tang sees him eye him uneasily, almost as if he cannot believe his eyes.

Keng coughs. 'A lot of new people come here. It's not only the writers or would-bes that come, but artists and pop musicians and tourists. They're bringing foreign writers that are here for some festival or other, to entertain them. I've seen the Minister of Arts eating here with a couple of foreign-looking people.'

'Uh, yes.' Tang reflects how little the club affects him or the concerns of these members, how empty it is.

'Empty, no, I'm sorry. I didn't get what you were saying?' Tang sees Keng staring across at him.

Keng is still babbling on. 'A romantic ideal, don't you think? The writer as the outcast, as an exile doomed to wander the world. Ha, ha. We don't have the space for nomads. Physically and spiritually. We are too modern.'

Tang sips cold beer, which the waiter has brought. Keng's words enter and leave without much trace. He finds his thoughts drifting. Keng looks down. There is a silence. Tang's right foot, crossed over the left knee, is shaking uncontrollably under the table, which happens whenever he is bored or tired or nervous. He hastily adjusts his feet.

'How's the wife?' inserts Keng into the pause. Tang replies briefly.

Another long pause. When the waiter arrives with the food, they welcome him with relief. After a few mouthfuls, Tang begins to feel more at ease.

'You know to go back to what you were saying, only poor souls congregate. A writer has to be outside of any group. Or he will be blinded by the group's prejudices. How can he have the perspective to see? They're (Tang waves his hand towards the other lunchers) all too busy licking boots.'

Tang gulps more beer, and comments expansively, 'We are all dead souls here.'

Keng mutters, 'Take your mind off what's happened, for god's sake. It happened to all of us. Life still goes on.'

Tang stares. 'Do you think what happened makes no difference?'

Keng grimaces, and averts his gaze. 'Why don't you just finish your drink? We'll get another bottle. Hey, waiter!'

'Oh yes, drink and forget.'

Then Tang thinks, *He has brought it up. He has brought up the subject of our arrest. How does he propose to speak of it? How will he justify himself?* Tang feels an immense weariness. He does not want to listen to excuses. Feeling superior, Tang leans back and almost glares at Keng.

Tang thinks, *I, at least, betrayed no one as you did.* A shadow of doubt nudges the back of his mind, but he quickly blocks it out.

'What I said I said without intending harm to anyone,' Tang corrects himself. 'I only said what I had to.' He awakes to the fact that he has shouted the last sentence aloud and that the surrounding diners have turned to look.

Keng looks miserable. He pours out another bottle of beer into both glasses. The glasses clink as his hand knocks the bottleneck against the rims.

The light is too bright. The noise too close, Keng too familiar. There is a stupid fly buzzing around Tang's head. Tang waves his hand vaguely. Sounds that were previously normal to his hearing have amplified.

The colours exaggerate grotesquely: the red bloom of the flame of the forest in the garden, the sunlit tops of the lalang, the wide-petalled hibiscus with its insolent tongue. He blinks as the light dances.

Up in the blue sky, the sun-woman drives her babies across the heavens towards the ruo tree in the west, which they will set alight with fire flowers.

The pellucid light swells and pulses, turning the landscape glasslike. Blinking, wild recklessness after his third glass of beer makes him declare, 'There, that's a poem for you.'

He points to the flame of the forest flowers, which have

littered the ground, among the brown skeletal leaves. At the moment when light has intersected with the living world, the remnants of death are visible. Each dead flower is a stillborn poem, tender and null, its life inevitably short.

'Yes,' Tang thumps the table. 'They have lived and they have died. And we?'

A moment's pause while Tang recollects that he is a recently released political detainee, that it is wiser for him not to draw attention to himself, that it is better not to make a scene. At other tables, some of the writers have turned to glance. Some snigger. He does not want to be disagreeable. He will lie low.

'Poems,' Keng exclaims, picking up the thread of conversation, 'out of this land?'

'All things are possible,' Tang slurs.

Then Tang is reminded of a scene that took place during the arts festival only a week ago. A performance artist, suddenly stepped out of his ritualised tying of his body to a tree trunk, and pissed … into a styrofoam cup. After this act, he picked up the cup and drank from it, shouting, 'Celebrate art!'

It was sad. Really sad. What was worse was that the media – normally silenced in all important aspects, sycophantically toeing the government line in their series of hectoring and lecturing articles aimed at elucidating to the citizens the benefits of the Chairman's government – took up cudgels for this artist, this expression of free art, free speech, freedom.

There was a great outpouring from these repressed pens on the freedom of artists, on the merits of drinking one's urine, of modern art and the spirit of Dadaism, and in other words, telling the common citizens expressing moral disgust to get stuffed because they know nothing about what constitutes art.

Behind all this was the simple irony that they could rant and rave as much as they pleased, the Chairman was disdainfully silent. They could rant and rave because they knew and the government knew it was over something inconsequential.

Freedom in art is paramount, but when the essential

oppressions are not tackled, the media critics become like the sightseers watching a naked Emperor parade and shouting defiantly, 'This is art. This is freedom of expression,' and all the while the average, the fearful, the inconsequential is celebrated.

'In an oppressive society, scum rises,' Tang cries. 'A city's literature is a reflection of its soul. What do you say of a country where the expression of what is art takes the form of a man drinking his own urine in public and being made an instant hero by the media trying to appear liberated, having a tacit agreement with the government on what issues it can blow up, and knowing full well that issues that are intrinsic to questions of how one lives, who one is, such as the fate of political detainees, are out of question? That where the real barriers lie, where real freedom should be fought, at the frontlines, there are no soldiers.'

'We cannot pretend to be artists in such a society, for in our art will lie complicity and lack of truth. Oh, yes, they are spending millions on the new arts complex. Hosting international artists. Urging us through their media to let a thousand flowers bloom. That should catch any wary artist by his throat, let a thousand flowers bloom. Why should any government need to say it? Art is natural.'

'Let all artists watch out, for when they start confronting the malaise at the heart of their art, their bloom will be crushed mercilessly. The ones stupid enough to take their word explicitly will be the ones to feel the rewards! All that we can produce is scum and that is the way they want it. Timid souls and over-fed stomachs, mere puppets that pretend to rebel but deeply acquiesce – how can art grow from such soil?'

He has said too much, is aware of being lugubrious, but finds he is unable to stop. All his pent-up frustration, Ching's apparent disloyalty, complete with the realisation of his inner weaknesses, have overwhelmed the stopper in his brain. Keng has fallen silent.

Why am I here? Tang thinks angrily. *Watching them. The curlicues with long tails like cats, squatting on their haunches, licking each other's arse-ends. They cover up their talk with persiflage. There's no freedom here, our press is muzzled, we are muzzled. No one wants to hear our side of the story.*

He seems to see in his mind's eye the interrogation room and the moment of his collapse, when he realised that nothing was of value. Even hate becomes too strong an emotion.

Was it a year ago over a lunch at the club, that Keng assumed a serious position and said, 'You want to get somewhere, you have to know the right people, pull the right strings?' In all seriousness and faith in the importance of his own position in society. But alas for him, and his well-made plans. His amazing naivety in the face of their power which he had not understood. The only strings that were pulled were the drawstrings of the pyjama trousers which they had made him wear and which someone undid during interrogation. When the trousers fell, he stood before them naked while they mocked his spirit.

This is a different man from the one who had thus instructed him. Here is a man who has known defeat, though there are certain sorts of defeat no man can face up to, because the price is his cherished ideals, and his conception of himself.

What happens when you know you are worthless in their scheme of things? Because he does not play their games well, they have cast him aside. There is no room for those who are not of their kind, no room for those who do not agree with them. An interruption occurs. A couple of young writers have started squabbling, three tables away. Their voices rise raucous and ugly. People begin turning their heads to watch them. One writer suddenly climbs upon a chair and begins to gesticulate. Some of the people start to boo him.

'Hey, people,' shouts the young man on the chair. 'Listen up. I have been told that I am not to write on an art exhibition of stone phalluses!'

He sways on the chair. His companion tries to pull him off

the chair. The chair turns over. The young man falls to the ground, mumbling, 'Do you call that fair?'

Raising his voice, Tang turns away from the scene and remarks shrilly, 'How can a crow teach an eagle? Can the crow, with his different worldview and being, instruct the eagle? Is there one infallible way of being in the world? Are actions the only criteria for judging the man?'

Keng's face reflects despair.

And then Tang thinks, *They sit up high and make a mockery of me, the small man who struggles to comprehend the rules they set for the world I have to live in. They deny there is an inner man. Man shall be judged by his externals alone. Look at your neighbour with his huge mansion, his Porsche and Mercedes-Benz, his beautiful wife, his servants.*

'Another beer?' Keng is asking. The noise has subsided. The two squabbling writers have retreated from their defensive positions to lurk behind plates of steaming rice.

Keng calls the waiter over and adds an order of *rojak*.

'You don't mind?' Keng takes out a cigarette.

He lights it, inhales and leans back in his chair. The smoke slowly rises from his lips to curl into the air.

Tang is suddenly afraid. He knows he has made a serious mistake to speak up, to stand up for what he believes in. It does not work in this city, in such a society, with people who do not have humanitarian impulses, but who believe that people are digits to be used or crushed, that the individual can be sacrificed for the greater good of the community. Perhaps he has believed too much in the people. He tried to speak for them. He finds they will bring to him their complaints and misgivings, but they are not prepared to stand behind or by him. No one wants to stir up the waters. No one wants ideals if ideals prove difficult. Perhaps they are right. Tang feels full and fed. He thinks, *Why dream, why desire? I don't have what it takes anyway.*

Voices commence speaking, breaking into his thoughts. From the next table where two men are eating, Tang overhears snatches of an animated conversation. 'Horrible! A great shock.' Then their voices lower, till, 'What! Without his guts! Eaten!' More protests.

Then clearly, 'We are going mad in this city. When even the Captain … what a frightful end!'

From what Tang can gather as they continue speaking, the Captain, presumably the Captain of the Red Guards, has been found by a cleaner, dead in his office. He was lying on the carpeted floor in front of a mahogany desk. His throat had been cut from side to side. A long cut extended to his groin. The great wound gaped. What was worse, they could see no entrails.

'In the morning … visitors. The guard let them in. He would be in for questioning, but he's missing. Strange-looking people. A woman.'

'A woman! It'll be on the news.'

'I reckon they won't say much. Not about the missing entrails. Looks like an act of revenge. He'd have many enemies.'

'Oh, I wouldn't say that aloud … what are they doing about it?'

'Questioning the staff. I was lucky to get away this early to meet you. But I hadn't been in the building that day, thank heavens.'

Tang is listening intently, bemused. Who could have committed such a fiendish act? He would not wish it upon his worst enemy but … a flood of relief passes through him.

August is the month of death, hungry souls from purgatory are released to roam the earth. The streets fill up with the smell of burning incense, prayers dancing upon the wind, bits of burnt red paper. Old men and women, holding their grandchildren, are squatting by the roadside, waving joss sticks. *Wayang* performances take place nightly. The evening splits with high cries and crash of metal cymbals. *Tock, tock, tock … cang!*

The journalists at Times House are chattering in their canteen. Then the peace is abruptly shattered. There is new information. At the Hotel Orient, a new corpse. In the Botanic Gardens, another. Then the cut up pieces of a man are discovered in a curry that has been dumped into a garbage bag and placed into the bin, which the garbage man finds too heavy and suspicious.

The newspaper headlines in four languages scream: *Curry Murder!*

Sixth corpse found in three days. Police ask for information. Anyone vaguely seen in the vicinity of River Valley Road, dumping a garbage bag, who may or may not be a resident, acting in a furtive manner, etc. But it is no joke.

Roxanne comments to her colleague, 'What next?'

Getting up in the mornings, the city's people wonder what fresh assault they will read of. The once-tidy city is coming unravelled. Everyone whispers his or her notions. It is possibly a gang. Of four or more. Possibly the communists. The Catholics. The Triads. The mirror people.

In the marketplaces, huge roasted red-skinned pigs lie in state on long trestle tables as offerings to appease the vengeful ghosts. Thick gaily wrapped candles burn into smoke.

Tang

This morning Keng calls to let me know the details of William's funeral.

It is a gloomy place – the cemetery. Perhaps I colour it with my own feelings, or it could be the weather. By the time I leave the cemetery with Keng beside me, strong gusts of wind signal an imminent storm. The death of this man subdues me.

One of us.

One of those the government had detained. Like myself, he had been a contributor to the Catholic journal. Death comes unexpectedly when one is in one's prime. The man left behind two small children. He and his wife had divorced some time ago and she had remarried. They came to the funeral: the man's old mother weeping unstoppably, his ex-wife, and the dead man's children, pale, strained and frightened on behalf of the father who had crossed over.

Death. He had gone to meet her. Torn himself out of human society, and launched into space, from the top of a building in Chinatown.

He was a nice fellow, a good chap. Had I talked to him only two weeks ago? The shock will subside, death in the past tense becomes easy to accept, even the family will put aside their mourning and continue with living. The dead are seldom remembered by the living.

But the funeral leaves an impression I do not find easy to shake off. It's closing in on me like a net.

When I get home, I can hear Ching's high voice upbraiding the amah in the kitchen. Her voice grates painfully on my nerves. I do not understand her nervousness. She leaves me to my own devices often these days while she attends to her own matters. Rain starts to pour.

48

Ching

Some people are hypocrites. I comb my hair before the mirror and contemplate my recent power. I am not so stupid that I do not see. How funny that the very same people who during my childhood or acting days should have snubbed me because I was different from them: too poor, too unsophisticated, too ambitious, or simply that they felt my nature to be different from theirs which made them uncomfortable, these very people who called me names or cold-shouldered me should, now that I am at the height of power, greet me as a long-lost friend, as though they, of all people, have always believed in me, thought well of me, were concerned for my welfare.

Take this acting colleague I worked with before. When I first met her, the woman was the centre of a coterie. We had to work in the same play. She took a dislike to me, then a new and young actress. She and her group sniggered when I came by. They made little caustic remarks that they overlaid with honey. They overpraised my singing voice. They remarked on my lack of background in mock-sympathy.

Yesterday I met her, that same woman, on the streets near Orchard Road, the heart of the shopping district, just as she stepped out of a boutique.

'Ching!' she greeted me, throwing her arms around me as if I was her greatest friend. She began to talk non-stop. She wanted to invite me home to dinner. She invited my confidence. I had none to give her.

I stepped back from her embrace and said cuttingly, 'Do I know you? When I was no one, did you not pick on me? Were you not the one who turned the group against me for no reason other then to show that you had the power, that you were more popular? Leave me alone now.'

I could see her mouth drop. That painted face turning ugly as her real self surfaced.

But it was not what I said.

Unfortunately, instead of seizing the chance, at the moment, instead of truth, I spoke to her with some courtesy. Why? I do not know. Perhaps I could see her with her mask slipping. It showed an older face, a face worn out by her wormlike nature.

Perhaps, after all, in her pitiable state, she reflected to me my face, the face of the woman, the face of Madame Mao, and I was seized by a sudden fear.

'I will be your right-hand woman,' I say to the Chairman, as I caress his body in bed. 'I know all about the theatre. I will rewrite history for you.'

To prepare myself I begin by demanding back all letters and photographs from those who knew me in times past. Unmindful of Tang's warnings, I plunge into the revolution, as if it were made for me.

'I want my letters back,' I say to old friends. 'All of them. I cannot allow you to hold onto the things I once wrote and said. That was a past self.'

'Now,' I continue to my victims, 'people look up to me. Can I let them down? I want all letters and photographs you have of me.'

And when I do not trust that they have returned them all, I order that they be tried as communists, and imprisoned. Many of my former friends and foes go in that fashion.

It is a time when you only have to whisper so-and-so is a communist or mixes with communists or holds Marxist ideas and all his friends will disappear. Alone, he will return to face the Red Guards who have rampaged through his house, overturning desks and drawers and upsetting bookshelves for evidence, which they may find even in an innocuous letter about to be sent or a wedding photograph.

Years later some were to say it was incredible, a great explosion of self-destructive energies. It all seemed so pointless. The lives sacrificed. The stoppage of industry. Philosophers and politicians scratched their heads. 'Why?' they asked. 'Why did it happen?' How was one to explain mindless or not so mindless violence? And the old men and women resting their feet upon stools in dimmed corridors would talk of it, and wonder at its ineffability.

'There had seemed a point to it,' murmured a former Red Guard. 'At that time. It seemed so clear that it would be the inevitable path. Now I wonder if I understand it myself.'

Early February. I find myself upon a stretch of road in Little India. I study the street signs intently for a clue. I move like a man sleepwalking. Down narrow alleys, past open doorways with fragrant hanging garlands of roses and jasmine, strings of mango leaves. Through glass fronts, I peer at the silver and brass figurines, bottled essence of herbs and flowers, the colourful pictures of Hindu deities: blue-skinned Krishna with the milkmaids, Shiva performing his fruitful cosmic dance, Ganesh with his elephant's head, which the god obtained only because his father had mistaken him for his mother's lover, after he was a long time away from home. 'Ah, my son,' cried the distraught father, after cutting off his own son's head. He seized the closest replacement at hand, which happened to be an elephant passing on the street.

I walk down the street towards an approaching woman whose face is partly hidden by a veil. A dark and dainty woman in a sari with a black *tilak* painting her forehead. She passes me like a piece of music. I feel a sense of time passing. I swing around and watch her silent back going up the street.

Further along, I stumble upon a scene, straight out of biblical times.

'Oh, my god!' They have crucified them like birds transfixed. Figures with their arms spread wide, their heads drooping to one side. Red Guards.

His mouth is slightly ajar, and you can see they have forced him to drink of some liquid before his death, and dripping from the corners, his saliva is thick and ugly.

The other Red Guard strung up beside him grins maniacally, his features set into a stony mask, his stomach gapes wide, there are no organs within. Someone has removed them. Dark heavy flies buzz uncertainly upon his wound. No one goes near. But

I, trying to overcome my disgust, approach the immobilised body, reach up a hand and touch the grey cold flesh of the face.

It is the face of one of my interrogators. I am sure of it. I break into a smile and then I spit, and my spittle runs gently down. I start laughing. I hold my stomach. As my spit touches the man's face, the skin seems to absorb life. Like a crimson flame of the forest the gaping wound of the body blossoms. It becomes, instead of a sacrilege, a fount of life. As I look, it seems to me that the blood begins to throb from the gap in rhythmic drops like rubies. The bystanders gasp and crowd forward. They reach out with eager hands, palms open till the blood has filled them with riches. Their voices shake and swell around the crucifixion. Someone picks up a pebble, flicks it towards the dangling corpse. There is some laughter. Then I turn away abruptly, for the heat and stench of the corpse and the perspiring crowd around it has sickened me, a sense of my unfair act against a corpse in my heart.

'Well, what can you say?' I damp down my sense of compassion. 'Father, forgive them …?'

I recollect myself. 'Hey, stop pushing!' I say, giving my neighbour, the little man who has shoved me, a sharp nudge. The man has been pressing ahead, but now turns quickly, with a mumbled apology.

Then unexpectedly, on catching sight of my face, he starts to shout, 'You are the one. You! I saw you on TV. I know you!'

I am surprised. I stare into the man's round face. I retreat. I cannot describe what I feel at that moment. Then anger wells up.

I shout back. The little man glares at me with hatred. It seems that we may come to blows, but the approaching sounds of the Thaipusam procession reach the crowd.

'Get out of the way!'

The chanting gets louder. My accuser and I are separated by a wave of people struggling to get off the road.

Losing my assailant, I find myself standing confusedly on

my own. I enter Komala Vilas, a vegetarian restaurant a little further away. I mop my face with a handkerchief, and order a glass of sweetened yogurt to cool my temper. As I sip the thick liquid, and think of what to have for lunch, I watch the dancers of life and death pass by in the procession, slim shadows extended.

Watching them, I drum my fingers against the Formica-topped table to the rhythm of their steps. Today is the celebration of the Thaipusam, the feast of the Hindu god Subramaniam, son of Shiva, who triumphed over evil. The devotees are making their way from the Sri Srinivasa Perumal Temple in Serangoon Road to the Chettiar Hindu Temple on Tank Road. The devotees are carrying arches of steel, *kavadis*, as penance for their sins.

They chant wildly, with painted hands, faces and feet. There are the towering shapes of the *kavadis* above their heads, iron hooks and spikes protruding from tongues and chests. In each centre of pain is a man, eyes glazed, staring before himself at a point beyond, each step, tentative or otherwise, taken on the way to purification.

I feel a deep heat flare up in my spine, a sunflower bursting. The sun descending on the heads of devotees, the flame bird encircling their heads.

Ching

I am in the crowd, hurled along by the tide of spectators, and I see Tang standing a little apart. I do not call out to him. It would be useless, he would not hear me. Out of nowhere, there are three mirror people by the roadside, watching as I am, mocking all that men do. What is it worth? Salvation? Eternity? Only they among us know what it is to be immortal. Then the crowd pushes me against Roxanne.

Roxanne

I have come to Little India to write up the Thaipusam. A bump against me, and Ching's voice, 'Roxanne!'

It is not what I would wish. I have not felt like seeing her of late. But, 'Ching!' I say. She takes my hand and we move out of the crowd.

'I've been wanting to talk to you,' she exclaims. 'You have been impossible to get hold of lately.'

'I've been working late,' I reply, lamely.

'Such a great deal to do. The ever-dedicated reporter,' she says.

I feel she is mocking me and remain silent. When I do not respond, she is concerned and changes her tone of voice.

'Tang has been very gloomy. He suffers so. I keep telling him, "What's done is done." No one thinks the worse of him for his confession. It was the sensible thing to do!'

She shakes her head. 'Roxanne, my friend, how I have missed talking to you! You are the only person who understands me.'

She suddenly repels me. Her charm? I feel that all the while she speaks of Tang and his troubles, she does not feel them as she should. She is dramatising herself. The pity she feels is more for herself than for his plight, or rather, she feels pity because of the role she has to play. She has no real sympathy for his cause, no wifely sense of duty and support, she is terribly unfeminine despite her feminine *charm*.

And she repeats this charm every time I see her. Of course she is the same as she ever was, but why did I not notice it before? Why did I admire her? I thought I knew her, knew her soul, but it was only her power I felt, the power she holds over her audience and me.

'Stop acting,' I say, harshly. 'Why are you always pretending?'

I am shocked by the words that have come out of my mouth. But she takes it lightly.

She laughs, 'I'm not acting. Why do you say that?'

When did this malaise start to creep over me? When came this sense of wanting to avoid her? What sparked it? Was it her behaviour towards Tang? Was it that when something real happened, then only could I sense the falsity of her act? Or is it me, tired and depressed when I see my husband for the mean man and traitor he is? Did my disillusion with him lead to my disillusion with her? But I did not think all these things clearly at the time. I only wanted to stay away from her.

Ching

Roxanne leaves me standing by the side of the road with her excuse of going back to the office. How strange she is! To accuse me of acting. And it came like an outburst!

50

Days later, a tremor passes through the earth. Tang hurries downstairs, and is met by a crowd. The people are attracted like ripples to a river-dropped stone. It is still early, around four in the morning, but no one sleeps nowadays. At least Tang doesn't. Revolution rocks the city, and acts of vengeance are carried out daily.

A sense of other worlds, like the cold fingers of a wind down the neck, creeps into people's lives. In some areas the earth breaks apart, becoming flaccid and unhinged. There is a little upheaval of red soil. Superstitious, some hear the susurrant swishing of a tail underneath the earth they stand upon. They suspect a dragon.

'It's swishing its tail in anger,' a woman addresses the crowd. Tang is among them. He welcomes small interruptions, grown dull as he has to the effects of wonder.

'Dragon, huh?' Tang comments.

The prophetess has drifted away. Under the streetlights, he observes her age. The voice has deceived him. He has thought her a young woman but now he sees clearly that she is quite old, with a bent back and greying hair coiled in a bun. *Maybe when I get to that age, I too will grow senile*, Tang thinks with a coarse laugh. He retires to his apartment.

'Nothing. Just the earth shaking.'

'We are not in the earthquake zone,' Ching remarks.

He shrugs. 'Maybe it was a dragon.'

Tang lies in bed, unable to sleep. He talks to Ching aimlessly about the Thaipusam procession he has seen, and the news on TV – new car taxes, a minister opening a new building, who got killed, who was robbed, what new government campaign is being launched.

'I think I'll have a small glass of something,' he says, getting up. 'Maybe a drink will help.'

He weaves a path to the kitchen. Ching picks up a book and

starts turning its pages. She is just putting aside the book and getting ready to snap off the light, when he returns.

He pulls his feet in under the blanket. 'I'm tired,' he says. 'Every day it's bloody crap on TV. Bloody movies. Bloody books. It's all the same.'

He turns to one side, and his breathing falls quiet.

Ching

Poor Tang. I think he begins to hear the director's voice speaking ever more clearly in his head.

I can see it. The director is a rotund man. The director's voice is frequently gruff from shouting. Even though the director issues stage directions and prompts cues, few of his staff have seen him face to face. He is like the boss, Charlie, in *Charlie's Angels*, the one in the swivel chair, back to his angels, issuing commands, which are implicitly believed in, and obeyed. He is just a voice, just a shape.

The master in Zhang Yimou's *Raise The Red Lantern* never has his face shown. That is part of the strategy of control. To obey what you do not see is more mind-numbing than to see what you obey. The unseen/unknown is by virtue the dominant, as the two assassins find out in Harold Pinter's play, *The Dumb Waiter*. Buried deep in his leather chair, the director chuckles.

I get carried away. Perhaps Tang sleeps peacefully. No dreams haunt him as they do me. I envy his steady breathing. I turn on my pillow, catch a glimpse of the time, try to force myself to drift.

51

I cannot go on like this, Tang reflects, burying his head in his arms, upon the pillow. *I am like a dead man.*

A dim notion takes hold. A wild flickering of an idea. Gandhi. A hunger strike. It will be something. Instead of being passive, he can show them that he is not cowed. He will show the world the stuff he is made of. His family name depends upon it. The scholar makes the headlines in the newspapers: *Former Detainee Goes On Hunger Strike.*

'Why?' Ching demands. 'Why can't you stay out of it? Hah! Do you want it to start again?'

'You don't understand.'

'No,' she says, flatly. 'What are you trying to do?'

He closes his eyes to her anger, the look in her eyes, his own pain. Lying in bed, he thinks, *Father would have approved, I am sure. Mother would have defended me.*

Tang father's room was a bright unknowable territory crammed with books. He lived in a rarefied atmosphere of learning. That gentle man had lived the life of a coolie as a young man, then as a plantation owner and with his wealth built his house and study. The scholar's father had come looking for a world where he could be free to work without being harassed by feudal overlords. He opened his eyes, sharp and black as knife slashes in a pale smooth face, and stared into a white ocean on which the morning sun was hanging. The vessel sailed. His journey pointed forward. He was the intrepid traveller. Like the intrepid traveller of a far earlier age. A scholar by the name of Wang Ta-yuan.

Reflections made by Wang Ta-yuan, on such a day and month in the lunar year, in the year known now as the early half of the fourteenth century: I made several trips in the southern seas in a period of twenty years altogether. This region was the Nanyang. I wrote of rocky bays and dragons and pirates lurking in murky reefs. I wrote of jungles and blue skies and an always-humid spirit wrapping the land, bringing typhoid and malaria.

Unlike many others of my class I am not too particular about my status when travelling. I am a gentleman and a scholar, the two going together, which naturally enough means that I am also a writer and artist. I have always been curious. It is not enough for me to know that the Middle Kingdom is the centre of the world. I want to know what lies beyond this reference point of civilisation and culture. How do others live? Who are they? Stories floated down through history from itinerant strangers to my country – of exotic trees, birds and animals, blue skies and hot thick jungles. I wanted to see these lands for myself. I persuaded the emperor of the necessity of setting forth a sailing vessel to look for vassal states. The emperor agreed.

On the day I set out, the signs were auspicious. I arrived at a little island called Temasek between the sharp teeth of a dragon, a narrow strait of water with two outcrops of rock at the entrance. I wrote in my journal: passed Dragon's Teeth Gate today.

That gap-toothed dragon led the way inwards to a small settlement where the people, perhaps a hundred, lived off piracy and fishing. The soil was poor and unable to sustain heavy agriculture.

When Wang Ta-yuan sailed into the Nanyang in the early half of the fourteenth century, the island which was to become the city was mostly jungle. The population was mainly *orang laut*, or men of the sea.

When the Chinese migrants came, they were escaping the civil wars, famines and oppressive regimes of the motherland. They were rebels fleeing: a succession of refugees of the Tai Ping Rebellion, the Boxer Rebellion, the several kung fu schools that had been closed down.

Some who came were simple peasants and merchants seeking a better fortune. They came from coastal seaports in droves, on boats that would take them to faraway lands where they could make their fortunes.

They drifted into countries in a great beyond, carrying with them heavy cultural luggage, which they unpacked in every place they arrived. In many places, their luggage was greeted with suspicion.

It did not help when the Middle Kingdom asserted her cultural and moral authority over her runaways, proclaiming them to be always of the Kingdom. And for a long time, even till the present, the runaways find themselves compass-pointed to the great motherland when they go in search of an identity.

A term was coined. *Sons of the Yellow Emperor*. Daughters too, naturally, though the Kingdom had been slow in acknowledging them. Perhaps then, it was easier for the daughters of the Kingdom to detach themselves from a heavy cultural burden, since they were ignored, and to strike out on paths of their own.

★

Tang sits gazing sourly at a teak and mother-of-pearl chair, a family heirloom. He is permanently listless these days. Ching, her hair done up in a bun and in a light blue cotton dress with a Peter Pan collar, stops on her way out.

'Come,' she tells him briskly.

Her eyes rest on me as if on some unwanted furniture, he feels.

'Will you stop moping? Why don't you go for a walk?'

The scholar stirs, 'I'll stay in. I'll write a poem. Something just came to me.'

She gives him a look of suspicion. 'I'll see you later.'

Window encrusted with snow
Waking, eyes covered with sleep

Shreds of the poem have stayed in his mind since the morning, as he haphazardly awoke and blinked at the wall. He has dreamt a poem. Two lines of which he remembers. Romantically he thinks of himself as a sleeper in the snow, misty-eyed, still dreaming.

The scholar's father became a rich man with some luck. Tang grew up in a house with seven bedrooms and almost as many bathrooms. Even the maid who slept downstairs had her own bathroom next to her sleeping quarters. The house was filled with fragrant camphor laurel, rosewood and teak furniture. Some of the black lacquered chairs had been inlaid with mother-of-pearl on their backs, seats and arms. Upon the wood were carved flowers, birds or gentle landscapes. On the legs of the chairs, his father's and mother's names were inscribed in flowing calligraphy. The chairs were uncomfortable to sit on, but beautiful.

The scholar's father made his journey across a sea of milk-white waves; his boat sailed to the Nanyang. One day, a sudden feeling made him scrabble among his clothing and fish out the jade piece on a chain his mother had given him. He put it around his neck. Then he breathed in deeply. Before he sailed into the Nanyang, he had thought of himself as a Chinaman with thousands of years of tradition upon his back. But this morning, he opened his eyes to a familiar, yet unfamiliar, sky. He watched the four-cornered sails tilting. As his boat neared his destination, there was a shift of perspective. Something that had been slowly churning inside, some change of emotion, kaleidoscopic, dropped into place.

A whole day ahead. New faces. New landmarks. In his heart, he was afraid. He was only eighteen and the long journey sailing from his home port in Foochow to the sunlit humidity of the Nanyang had sapped much of his adventurous spirit.

He had heard that one would have to have one's name changed to suit the tongues of foreign devils, that one had to talk face to face with them, work for them. He heard the women of the Nanyang were dark-skinned and wore only cloths around their bodies. He heard of heatwaves, cholera, dysentery and malaria, and men dying like animals in small cramped dormitories, packed ten to a room, uncared for.

'Only a few years, then I'll go back,' he promised. 'I will buy my way back on a boat sailing home.'

He knew though that going back was an impossibility, that his parents' farm was a ruin, and that only here he had a chance to make money to send home, perhaps even to buy his parents' passage over, or at least his brothers'.

He shattered the panes from his eyes with a tremendous yawn, stretched, and swung his legs abruptly off the pallet, rapidly pulling on his clothes. He sat on his clothes chest, his only possession, and waited. He had spent the past weeks cramped and tired.

'When you are rich, remember your brothers and sisters,' his mother had said at parting.

He vowed he would send home money regularly. Some years passed, he met a girl. The scholar's mother was a Straits-born Chinese. Her father was wealthy, a philanthropist who had funded the building of a girls' high school in Penang. The scholar's mother was highly educated, a teacher.

The scholar's father saw her for the first time during the Orange Throwing Festival, when girls from high-class homes rode out in horse-drawn carriages to the river to toss oranges into it, in hopes of being seen by a prospective husband. It was an occasion to be seen.

The girls were allowed to show themselves in public once a year. The men stood amongst the palm trees watching. If they saw a girl they liked, a marriage broker would be approached and the girl's parents would be offered a proposal of marriage.

The scholar's father was of lowly origins. His parents were from the peasant class. He despaired of winning the girl's hand. But fate that tied prospective lovers together proved stronger than reason. He had a little money saved up. So the scholar's father decided to return to China to get a university education.

When he had earned a university degree from Shanghai, he returned to propose and was accepted.

The scholar's mother was a beautiful and intelligent woman. She spoke Mandarin and English fluently. She taught English at a girls' high school in Penang. She played the guitar. She was the President of the Chinese Women's Association for ten years. She was by her husband's side when he began to host parties. She made speeches on behalf of charities.

The scholar's father had become a rich businessman, and sponsored his brothers over to the city. The scholar's father and mother danced at charity balls, and lived in a big house on Northam Road.

But she was to die of tuberculosis at the age of forty-eight. Tang Na Juan was born seven years after the end of the Second World War into circumstances vastly different from what had been before. Tang's father lost all his land and money during the Japanese Occupation. He never managed to recover his wealth in the years following. What little he still had was spent on physicians, when Tang's mother fell ill soon after Tang was born. After the funeral of Tang's mother, they had even less money. A rich widow came to Tang's father and offered him marriage. He refused her. He would live with his memories of his wife till the end of his life.

There is a photograph standing on the cabinet: a black and white print of Tang's parents. His mother is clad in Peranakan garb, her slim figure enhanced by the sarong, her eyes alight with impish laughter, her body bending like a willow towards the scholar's father who is standing stiff and straight and sombre in Western tails.

Tang's father owned many rubber plantations in the Malayan hills. He read widely and with great interest books from all over the world. He could speak at least four languages with some degree of fluency. He read in English as well as in Mandarin and spent his time translating his favourite English texts.

He practised calligraphy. He painted and wrote poems. Because of his great civility and kindness, he was often taken advantage of.

Once he was robbed of his best pair of trousers, which he always hung behind the door before putting on an old pair to go out to the fields. In the back pocket he had left his wallet. The scholar's father knew it could well be one of his employees who had stolen from him. The next day, he brought the coat that went with his best pair of trousers. He hung it behind the door. He meant it to be stolen. His theory was that the coat was no good without the trousers and he would give the thief his coat.

All his men saw his action and thought him a fool. All except one. At the day's end, the guilty one came to him. It had been Ah Lim, one of his poorest workers. He knelt before Tang's father. But his master raised him to his feet. He told him gently that he had already given him the coat and trousers. They were his.

The thief gradually became one of the best workers and eventually a manager overseeing the estates. Perhaps Tang's father was not such a bad businessman after all. Or perhaps there was honour even among thieves in those days.

Tang had a background vastly different to Ching's. Perhaps it was what had attracted him to her. She had nothing in terms of status, family name or money, only a fierce will. He had found her immensely attractive. He had proposed to her two months after first seeing her.

But the legacy of his family remains. 'Ching thinks I am a fool, because she only considers what she can get out of anything,' Tang says to himself, with a note of anger.

Ching

The Monkey God thought it could outwit the Buddha and leap beyond the palm of the Buddha's hand in which was held the whole of creation, all of life. So he jumped and it was a good long jump, the Monkey God being an immortal, and he found himself at the outermost edge of the world with only five pillars standing solitary. The Monkey God chalked upon them little red marks to say, 'I was here!'

As every railway commuter has seen – those personalised graffiti that shout to an indifferent world, 'I exist!'

And then he leaped back from where he had come. Before him was the Buddha's smiling benign face.

'And how, little one? Have you reached the end of the world?'

'Of course,' boasted the Monkey. 'And I have marked upon it my signature.'

The Buddha spread his fingers wide, 'Climb into my palm, little one and see, your marks are upon my fingers.'

The Monkey God saw that what he said was true and experienced crushing despair, for he realised then that no matter how he tried, in his limited capacity, he would never be beyond, he could never get outside, that there existed for him no other world he could escape to.

I have ridden once on the back of a whale and it told me that it would give to me a stone that contained the secret of this earth. I held it in my palm and on the stone I saw the world, all crushed within the fine rock material, crushed and blurred and not terribly important, and that was what it should be.

I have known only images. The world remains as frightening to me now as it did when I was a child riding the whale, perhaps even more so because now with developed intellect and reason, I know it is still inscrutable to me and that no matter how much I grow, I will never grasp this life and its horror and my soul or something inside will still resist my living in it.

Sometimes you make do with what you've got. In the end, life is short. Confronted with death, everything else falls into perspective. Many a time I've asked myself, 'Why was I born here, in this small city, so small it is sometimes not even shown by a dot on a map? Why here? What forces of circumstance? Kismet?'

> *There is a long slow waiting*
> *between the pavement slabs*
> *an upheaval of grainy sand*
> *a tingling pause in the mind*
> *knowing that beneath it all*
> *is a world in silence*

'Are you sure this is what you want to do?' I ask my husband. 'Perhaps,' I suggest, 'you could pay more attention to your bonsais.'

'Perhaps,' Tang says, 'I might as well lie down and die.'

When I see how he is determined, I lose all motivation to make him change his mind.

'It is your life,' I remind him. 'Your decision. I am only telling you how useless it is, what you are doing.'

52

The scene: the bedroom. Tang sits up in bed, blanket over his legs, busy composing a letter to the editor of the daily newspaper. The words come unimpeded from his pen.

I believe in a world where justice prevails. Where the voice of a single man will be heard. I believe that I have been misjudged. I have had no trial. I have been treated without justice. Fear implanted in the minds of the citizens serves as a potent form of inhibition. No one dares rebel or express a different opinion from that of the government's.

The time is about nine in the morning. He writes away fast. His words flow smoothly but inside his head is pandemonium. He rubs his temples and glances up.

The spirit comes to Tang on the first day of his hunger strike. A woman with a sharp face and rather unusually long toes, a bit like an animal's, sits at the foot of his bed, upon his blanketed legs. She is almost weightless. Tang exerts some energy to move but is held fast.

She hoots, rocking back and forth, shaking her round head in merriment. In fright, he roars, 'Who are you? In heaven's name, who are you? Are you a ghost? Or a thing of my past?'

The thing, whatever it is, leaps out with two hands to clutch his throat, no longer laughing.

'You are a devil from hell?' Tang squeezes out a cry.

In answer, the spirit woman tosses a brown furry head, soft enough to stroke, and sticks her tongue out at him, showing him its warm pinkness and the black back of her mouth. He shudders in revulsion. A smell rises from the woman, a hot potent smell of an animal of the wilds: a fox woman.

He screams, 'Go away!'

The fox woman holds fast; she laughs in great cackles; she rides his ankles as if she is upon a stallion.

It has often been recorded, Tang tells himself, *the meetings between men of learning and these fox women who are evil and intend only to capture the mortal souls of men.* Why it should be that it was primarily scholars of ancient China who met with these women, it is hard to say. Perhaps learning befuddles the brain and opens it up to delusions. Reading allows the mind to travel to distant vistas, to worlds never seen by visible eyes, into other souls and points of view alien to one's own, hence the dangers. Maybe scholars of ancient times dreamed far and wide and sought for their temptations in the fox women.

Tang has chanced on books that tell of fox women who fall in love with mortal men and repent of their evil ways. In rare cases, they may even live together happily as man and wife. But by and large, the fox woman is a free spirit, roaming the land in search of a foolish man who will give her back her mortality.

Hanging over the ditch are wildflowers whose names Tang, with a wrinkle of brow, recalls. He moans faintly as he tries to raise himself and waves of nausea hit him. With his lips, he reaches wetly to one of the flower petals and pulling, begins to chew. The taste is sweet, unexpected. He shakes his head to clear it.

From the jungle, he hears a roar. He imagines lions and beasts. No, he is a beast. Lower than men. Lying in mud upon his back in a narrow ditch. How has he come to be there? He, a prince? What robbers have done this? But as he remembers carrying no money, it is not possible. His clothes are still upon his body, nothing has been taken, he can think of no attack, nothing.

Uncertainly he peers out of the ditch. Interlacing branches of overhead trees create a shadowy canopy, although bursts of sunlight seep through to the ground and where they alight, there spring stunted bushes and wildflowers. Once his head stops throbbing, he thinks, he would recover his bearing.

But instead he dreams of a prince – or is he the prince dreaming he is Tang, the scholar?

When Sang Nila Utama, a Sumatran prince, awakes, his head is fit to burst. As if a hammer has attacked him. Around the boat he is in, a wind springs up, the water hissing and sucking at the gunwales. His crew panics. 'Sire, the boat sinks, we die.'

But he replies, 'Take my crown and throw it into the sea. It will appease the waves and sea-monsters.'

They do his bidding and the waves subside, and they continue on their way with fair weather. Their load is also considerably lighter. The light boat speeds along and the prince looks keenly for the first sight of land. Into view it comes. A stretch of palms and white beaches.

'This is a good land,' says he, stepping off the boat. Then, a roar from the depths of the jungle and a magnificent beast with red mane emerges.

'A lion,' shrieks his crew, and fall upon their faces in terror.

But the prince eyes the beast calmly, 'Let this land be known then as Singapura, the city of the lion.'

With these words the beast vanishes into the jungle from whence it has come. The prince and his followers stay to help themselves to the wild coconuts fallen from the trees.

Tang walks along a path in a jungle. The fox spirit trots by his side. As he passes under the giant trees, yellow flowers like sun-kissed drops begin to fall out of them. Soon they cluster on the ground so he treads upon petals. By the pathside, the wild lalang sways. Wind blows bleakly upon his face.

Soon they come to a clearing. At its centre is a giant mirror. The fox spirit calmly walks into the mirror, which turns into a pool of water, and disappears. The scholar is held back by his fear. A sense of evil pervades the place.

He says to empty air, 'This is the place where men's souls are lost. It is better if I were to die now.'

He waits for some response from the silent jungle. Time passes. He feels as though he has been in this place for a long time, as if time has stood still, and his sentence commuted indefinitely.

'I am not in the city,' he remarks, feeling some certainty in saying this. He senses the form of a prison upon this tiny place. It is an island, only smaller.

In his spirit, he feels himself as the city's longest serving political detainee. Unbidden, the director's voice comes, 'You are on Pulau Blakang Mati.'

'Pulau Blakang Mati!' the scholar exclaims. *'The Isle Beyond The Dead.'*

Tang discovers that he has never been out of bed. Was it a dream? He does not think so. Even if he had been asleep, his soul could have emerged from the open chakra in his head to wander the world. Its adventures were as real as anything that happened to him in his mortal life.

'And how are you?' Ching asks, coming to his bedside.

'You didn't tell me I was going to start hallucinating!' he replies, his voice rising in surprise. 'Why didn't you call the doctor?'

The rest of the day passes in weariness.

His mynah screeches in its cage. If he does not have more serious problems to think of, he may think of strangling it.

'What is it?' he curses. 'Raising the dead, are you?'

And outside the sky shines like lapis lazuli, while the Channel Eight television crew enters through the front door. Tang tosses restlessly.

Tang has miscalculated the nature of his oppressors. He thinks they will be softened, much as men may be softened by a weeping woman, but there are men who will gather to cast stones no matter how much the woman is to weep and wail. Softness cannot subdue them.

Tang thinks, *I have no other choice, for I am without power or political friends.* He holds his head in his hands. His room is once again empty of all others. The white curtains shift in the open window and the wind blows upon some papers on the bedside table.

When Ching comes in again, he says, 'In the *Analects*,

Confucius said that there are mistakes that may be made. *To speak when it is not yet time to speak is called presumptuousness; not to speak when it is time for one to speak is called secretiveness.* It is my time to speak, to act.'

'Three,' his wife says. 'Three mistakes.'

To his surprise she quotes Confucius, '*To speak when one has not yet observed (the other's) expression is called blindness.*'

She adds in a tired manner, 'I have read his *Analects*. That is correct, yes?'

Tang is frozen by her words and look and cannot reply.

Roxanne

I persuade my editor to let me do an article on the hunger strike. But it is a week later before I manage to find the time, so busy has my editor kept me with other stories. I have not had the time to talk to Ching of late, except to call on the first day and ask how Tang was. She seemed almost bad-tempered. She said he was unwell. I advised her to gently induce him to give up the strike. I have been hearing things in the newsroom. Word has been passed down that we are not to take too much interest in the strike. They want to prevent sympathy. My editor is jittery over everything and keeps all our articles under tight scrutiny. Something must be in the air. I console Ching, and tell her that I will be down to see them.

Tang

Headlines on page three of the city's English daily. A sizeable paragraph complete with photograph on the front page of the Chinese press. A television news crew takes up residence in the living room.

After a week and a half of the hunger strike, as I lie in bed anticipating the return of the spirit, I am sure *a certain someone* is watching me. The long window has opened and two or three figures have crawled in and are standing at the foot of my bed, quite near my coverlet.

My bed is a boat and the waves are rocking about me. I feel horribly nauseated. I squeeze my eyes into slits and try to focus.

'Hey? You have some business here?'

A pink melamine bowl filled with pap appears by my bedside with a spoon. In the bowl of the spoon, I see my distorted reflection, and then look up to see grey shapes.

'Eat,' the shapes urge. 'Eat.'

A mild twitch begins in my left eye, I feel tremendously hungry. Never before have I gone without my meals. My former exhilaration seems to have passed.

People have been coming in and out of the room to see me – old students, current students, a few friends and relatives and a few well-wishers who support my stance. Ching's good friend, Roxanne, has come to do an article. Perhaps these men are my well-wishers.

'Well, I'm on a hunger strike. I can't. It's important for me not to eat –'

The aroma of the pap before me rises to my nostrils, tantalising me. The pap seems vague in shape and consistency but delicious, oh, yes, definitely delicious. Before I can stop myself, I have taken a mouthful and then another. The grey shapes standing at the foot of my bed materialise presently as three men with heavy nondescript faces. Vaguely massive. Whitish uniforms on their bodies. They watch me as I eat.

'Faster,' they say. 'More.'

I eat and drink and wipe my mouth on the sleeve of my T-shirt. I try with grim expression to fulfil their bidding.

I am surprised by the lights of the news crew. The three men are no longer there. Before me is the television news crew from Channel Eight. The light blinds me.

In the evening news: *Hunger Strike Fails.*

There are headlines in the papers. The media reports mockingly, *How long suffering, this champion of the wronged.*

Ching comes to the bed, her face drawn. She looks as though she has suffered much. I quickly take her hand.

She says, 'I've just picked up the phone. You've lost your teaching post at the poly. The polytechnic is firing you. They'll send a letter.'

I am too weak to object. I turn my face to the pillow and think of the friends and supporters I have lost, and the lifelong enemies gained.

Roxanne

Tang is calm and resigned to his fate following the unfortunate hunger strike. Ching calls me the day the headlines appear. From her bitter tones she sounds almost as though she accuses me of complicity. I suspect the Chairman had a hand in stopping the strike. Why should there be such headlines about Tang's hunger strike when we were told to keep it low? Why the build-up in the media, and then the ultimate humiliation for Tang?

I find it hard to regain my trust for my editor. He hurries past my desk, and hardly says a word to me.

53

'Comrades, you have got it all wrong,' the woman's shrill voice was loud and threatening. 'You have strayed from the path of the revolution. You are all fat and satisfied chickens. Not one of you has any guts. When the government says take this, you take it. Do this and you do it. Is all that matters to you your stomachs and your purses?'

Someone replies, 'But, comrade, in a materialistic society, we have little choice. We put up with the division between rich and poor. We put up with being told how to conduct our private affairs. As long as the government provides for us, it is enough.'

'Silence,' thunders the speaker. 'Do you not admit that class snobbery has arisen? That money determines rank in this city? That our children are streamed at the tender age of nine according to their examination results? That the English-educated hog the jobs? That the poor lose out because they cannot afford tutors for their children? That the downtrodden of society are hidden from the public eye? And that your silence and complicity are bought!'

There was a loud murmuring of agreement from the audience.

'But what can we do?'

The woman speaker has calmed down a little.

'It was not the Chairman's wish that such a situation should have arisen. We all know how much he has himself personally sacrificed to build up this city – it is the doing of some in parliament, some whom I will not name, holding high ranks. They have been born with silver spoons in their mouths – it is they of whom I speak.'

Again there is applause.

The woman draws in a deep breath and lets loose a battle cry, 'Shall we allow these people to destroy what has been built up? Shall we forget the ideals of our city – democracy, peace, prosperity for all regardless – how many of *them* belong to a certain class, a certain language group, a certain religion? Comrades, there is a need for revolt.'

It does not take much to stir up a crowd. Dissatisfactions there are aplenty. The woman – Comrade Chiang Ching – makes herself an instant hero with her rhetoric.

'We will bomb the national monuments,' hisses one.

'Let us call together the cabinet and cut them down to size,' cries another.

'Why is there such a heavy-handed and hierarchical bureaucracy in this city?' shouts a third.

'My boss is a tyrant.'

'Car prices are outrageous.'

'Taxes have gone up.'

'My children can't afford housing these days. They are all staying at home, though they are in their thirties and all professionals.'

'My daughter works too hard. She doesn't have time to find a husband.'

'What's going on?' An agitated colleague addresses Roxanne. The journalists are working late.

'I hear there are strikes and riots happening. I thought strikes were banned.'

Roxanne stops typing her notes. 'I don't know,' she replies, 'but many strange things have been going on. The Minister of the Arts was hauled before a crowd of egg-throwing protesters for having censored a play that made fun of government policies. It was a silly play. I wouldn't have thought it worth banning. But he did so, and now the play's actors are heroes and the playwright is running around as a spokesperson for revolt.'

'The Minister was forced to stand in the centre of the crowd wearing a paper hat that had the word DUNCE written in large letters, his arms were forced behind his back in the position of an aeroplane about to take off. The crowd jeered at him. He was forced to apologise.'

'The editor says he doesn't know whether we should run the news. If we don't, people will hear of it anyway through word of mouth and then we would really look like the sycophantic press we are, but if we do, he is afraid of government crackdown.'

'Huh, why pretend we have freedom of the press when we don't?' says Rajan, overhearing. Rajan is a senior reporter and has been working in the paper for over a decade. He stretches his tired fingers.

'Actually, one doesn't really know. One can only test the limits, like a ship at the edge of someone's water borders,' Choon says. Choon is a Political Desk journalist. 'Then when they crack down, you know you've gone too far. The problem is that it simply creates an atmosphere of uncertainty. The journalists themselves do not try, do not wish to report on anything that may be perceived as sensitive. It's more a case of self-censorship.'

'It's diabolically clever,' interjects a colleague.

'You can tell me!' Rajan says.

'I wish,' comments another reporter, Fatimah, who has been quiet during the discussion, raising her gaze from her notebook to join in, 'I wish I knew where the Chairman stood on all this. I wish someone would tell me.'

The journalists in the newsroom are kept busy. To complicate matters a series of strange murders are taking place, with the victims' bodies found devoid of their entrails. It is a hectic and stressful time.

'Do you suppose it's cannibals?' mutters Will Reutens, a reporter from Crime Desk.

'Who cares?' sighs Rajan. 'It's past nine and my copy's not cleared yet and I need sleep.'

'Maybe someone should murder the editor?' suggests a listening colleague.

They raise their eyebrows while he giggles nervously, 'I'm just joking.'

'Whatever's happening … I wish someone would get to the bottom of it soon,' says Will, yawning. He pulls on his green cardigan. 'Anyone want to come with me to grab a bite to eat somewhere?'

'Hey,' says the editor who has come in looking excited, 'good, you're still here. I've got news. The Chairman stands behind the revolution.'

'Oh my god,' says Rajan, without thinking.

The editor hands them the sheet of paper he is holding. It is a letter from the Chairman to the head editor. The journalists all look at one another silently, no one says anything.

In the evening, one zealously hardworking journalist bumps into a man acting in a furtive manner around a national monument, the statue of Sir Stamford Raffles, by the river.

'Hey,' cries the journalist, catching hold of the man's sleeve. 'What do you think you are doing?'

The man utters a sort of squeak, drops the parcel he is holding onto the ground, and powers his legs away. The journalist touches the parcel cautiously with the tip of his shoe. He decides rather than risk his life opening it, he will call the police. When he is gone, a Red Guard enters. He, too, is acting suspiciously and is clutching a parcel to his chest. He sees the earlier parcel and stops to stare at it. The journalist comes back.

'Hey,' he says. 'What do you think you are doing?'

The Red Guard looks him up and down.

'Can you keep a secret?'

'Yes,' says the journalist, automatically.

'I'm going to bomb the national monument.'

'But why?'

The Red Guard looks puzzled. 'Why not? Isn't that what a revolutionary does?'

'There was someone else here before you,' says the journalist, indicating the first parcel.

'So I see,' says the Red Guard. 'Why don't we check what's inside?'

'It's probably a bomb, I'd rather not. I've just called the anti-bomb squad. They'll be here shortly.'

'I want to know,' says the Red Guard, obstinately.

He bends down and rips the parcel open. Inside is a crude bomb.

'I told you,' squeaks the journalist, backing away.

'How clever,' says the Red Guard, 'looks like I won't have much need for this.' He looks at his own parcel absently for a bit, then crosses to where the railings separate pedestrians from the river, and drops his parcel in.

He hears the sounds of people approaching and quickly takes to his heels. The journalist follows.

'It hasn't gone off,' says the man who dropped the first parcel. He stops at a safe distance with the companion who had been waiting for him in their getaway car.

'Of course not,' says his co-conspirator. 'It was just a dud.'

'But why? Why was I sent with a dud bomb?' he asks in injured tones.

The companion shrugs. 'To test your mettle?' he suggests. He picks up the open parcel and crossing over to the railings, drops it into the water with a splash.

'Hey, wait a minute,' says the first man. 'What are you doing? What is this all about?'

His companion is about to say something, then cries out, 'Quick, the police, run!'

The two men speed off.

The police enter. 'Nothing here.'

He looks around. 'Thought I heard people running away.'

'Must have been a prank caller.'

'Look, there's the statue intact.'

They walk around it.

'Well, all's quiet.'

'Let's go,' the other one says, disgusted.

54

Certainly the Chairman is behind the revolution. The next night, the Chairman's face appears on the nine o'clock news on the TV. Roxanne has just returned home after work. She stands behind Jeff's chair and both watch silently.

'I condemn,' says the Chairman, 'the actions of a riotous group of people. Traitors to our harmonious society. You know how easy it is to fracture this multiracial, multireligious, multicultural society of ours, and some persons have sought to do so by promoting chauvinism. Some people have sought to impose their religious views. Some have committed crimes in order to intimidate the rest of the populace and convert it to their ideology. This is wrong. We cannot allow it to happen.'

As he continues, he praises the Red Guards for their courage in standing up to seditious elements within the society and within their own ranks.

'He is so reasonable,' Roxanne exclaims. Jeff does not comment. He sits silently, his face looking wan.

Roxanne refrains from further remarks. Their relationship has been much strained. Roxanne cannot tell if he still feels the way he did towards the Chairman, respecting him to the point of placing him upon a pedestal.

When Roxanne has had a bath, she goes to the fridge and rummages for food. She piles leftover green mango salad onto a plate and makes herself a coffee, before sitting down again before the TV. An excerpt of the Chairman's speech is reported during the *News In Brief*.

It begins to be obvious to Roxanne why the Chairman should stand behind the revolution, and why he is playing one group off against another. His power is ebbing. At the last count, his voter popularity dropped by fifteen per cent. Chaos unleashed gives power to the man at the centre, Roxanne considers. But speaking at this time when strange elements are roaming the streets! It is unwise to provoke. But perhaps he has faith in the Red Guards!

55

Tang

My bed is a warm blue, rocking me, ship-bound in a turbulent ocean. Outside the closed window of my room a storm is brewing. Between the world and me is endless nausea, a black wind blowing. Nothing stands between me and what lies without, nothing except eternity. Chased by the storm, a moth outside flutters against the glass pane. Two moths. A small white one intimately pursuing a large dark one. Their wings make frantic beating sounds. I hear it said that the small white moth frequently seen in company of a larger dark one is a dead person's soul. The dark one is death.

I have begun to think that I am developing a form of paranoia. I hear the squeak of shoes. Little sounds hang in the air. My toes tingle. I turn my head from side to side because I feel their presence. The men in white clothes are watching me. They have spies waiting. They want to see what indiscretions I will let slip, what move not in keeping.

I press on the radio. A song laments out. A song I recognise as written to a poem by the poet-general Yue Fei of the Sung Dynasty (AD 960–1279).

With anger I leaned on the railing, to the patter of rain.
Raising my head I howled with passion my great aspirations.
My thirty years of career and honour are like dust and mud.

The resounding call of the song beats waves around my bed to a fury. The waves rock splashing against the sides of my bed, while I huddle beneath my quilt.

No soldier, I. Only a mouse, no, worse, an insect. Scrabbling about underground.

Yes, this is what I am, without even the victorious modesty

of an Ah Q, who each time his pigtail is pulled and his head knocked against the wall would, a few seconds later, crow that he was the winner!

No, I do not even have the pride to do that.

Their weight sits on me. Sometimes I feel them in the pit of my stomach, at the base of my throat. They want to know everything: where have you been? Why? And more importantly, what do you think?

Thinking is dangerous. You have to be careful not to fall into traps. You can simply think like them, trap one, or more insidiously, think unlike them, trap two. Because that is what they have pushed many of us to do, thinking the opposite. But their ends are good ones, and if we reject all they say, we reject even virtue.

But now I have to be careful. While their professed ends are virtuous, surely their means are not? But are you saying that they should have no authority? See how tricky thinking becomes?

Kahlil Gibran. *The Prophet*. On freedom. I do not remember what he had to say exactly but I remember it is to the effect that freedom is not when you are without difficulties, but when their weight binds you like a chain and you rise above them. Firstly, be rid of the tyrant who is within you, before killing the tyrant without.

But what if they have planted the tyrant within you so you live in fear? Even Kahlil Gibran may not understand the position of mice and insects.

I have spent almost all my energy resisting … what? I am not clear. The pressure lines pull at my temples. It is a familiar throbbing. I am wondering if I should summon up my courage, take the plunge – step out of bed. But then why should I? It is warm and safe where I am and beyond me stretches an endless sea. An insect is doomed.

What if I should get my feet wet? What if I should be held

responsible for the chaos which might erupt – the waters parting. I am not a Moses leading the Israelites.

The door beckons. There is a stain on its cream colour. The other night I squashed an insect against it and it left its dark stain.

Maybe these are mere excuses. What, after all, can an insect do? Simply to survive is bad enough. One has to be on the alert at all times, to make sure they don't realise, no, that they will not suspect, any lack of will in you for their proposed schemes and goals.

This is no place for the weak, the idle and the stupid. Because if the least hint comes through, their faces turn wary, they turn from you, they leave you alone. Surely it is not a bad thing to be left alone, you say?

But the loneliness of it … so utters the insect that would rather speak their interests, their lingo, than to be left alone to think profitless thoughts. Insects delight in company.

How often when I am reading by the lamp, does an insect settle beside my book, pleasurably hanging onto the edges of the light, grooming its wings and waiting. And the other night, growing impatient, I chased it away where it settled on the door.

A monstrous urge came over me and I closed my book and smashed the poor thing against the door. It is hard to be constantly reminded of the sort of creature one is.

So I have done it, dangled one foot over the edge. Go on, put it down. Yes, I know a journey of a thousand miles begins with a single step, but if I take a step, it will lead to another and another and another and soon I will be on a journey going I know not where.

It is better to go of your own will than to wait for them to come. Well? I am waiting for their footsteps.

In this world, we live with the hustle of every other person grabbing some limelight for himself to assert, 'Here am I, surely I exist,' in a sort of mild panic, as if one is no longer sure.

In this world I only hope to sink into insubstantiality, to pass off as one of the crowd. I would rather make the ritual movements, speeches, and pass undetected so I can think my thoughts in secret peace.

But where am I?

Getting out of bed.

I grab my bedclothes before they fall to the floor. In my striped pyjamas I stand upright. I make nervous gestures with my fingers as if the arabesques I perform in thin air would transform into words of magic, spells to change destiny. My fingers waver, hesitate, drop.

I am nervous. People make me nervous, with their tightness, their categories, and impositions upon me. All, all of them, even the one who professes himself a liberal, a free-thinker, an open ocean, sometimes he is the most intolerant of all. I want to be rid of humanity.

I speak and then am sorry I have spoken. Words engendered within one's soul once uttered lose their preciousness; they become commonplace because they fall upon commonplace ground, upon minds that know only how to categorise. *Poor man. On the verge of a breakdown.* I want only to be alone in the world, beholden to no one, owing nothing, wanting nothing, just myself and the world, a potentiality stretching out before me.

I make my retreat to the toilet.

To be alone, completely alone, one has to be mad or dead. The thought of death fascinates. Death. Is it final? Is there a beyond where I will travel? I have been to the other world and back. Because of the betrayals I have suffered, I have gone to the edge. My mind has been battered under the cudgels of their authority.

I cannot think further. This is the furthest edge.

I find myself drifting in my thoughts. When I jerk myself into a semblance of life again, I find myself in the same jungle

I had visited before at the time I was on a hunger strike. I shudder upon recognising the place.

'*The Isle Beyond The Dead*,' I whisper. I wait for a cue. None arrives.

'The director is slack tonight,' I murmur, following the pale moonlight towards the giant trees. An extensive bird's nest fern bulges out of a tree.

In the light, the body of a carnivorous pitcher plant leers grotesquely at me with florid lips. There is a whirring of insect wings playing at a pitch. In the shadow of the jungle, each step makes me nervous. The twigs crack, the leaves rustle, whispering tendrils grope downwards, and I feel spiders run over my face.

In the centre of the clearing I come again to the pool of water. The waters are murky as though stagnant. A large angsana hangs over the pool. Though it is dark, my eyes soon make out a wooden chair under the tree and a rope tied around a branch.

Is it for me? I have reached the edge of time, I have come to my last chapter, my history is ending.

The shadows mock me, taking on the forms of my interrogators, hissing in contempt, 'Coward.' Loud laughter rings in my ears.

When I die, will it all end? Does my broken self follow after me? Will I live in permanent torment? What drives a man to kill himself? I think, fascinated. I have heard of a man who before jumping from his HDB flat on the tenth floor, scrawled *I Love You* messages on all the mirrors in the flat, just a farewell thought to his wife and children. He must have known they would care.

I liken choosing death to crossing the Rubicon. I step over to the chair, which is of poor quality and much used, pull at my trousers, and climb on. I sway, stand, one hand upon the rope.

'Is it for me?' I repeat. 'I have not said my farewells yet.'

Then I think sadly, *No one will regret my leaving*.

I pull the noose towards myself and slip my head in. I tighten it. A long pause as I watch the shifting shadows. The supposed beasts of the jungle making noises of loud and clamouring varieties, the flap of a bat's wing overhead, the pad of a tiger's paw, and the cricket singing at my wake. My senses are much awakened. I have an immense sense of the suffocating beauty of the jungle, of the heat and the closeness of the trees, and here and there the iridescent patches of luminescent bacteria.

Great and small are beautiful. They choke me to the point of nausea. I will regret nothing. Not the calm orderly life I once had, the chaos that followed my writings or the hunger strike.

I feel a pang when I recall my cowardly confessions over television, but my mind forbids me to dwell on them.

We all make mistakes.

How alone I feel at this point, contemplating my next manoeuvre. The wind blows gently across my face. With a sudden move I kick away the wooden chair.

56

In the bedroom the last strains of the song over the radio cries out to empty ears. In the toilet the scholar's hanging body waits for someone to discover him.

I do not know who is right, Tang had written in his last entry within his diary. *They have a barrage of lawyers and the law with them. I know only I am afraid, and in this fear, there is at its core, something wrong, something evil in this city … against which I am impotent.*

57

Ching

As I reach the front door of my apartment, I hear the notes of an opera, hesitantly sung, as if from behind the closed entry. It is my own voice, layered by a chorus of others, rising in melodic intensity.

I pause, with my hand clasping my handbag, nervously, as the faint sounds of presentiment come to me. The amah, in reply to the doorbell, swings open the door with a wild gesture.

'*Ah Yi*, the master die.'

It is a stage, only a stage, a makeshift affair, a drama of the mind, laid open like a proscenium arch theatre with one wall missing, the hole through which they may enter. There's no one selling the tickets, there's no backdrop except the trees and its branches interlacing the sky. There is heavy knocking on the door which swings open. Easily broken timber. His aspect framed in the doorway. He is dead, his feet dangling off the ground, shoes knocking against the wood, face purplish, his eyes wide open. The doors of his body have opened, to release his soul. He is dead. The knocking is only the wind. Or the sounds of the neighbours. Perhaps the rain hammers down like blows on the parched etiolated face of the land, my husband's ghost, shadow thin, is roaming within the city.

PART THREE

58

Ching

The Red Guards have not been idle in hunting down the mirror people. The chief of the group who had called on the Captain, the mirror woman in the halter-neck, was found, taunted, and made to undress. Her bruised body was later found floating in the muddy river. I was among those who tortured her.

The Chairman continues poorly after a stroke. The people of the city seem restless, infected by some disease. I sense an upheaval. They are dissatisfied after all these years with the Chairman. They demand changes. They want to be *listened to*, consulted, made important. Fools and dolts. Who listens to the masses? Do they have minds of their own? Only the Superman can govern, the rest shall follow as sheep. Yet even the pettiest aspires to heights beyond him.

I think the Chairman made mistakes. Now that the Red Guards are losing prestige, people are saying, 'The Chairman should have disassociated himself.'

Sometimes when I see the Chairman, I see an old man looking for immortality.

Some time in 219 BC, the First Emperor went roaming the shores of the Eastern Sea, because he was seized by a fear of death. He made a gaunt figure, flapping in yellow robes, as he sought for the Eight Immortals and their secret: the elixir of eternal life.

He made sacrifices at significant sites to the snow-capped mountains, green rivers and Eight Immortals. When his singular quest produced no results, he employed his underlings for further tasks.

'Go,' he told one servant after another, 'in search of the three blest isles where the Immortals live.'

They did not return. In some stories it was said that the

travellers found their way to the country we now call Japan and remained there to intermarry with the native folk.

In his imperial court he gathered scholars, magicians and itinerants.

'Tell me how to live forever,' he ordered them.

When they were dumb with horror or ignorance, he sentenced them to be burnt to death.

'I get the same inane replies again and again. Do the scholars know nothing?' he shouted.

Ennui? Revenge? Or self-glorification? Whatever the First Emperor's motives, circa 213–212 BC, he launched a massive campaign of killing scholars and burning all books (except for those on agriculture, engineering and the law).

'History begins at this point,' he told the dumbfounded court. 'I am the first.'

In the garden the trumpet-tongued hibiscus, the 'rose of China', sways upon its stalk. An air of calm pervades. The Chairman sits in a bamboo chair in his garden, at times gazing towards the road, and beyond, at times wrapped in his own silence. He seems almost diffident. Such an alteration to his manner! Slowly he stirs a cracker in his cup of tea.

The evening is hot and moist. A storm threatens. The pong-pong trees' smooth white flowers are dropping into the storm drains by the sides of the facing road. The birds descend chattering from the sky.

It is late March, 1990. Around this time the Chairman takes it into his head to attack the pigeons. The pigeons have been gathering and nesting in his courtyard, attracted by the loose grains of rice so often spilled through the seams of the gunny sacks by his servants carrying them into the kitchen.

'Pigeons,' he swears. 'Shitting pigeons.'

I think his obsession shows his deterioration. He devises a plan. He calls the servants and instructs them to stand in the courtyard, clashing kitchen woks with metal ladles. He explains that this will prevent the pigeons from landing. As time goes on, they will grow exhausted, fall to the ground, and the servants can then bash their heads in.

The servants agree enthusiastically as it will give them the day off from their usual hard chores. Chattering and laughing, they stand scattered about the large courtyard, but fall silent when the Chairman appears.

Weakened, recently, the Chairman limps in with a stick. He shouts, 'Are you ready? Begin!'

The servants start up a frightful din, clanging and banging. I cannot take the noise and hurry to my bedroom. Even there the noise follows. In the end I go out for the day. When I return, it is almost night, and the courtyard is deserted. There are no signs of any pigeons, dead or alive. But as I cross, I think I see a shadow lengthening over the paving stones as if some great bird is flying overhead. I decide it is my fancy as the birds, if still alive, will be roosting at this hour. Besides, the shadow is huge. What can it be?

I meet with a servant in the hall.

'How did it go?' I ask.

His face looks embarrassed. 'Birds flew into the trees.'

'They did?' I say.

'Yes,' he says. 'And then they try again to land. Went on and on like that the whole day.'

'So none were killed?' I say.

'None,' he says.

That was all the conversation I had on the subject of the pigeons. I do not mention it to the Chairman, diplomatically avoiding it when we meet. He, too, says nothing. We take our usual seats in the dining room, and eat a good meal of braised duck. I talk lightly of the purchases I have made during the day's shopping.

'Do you think you will be going home soon?' he says.

The festival of the Ching Ming is drawing near and I will return to my childhood place to tidy my mother's grave.

'I have considered it,' I say. 'Do you want me to stay?'
I ask him because he appears frail to me.
'No,' he shakes his head. 'I will make do.'
'Very well,' I say. 'I will make the necessary preparations.'

The pigeons line up. Rows of them, dryly chattering. They are bold, coming closer for scraps. They eye me with hostility. They have flown down from the trees and telephone wires to the earth. They shift from one clawed foot to the other, dust their beaks against their wings, and all the while that he thinks he has defeated them, the flock is outside the door, waiting for entry.

'Go away,' I hiss, banging one hand against my thigh to startle them.

They cock their heads, mock me with beady eyes. They know I will be leaving soon, and then he will be alone with them. I feel a sense of inevitability. There are moments we are powerless to put off. Like a heavy rain cloud they will descend and burst above his head.

I have many preparations to make for my journey. With the Ching Ming coming, I am not in the mood for quarrels with him or any other. I think of my mother and her life. It seems a very long time ago. I try not to think of Tang.

The Ching Ming or Pure Brightness Festival in early April celebrates spring and renewal. It is a time to conduct ancestor worship.

I will go to my mother's grave to tidy it from the weeds, the dirt, the accumulation of time. I will clean the tablet in her memory.

Mother, how far away you seem now.

I will tie yellow ribbons onto the end of a bamboo stick and I will put that into the ground by her grave or prop it with a stone on top of her tomb to bar wandering ghosts that come in search of a home. Mother will be pleased by these attentions.

I have a presentiment. It comes one night when I am unable to sleep and take to strolling in the garden. I sense that I will not be seeing the Chairman again, that I will be leaving this place for good. The feeling is so powerful that I become afraid. I think in the morning I will call up my old friend Roxanne, whom I have not met since my husband's funeral. I feel an urge to be in touch with someone who has known me in that phase of my life. I do so when morning dawns, and she seems surprised and agrees a little reluctantly to meet with me at a café on Boat Quay by the river.

59

Ching

Light pattering sounds. It is raining. It is ten minutes to five in the evening, as I see from the wall clock. I click on a lamp. The contrast sinks the rest of the room into even greater shade. A host of small objects crowd into the light. I blink. I am almost blinded by the shadows at the purlieus. I glimpse my vague face in the reflecting glass of a distant cabinet – the odd juxtaposition of objects which my eye falls upon: a large stuffed doll seated on a cushioned rattan chair with a rounded back, a silver Selangor Pewter vase with a single rose in the centre of a glass table, a glass bottle with an unfurled ship inside, the television set, a basket of extravagant wax flowers and fruits, and around me the cream-coloured walls of my apartment.

I am most certainly at home … yet … I have the strangest feeling, I think for a moment that I am not myself. No, more a feeling that I am drifting … in and out … of this body I have called mine. In the silence I can hear the clock ticking.

I cannot understand what is happening to me. Of late I begin to feel my life has little to do with others. Their concerns have little to do with me. I begin to think of emigrating. Hui called last night. I do not know why. He said it was to find out if I was all right. Why should I not be all right? Oh, no, no. I bear up. I am strong, am I not? I told him he needn't call again. I said people would talk about us, especially now with my husband dead. He said there wasn't anything to talk about, but that he was my friend if I needed him. I said fine, let's leave it, shall we? He said we would be doing another play next year. He wouldn't be putting on *Madame Mao* again. He said perhaps a comedy. I said all right, I liked to laugh. My voice was almost cracking by then. I told him I was expecting a visitor, so he rang off. I do not want to speak to him again.

The rain begins to beat down steadily creating rattling noises upon the roof. The wind whistles in and licks my calves. I quickly shut the windows. From window to window I go in turn, shutting the panes. Sheets of water slosh down from the sky. I feel like a fish imprisoned in its aquarium, looking out.

The wind is shaking the round-headed pong-pong trees by the road, but the room is peacefully aquatic. Only five o'clock.

Across the road where the cemetery lies, the great angsana trees bend and sway.

The amah enters the room with a note in her hand. It is from Roxanne. Roxanne who had not come to Boat Quay as we had arranged. I had been too tired, perhaps too filled with a sense of oppression, to think of calling her for an explanation. I decide to ask the amah for a cup of hot Nescafé, curl up on the sofa with my toes tucked comfortably underneath me and read it.

The smell of the steaming coffee is good. Strong and black with two teaspoons of sugar. I slowly unfold the note from Roxanne.

Dear Ching,

I thought it would be easier not to turn up for our appointment. But I think you will not be put off. Do what you will, and let me live my own life. For too long, perhaps, I have been in your shadow, seeing you but dimly, believing the fantasy you created around yourself. Let this be the final cut. I will return to you all letters, photographs and gifts, I am sure that you will demand them.

She thinks to separate her life from mine as neatly as that. She will discover that the ties which join us, all of us, are not so easily severed, that we carry with us the burden of history, of having lived through these times. I read Roxanne's note through again, swallow my coffee, and place it carefully upon the accumulating pages beneath my hand.

60

Chorus: footsteps again
do you hear the footsteps?
The tread of the dead man's shoes
the footfall of a lonely stranger
the approach of Christ at the door.
She thinks she hears a sound in the garden
signalling
a bat wing of suspicion
a whiff of fear
the kitchen knife at the throat
the chain at the door
the hangman's rope dangling
tripping her at the entry
knocking her out cold.
She hears the footsteps of the enemy
the soft shuffle of the Red Guards.
She hears betrayal.
Turn your palm upwards
and let me read your fate
in your hand I see
wait … they are at the door.

In the Chairman's house. She senses danger. Who knows when the blow may fall? As always when the prey is weakened, the tigers move in for the kill.

Tonight, the moon is full. As she climbs into her solitary bed, she has one wish that if they come, they do so quickly. She is too much of a coward to wait night after night for the advent.

Is that a noise she hears? In the garden? Footsteps. Light ones. Will she hide? No, why should she? She will wait for them. There! Again. She is not mistaken. They are there, foraging through the dark corridors of the house.

Ching, lying sleeplessly in bed, is jarred to her senses by the creak of the opening door of her bedroom. A shaft of light peers in, then a torch beam turns upon her. Men in a bulk stand at the entrance. She springs out of bed. In that light, her nightgown is a mere shadow shifting, her body, which has never turned hard in spite of years of travail, wavers under it.

'She was only a paper tiger,' Chairman Mao said of the woman who had run his revolution. 'Blow upon her and watch her collapse.'

'I am innocent,' Ching cries.

Dishevelled bedclothes. In her loosened nightgown, she is a dramatic figure. She falls to the floor. They haul at her arms. She crumples, sobbing.

'Prove it,' say the men. 'Prove your innocence at your trial.'

'There is no one?' she says. 'No one who will speak on my behalf?' They have produced ropes to bind her hands.

The men say, 'If there were, they would be here with you now.'

They lift her to her feet, and drag her to where their cars are waiting outside. It is a cold night, and look, the moon is a coin shining falsely in the sky.

They come the night the Chairman is away in a hospital. The house is empty, save for the servants who have obviously betrayed her.

She mutters under her breath, 'And yet they dare to say, "We do it all in the name of the Chairman and only for his sake." Do they know what he wants better than I do? Are they mind readers? He is only a decrepit senescent man they have made into an idol, into whom they all read their own intentions. He is their great mirror reflecting their philosophies to them, nothing else. Falsehoods. All of them, false.'

Women, we all know, are demons disguised. Yes, children, next door, a demon woman used to live. She howled for mortal flesh. The way to catch her was to show her her face in a mirror. Demon women are terribly afraid of seeing their own reflections. This is because underneath their disguises they are nothing more than the most hideous beings. The woman next door was one such being. But she has been taken away.

Behind cloth or lace curtains, faces partially hidden, the neighbours, male and female, children and elderly, observe the demon woman shrieking, and the car door slamming on her.

61

Ching

A hard band constricts my head! What can I do when I am taken like a conspirator in the night? Dressed only in a nightgown! The Red Guards! I see they turn against me. I am betrayed – I feel they hate me. Why?

I almost faint. My ears sing.

When I am taken to the court room, I see that it is but a stuffy box, no windows, only small vents, where the trial judges sit like wax figures in a mausoleum, with their cheeks still pink from cold, and pretending to be alive, while no heart is beating in their hollow chests.

I am framed in the centre of the room within a square of wooden bars encaging me, the she-monster on display to all and sundry, for each day's proceedings are televised live to the nation.

I think with contempt of the six hundred invited faces before me: there is Roxanne in the press gallery, her face white and strained (I almost feel pity for her), her eyes lowered to her notebook. She must have known the direction of the wind, perhaps that explains why she did not turn up at our planned meeting.

A row of hostile eyes in the public gallery meets mine: former colleagues, actresses, directors and the curious. The public. Why, there is Chian Yi, the theatre critic who has once written favourably of me, but who is now brother-in-law to the Minister of Culture. Haven't you known, seen it sometimes on the faces? With a sinking feeling I face them. That closure of expression, that almost too polite manner that signals non-acceptance, the lack of spontaneity. I have experienced it before and known the outcome: at interviews, auditions, meeting new people.

They have already decided about me beforehand and anything I may say is good for nothing. It makes me angry that I should waste my breath and time with these people. The moment I see such expressions, I wish to get up at once and leave, but they usually keep me talking, pretending an interest. And then again I cannot be one hundred per cent certain, and I have been wrong on occasion.

'All rise!' someone shouts.

A shaft of light from outside makes its way through a vent. Those faces in its path are lit up and seem like masks, eyes glittering behind.

This is no trial. There are at least five prosecutors, two of whom are women, and I alone as defence.

'Am I here to be targeted? Or am I here to be given a fair hearing?' I shout.

'Silence, Chiang Ching!'

My list of sins is read aloud.

'You can say I abandoned him. There can be no justification. I choose no line of defence.'

'Yes, I abandoned him. I let him die like a dog. Do I need to justify myself? Am I always to be asked to settle my accounts, explain my reasons, stand before a trial of jurors?'

'The city demands too much. I have always had to give account of my very existence. Has anyone ever spoken on my behalf? Everything I do is an outrage. Every step I take is out of bounds. You have spent years attempting to stifle me. I will not stand trial. I will not allow my self, my actions, my very being to be judged by contemptible and lowly people.'

'Do I need to say more? Do I need to speak?'

'I wish to go to the loo.'

'I have spoken.'

'I wish to go to the loo.'

'I wish to go to the loo.'

'She has been in the toilet for ten minutes! Bring her back.'

'Do not ask me to speak.'

'I was only a slave. When I was asked to perform, I did. What actress questions her director in these times?'

'I did nothing wrong.'

'Yes, I betrayed my husband. He was a fool. Does it matter if I loved him? I loved them both. Both of them let me down. I will not speak.'

'Why do you not let me go to the loo?'

'I have said I will not speak.'

'Why am I here again?'

'Why have you brought me here?'

'Again?'

'Again?'

'Again?'

'If dogs bark at a mountain, does the mountain suffer? Why do you blame me and not the Chairman?'

'It is because I am a woman who has transgressed the limits of your definition of a woman. For that you cannot excuse me. You turn upon me like tigers. I see the claws in your serious folded hands. I catch the glint of green eyes. Yes, you and you and you. You accuse me but you envy me too, my freedom despite your laws.'

'I only want to strike out, to do something that is real. And I find the only real thing is my anger.'

Light. Off-stage, lights frighten me, I prefer that the room stays dim, close, encasing me. I have no fear of the shroud, only of light and the corners it exposes, only of light and the shadows it casts, only of the piercing rays that illumine what lies hidden within. It is my habit to wear sunglasses when I go out and sometimes at home as well, it gives me a sense of comfort. I remember telling Roxanne that my eyes are weak, that they cannot bear the sun, but only I know the truth, that my eyes are afraid to see.

Imprisoned in the centre of the room, on display, framed in a square of wooden bars, this is the demon, the she-devil.

I shout at them, 'It isn't a crime to be revolutionary!'

'How will society grow if not for its wars and eruptions?'

'I have heard somewhere that reasonable men, when confronted with the world, realise its horror and adapt themselves to it. Unreasonable men (or women) force the world to adapt to them. They move the world.'

'But what reason is this for your crimes? What excuses are you making?'

Murmuring arises from the public.

'That woman is a tiger in a cage and he was her human sacrifice!'

'She is nothing more than a petty vindictive woman who tried to step out of line.'

'A witch!'

'We ask her to pay for the crimes of the Chairman.'

'On the Chairman there is only silence. If evil exists in one, it existed in the other.'

I scream, '*I am outside heaven and outside the law!*'

A grand statement succeeded by a long pause, while they collect their senses and try to think of a rebuttal.

It is a slow room full of pauses and sentences, full of the waiting intake of breath that signals the end or the beginning of life. The trial judges are arrayed like sculpture, only their mouths working; their faces and eyes are stiff. I spit on them.

'Do you confess to instigating a war?'

'I confess nothing.'

'Were you in touch with the mirror people?'

'I do not know.'

'You betrayed the Chairman. You betrayed your people.'

'My people? Do they claim me for their own?'

'You gave aid to the mirror people when they sought to invade the city. You quisling!'

'You insult me,' I shoot back, 'but you do not control my spirit.'

'Do you know,' I say dreamily, 'that once as a child I would hang lizards up by their tails on the clothesline and shoot at them with a hand-made catapult? I had caught them, still wriggling, in the palms of my cupped hands. Sometimes they dropped off their tails from sheer fright.'

Then I shout, 'Do you think everything I say to you is true? Look at you! Look at your staring eyes. Fools. That's a story the Chairman told me himself.'

'Enough, Chiang Ching! Keep to order. Do you admit to subversive activities? Do you admit to using your art as a covert tool for subversion?'

'All art, all of life is a cover-up for something *other*. In my case, it was only a means of earning my money. I was a poor girl.'

When I speak it is with a nonchalance that prickles their anger. One of the judges can contain her contempt no longer, and shouts, 'Fascist!'

When I look up into the public gallery, the row of capricious actresses is no longer meeting my gaze, they are silent and still, contemplating their fate, their own written sentence, not one of them will side with me, I know, the days when I could throw my weight about are gone.

The judge sums up the trial.

The judge speaking affects regret. In measured and serious tones, he says to me, 'You live in a dream world. You have sought to overthrow the boundaries of what should be, how this world functions. Your crime lies in your taking to yourself the law, the mandate of heaven, which is not bestowed lightly, and rarely on women.'

'You have made this world your theatre, your crimes are petty and full of woman's vindictiveness. Never should a woman wield power. Her lusts will not keep it well in hand.'

I am unable to remain quiet. I jump up abruptly and shout, banging my hand against the wooden bar for emphasis, 'Who is to say? Who is to say what is real and what is not? Who are you to judge that my world is any less real than yours, my set of laws any worse? All of you are guilty. During the revolution, before the revolution, you have all worked against ordinary people, exploiting those too simple and poor to know the ropes of your laws.'

'You grow fat on ill-gotten money and you dare to accuse me. What have I done that you have not dreamed yourselves of doing? What have I done that you do not do in your underhand ways, bringing suffering to those below you? Who has given me anything? All my life, no one!'

'Tell me, tell me one thing,' (Here I lower my voice dramatically as if I am rehearsing for a play, as if I am once again Nora in Ibsen's *A Doll's House*, lauded by the critics, the play that brought me to prominence, the play I wept over and raged over, putting my soul into playing the part, slamming the door upon history, upon authority, upon the law) 'one thing only – *who is to say which is right, the world or I?*'

During my outburst, I have one eye upon the judges and one upon the public for their reaction, then I see an actress yawning. I feel as if I've been struck in the face.

'Bitch,' I yell to the gallery, 'You, you bitch.'

The yawning actress stops in mid-yawn to purse her lips and glare.

'Quiet!'

I subside, the battle wind taken out of me. I have seen fear sitting in the audience, clean-shaven and thin, a poet, his wild eyes haunted, tormented, his face looking like Tang Na Juan's. For the first time in the trial I am lost for words.

When the trial prosecutors return to take their seats, their faces gleam in pinched satisfaction. The one who leans forward to inform the room of the decision speaks in slow deliberate tones.

'We say that the accused, Chiang Ching, has overplayed her role, beyond what were the Chairman's intentions. She has done great evil to our people. She has brought suffering. And for what purposes? Only she can tell. Only in her heart lies the truth behind her actions.'

'Her quest for power was unbecoming to a woman. Her actions were vindictive as a woman's can be. There is little we can say on her behalf, except that as the lover of the Chairman we will allow her a little time to repent. If at the end of two years, she does so, we may commute her death penalty to life imprisonment. This is kindness, for she deserves to die.'

I stand defiantly, chin up as my sentence is spoken. No expression passes my white face. No words escape my tightly drawn lips.

Murmuring arises from the public watching the trial on television through a shop front.

'They say she stripped during her interrogation to frighten her interrogators,' someone comments.

'Huh, what did they do then?'

'Oh, left the room, I believe.'

'I would leave,' says another. 'She is at an age where I would leave.' There is a coarse chuckle.

'Some woman, eh!'

'She was vicious, like all women.'

'Empress Chiang Ching! Well, that's the end.'

'Always in cycles,' says an old man. 'The wheel always turns.'

62

Ching

It is 1991, and the Ching Ming Festival approaches. I am still in prison. Through the solitary window I can see the flat dry land outside. Once I saw a few children in blue jackets running past at a distance, waving sticks in their hands. Birds visit me, chirping, perched upon the narrow ledge of my window. Sometimes sparrows, sometimes pigeons come. I am grateful. I do not ask them to stay. I do not tempt them with bits of sweet cake. They come of their own free will.

I ask the guard when he brings my midday meal when I can be free to pay a visit to my dead husband. I ask if I may visit Mao's mausoleum in Tian An Men Square. I am refused.

At the evening meal, instead of eating, I pick up a chopstick. I turn my back to the entrance. I ram the chopstick down my throat. The pain is terrible. It causes me to blackout. The guard, on returning, finds me lying on the ground. He will not let me die. He saves me.

I wake to find the horror of my walls around me again.

I am writing my memoir.

One day the guard enters my cell to find the mattress ripped open and shreds of white paper scattered in flakes over the floor.

I have torn up my memoir.

'Pick it up,' he shouts. 'Do it now.'

I raise my eyes to his, and gesture, 'With bare hands?' I start laughing, 'Does it not resemble *ten thousand miles of snowflakes*?'

'If I give you a broom you may attack me,' he retorts. 'Have you gone crazy?'

On one of the scraps of paper that the guard discovers under the bed, which is what remains of my memoir, he sees I have written, *Such a thought has come to me. I wonder if it is a premonition? I see a time of revolution when the mirror creatures will once again reclaim the land. The city lies dormant. Such a battle will ensue. It will go down into the annals of history. It will be like the end of the world. The mirror people …*

… here the paper is torn and he can read no further. The guard throws it at me. He shouts, 'What a crazy creature!'

He gives me a bin to put the scraps in.

Q: How does the Kitchen God travel to heaven?
A: The cockroaches get him there. They are his horses.
'Is that why his shrine is so dirty?' I once asked my mother.
'What is unpleasant to our eyes is of benefit to the gods,' my mother commented.

In my cell, I have the daily pleasure of seeing the black creatures scuttling over the floor. 'I think I may harness them and rise with them to heaven,' I mutter. Instead, I thwack these hard-backed insects with my slippers, and destroy my chance.

There are other means of dying. The time of death was 3 a.m., 14 May 1991. I had hung myself above the bathtub with handkerchiefs knotted together. Such an old body I could not have imagined. I looked seventy-seven years. My legs were skinny and blue-veined. In my face there was no peace. My eyelids were flung wide open. The guard went purple when he saw me. He swore into my face, 'Demon woman!'

He did not want to touch me. More guards came, attracted by the noise. They pulled my cold body down. Then they stood there, confused. I felt their fear.

Then they hid the news of my death from the world.

Epilogue

63

Sky very blue. Sun a trifle too hot. Roxanne in a Black & White Cab watches the landscape slip by. They drive past wide verandas and timber houses on stilts – 'Queenslanders' the taxi man says – purple trees, which are jacarandas, and palm trees that remind her of home, wide streets, very quiet suburbs, state schools, churches, and on.

In Ching's new abode. Sunnybank Hills. The taxi turns left just before Franklins Big Fresh. A few windings of the road and they arrive at Ching's brick house in Caprice Court. Roxanne jumps out and takes a look at the house, as the taxi man hauls her luggage from the boot. Chiang Ching comes out of the front door. And the bulbs in her garden wave their hands, seeming to feed upon the air. They seem to applaud her. They are her only audience, she is their star performer.

'Roxanne!' Ching exclaims. 'I thought you would never get here.'

In ironic contrast to her life, the numerous names she has gone by denote serenity: as a baby, Shumeng, pure and simple; as a child, Yun-ho, crane in the clouds; Lan Ping, blue peace, during her salad years as an actress. Chiang Ching, the name she and Mao Tse-tung thought up: Green River.

Madame Mao.

A rush of sentiment. Roxanne holds her hand and looks into her face. Ching has aged. There can be no doubting that her troubles have caused a deep mark to appear between her eyes.

'The plane was delayed at the airport, a passenger did not turn up and they had to throw out his luggage,' Roxanne says as she follows Ching into her house.

'You have a beautiful place. Such a big garden.' Some tendrils brush against Roxanne's face as they pass under a trellis.

'There's a pool, but later. Let me offer you something to drink.'

Madame Mao sits in the circle of stage lights, imprisoned, waiting only for the end to come, and until then there is the swimming pool and coffee and chicken curry for dinner. Ching calls out from the kitchen, 'Do you want tea or coffee to drink?' And all the little things that make life worth living, and the vines in the garden curling their way over and under the fence, holding out leaves like shovels, like blindmen's begging hands.

Roxanne curls upon the sofa, waiting for her coffee. She is settled upon a hump in the sofa, a slight cushiony rising, born of old age and long usage. She runs a finger through the velvet upholstery, lets the threads catch and weave a pattern into her hand.

Chiang Ching appears with a tray. There are cream biscuits on a plate and coffee cups on saucers. She places a cup before Roxanne.

'You look well,' Ching says to her.

'Oh, I'm older,' Roxanne says, touching the few greying strands she has found on her head but refused to pluck out, seeing it as a vain resort.

'I have changed?' Ching says, as she picks up her own cup. 'You look at me with such a look.'

'What?'

'Of pity.' Ching laughs to take away the self-pitying note in her voice.

'No, no. Yes, you are changed, not so much in face but manner.'

'I cannot stay forever young and vibrant.'

'No, no.'

Ching seems to withdraw. She sips her coffee, lost in some thought. She shudders.

The tendrils wave into Roxanne's face. She carefully avoids them, stepping a little off the path onto the grass verge, where black-eyed Susans are growing in little borders.

And there is the pool. She seats herself carefully on the edge, removes her slippers and dangles her legs in the water.

Over the days, Roxanne meets Ching's neighbour, Lynn Miller, a middle-aged woman whose husband Ben works as a real estate agent. Lynn's manner is always friendly. When she sees Roxanne, it's always, 'How are you? Nice morning, isn't it?' Or if it's raining, 'It's raining cats and dogs. You wouldn't want to be going out, dear.'

Lynn has passed Singapore on her way to England. Her plane made a stopover and she was in the airport for three hours. She didn't get to see the city, but she admired the airport. She talked of her travels and her children and the house her elderly mother refused to leave to move to a retirement home. 'If we can get a house with an attached little granny house, that would be perfect, but as it is, she would be better off in a nursing home ...' And the Tip-Top bread, white sliced or wholemeal, and the Vegemite and the strolls her old mother used to take in the evenings before the crime rate went up, and her fear of leaving her house for too long unguarded, and the water sprinklers going round and round in a dry garden and the garden path without gate, and the lettuce she grows, and sweet little daisies, and the neighbourhood, once a community, smiling, 'How are you?' and other pleasantries and everyone knowing each other. 'In my mother's day, everyone left their backdoors open, but now young crims enter and bash old women for twenty dollars lying on the table. The changes, oh, the changes, and new people moving in.'

Ching is of course one of the new people moving in, but Lynn Miller is not thinking about her when she says that. She shakes her head and sighs, 'Times are tough. Ben finds his job frustrating. But he can't complain, there are many without a job.'

Then, 'How would you like some lettuce from the garden?'

64

Roxanne rings the bell. The door with fierce amulets pasted on it seems to be closed for an eternity. But it opens.

'Is that you?' says a voice from within.

She replies, 'Yes, I'm here,' and wonders if there could be a self and an I and if the past could be the cool darkness of the open door.

The voice has retreated to deeper recesses and can be heard asking if she would like some tea or coffee.

'Tea,' she decides, and adds, 'a spoonful of sugar, please.' She seats herself crossing her ankles, leaning back on a red upholstered sofa with floral patterned cushions, picking up her cup of tea, Twinings of London, Earl Grey, with its distinctive bergamot flavouring.

'It's been a long time since your last visit,' the voice says. 'You look well.'

'Yes. I have remarried.'

'Yes, someone told me. She heard it from a relative on your husband's side. Wrote to me about it. You didn't write. But then you haven't written for some time.'

'Yes.' Roxanne knows excuses are useless between old friends. 'Do you know the Chairman is … ill?'

'I expected him to be dead years ago, after his heart attack, remember? He is a part of it, part of the thread, of what's real and what's not.'

The voice hesitates. Chiang Ching reaches out a hand to pick up her cup, drinks, scalding her lips, wincing. She looks at Roxanne with faint surprise.

Ching thinks, *Roxanne looks different. She's happy and confident. Look at how she dresses. She looks professional. She seems settled.*

'I wanted only to be real,' says Ching, in a slightly aggressive manner. The fire lights up in her dark eyes then fades as she sinks back into the folds of the creaking sofa. Although her manner is subdued, she looks attractive in a delicate blue dress of crêpe de Chine with a narrow skirt. Her fingers smooth her skirt in slight nervous gestures.

'And then I realised nothing I did was real.'

'None of us are real. How can we be in a city such as we have, created by an enormous effort of the will?' Roxanne says simply. 'I realised too in the end that we were pawns. You and I. Caught within a system that destroys. Nothing has changed. It continues, same as ever, the seeds of it lie in the deceit we entangle ourselves in. But it is the same in all worlds, in all lives.'

'In the end,' Ching says, bitterly, her lips twisting, 'those who win are the ones with the real power. Don't expect me to feel responsible for the lives of others. We all have only ourselves to take care of. Hah, if I had tried to take my husband's actions upon myself, it would have been a great weight. I know how I have suffered.'

'He was a philanderer,' her thoughts are starting to wander. 'An out and out bastard whose hand I licked, oh for years I flattered him, but he was weak, inside he was weak, and bad in bed, yes, indeed. I turned to other men. Did you think I would stay faithful to such a bastard once I realised his lack of prowess?'

Roxanne is shocked, *She cannot be without her role!* She reflects that she is no longer with Ching in her sufferings. She is detached, listening like a biographer, like a journalist. She tells her how much she respects and admires her. She tells her the truth and also lies. She lies to keep herself safe from her.

Roxanne remembers how a hysterical Ching came to her place some time after Tang's death to tell her that she wanted to confess.

'Confess! Ching, look you are not yourself … sit down,' Roxanne cried, filled with compassion and guilt because she had neglected her.

Ching told her that she blamed herself for Tang's death. 'I betrayed him!'

From Ching's garbled account, Roxanne gathered that she

had been the Chairman's mistress, that she instigated a revolution, and had been taken by the Chairman's rivals when he was in hospital and stood on trial, that she had lived in a cell, and when no longer able to take it, killed herself; only, of course, not for long, for here she was, resurrected.

Roxanne calmed her down as best she could. Advised her to rest. But no, Ching was here to say goodbye. She was leaving, immigrating to Australia.

'It had been Tang's plan,' she said. 'Of course, he will not be going with me.' She cried terribly at this thought.

Roxanne thought it best. A change of scene. It would revive her.

'I will come to visit you,' Roxanne promised.

Roxanne sips her tea warily. Then, Ching turns to her. 'By the way,' she says, 'I smelt fish when you came. Have you been eating fish?'

Roxanne stares at her. Ching leans closer, sniffing.

'Yes,' she says finally. 'It emanates from you.'

'My breath?' Roxanne says to humour her. 'Or my soul?'

Ching looks into the distance, still shaking with spasms of giggles. Her hair falls over her cheek, a gentle cascade. Ching's face sags.

'I wish only to be happy. I want to be peaceful and happy. I want to forget. Why do you come here reminding me of things I have forgotten?'

Roxanne reflects that Ching must be lying when she says she has forgotten.

And then Ching turns upon Roxanne with vehemence, 'Why do you come to torment me? Who do you think I am?'

Roxanne begins to protest feebly.

'I know you have always wanted to wield power over me. You with your words, you, the journalist. Leave me alone. I am not who you think I am. I am not even an actress anymore. My life is simple. I know few people. I eat, I sleep, I water my plants, I swim in the summer.'

Roxanne is shocked by her vicious manner. She gets up.

'I'll go. I'll call a taxi,' she says coldly. She slows down at the door as if she expects a response.

When the door has shut, Chiang Ching closes her eyes.

Lynn Miller is in her garden weeding when Roxanne comes down the footpath. She waves and Roxanne stops to wish her good morning.

'Been to see her, have you? It's nice to see you back. How long will you be staying?'

'Oh, not long this time, Lynn. I'm here with my husband. We're at the hotel in Queen Street Mall. Lennon's Hotel. We'll be on our way to New Zealand.'

'Well, have a nice time!' Then she says, softly, her eyes going bluer, 'Your friend is not quite well? I don't mean to be rude or interfering … but you know it's odd, some time ago, she told me that she was Madame Mao Tse-tung. Well, now. I don't know really who she is, I mean, Chiang Ching. But my husband, Ben, said Chiang Ching was Chairman Mao's last wife? That Chiang Ching, he means, the one that died. That's a fact. He read it in the papers years ago. She killed herself in 1991, he said. Anyway, she couldn't have been your friend now, could she?'

'No,' Roxanne says. 'She couldn't.'

'Well, why did she say that then?'

Roxanne hesitates, 'Well, she was an actress.'

'You don't say now. That's wonderful. An actress.'

'She played Madame Mao with a theatre group. That was a long time ago.'

'Well, that explains some things. I'll have to tell Ben,' she says. 'Poor thing! Some people find it hard to let go of their past.'

Roxanne murmurs something polite.

'Well, you have a nice time in New Zealand!'

'I will. Thanks, Lynn. Look … look out for her now and then.'

Lynn glances towards the house, 'Poor dear!' on her lips. 'Don't you worry,' she says.

As Roxanne gets into the taxi she looks towards the house, and thinks, *This is the last time. I don't think we will be meeting again.*

65

Ching

Stepping off the aeroplane in an unfamiliar city that is Brisbane, without Tang by my side. There are many people struggling through the airport. I was in Perth, yes, for a holiday. We took in the wildflowers, koalas, and cafés in Fremantle. It was summer and very hot. Over forty degrees.

This is a different world. Different fauna, flora, people. But Brisbane has some things similar to Singapore. The climate, for one. The fruit. I hear from my neighbour, Lynn Miller, that durians are grown in North Queensland.

But still a different world. Tang told me of a crack, the Wallace Discontinuity, separating the Asian and Australian biogeographical regions. A meeting of two tectonic plates in an imaginary line east of Bali. And on both sides of the line a distinctive vegetation, animal life, people.

I think of Tang frequently. It is hard for me to reconcile myself to his manner of dying.

Well, I am in Queen Street Mall. Fancy department shops flashing Sale and Genuine Sale and Half-Price Sale, shoes clacking down the mall, work shoes and sneakers, women in black skirts and men in ties, mothers with babies in prams and odds and ends in jeans. I head towards the one place which offers some semblance of memory: McDonald's. Clutching a brown tray with a cheeseburger and large Coke, packet of yellow fries spilling out, a Value Meal Deal, and making my way to an empty table, where I sit morosely, thankful to be out of the crowd. I bite into the warm bun. McDonald's is the one place that a person can find a measure of certainty. The buns are the same, no matter where you go to eat them. I wipe my lips.

I am an actress and I have managed to step across, from one

stage to another, in exchange for that elusive something one calls freedom or anonymity or simply to drift along the edges.

I am alone with myself. I mock my efforts to specify, to draw dimensions, to make sense of the new land. Only a memory lifts me above this void, this place where I am no one.

The new landscape repeats itself. Clusters of housing, K-mart, Coles, Franklins, Woolworths, Myer, McDonald's – add or subtract one or more. Mall, hardware shops, fish and chips, Chinese takeaway, petrol station. And then further on, the same. The pattern continues.

I wonder when the landscape will begin to make sense to me, to yield to me its codes of being. Am I doomed to wander on its surface?

In the new city I slip through the strange crowds like a ghost. I recognise the others of my old city. It is easy for me to pick them out, a way of walking, talking, gesture or inflection of voice.

When our eyes meet, something inside tells us instantly and we acknowledge silently a hidden bond. Sometimes it is not a bond the other wants to assume, and then he or she will turn away with a slight gesture. They have not been treated well in their past. But others will look and in their eyes there is a hunger. Mostly they do not smile, but you know and they know you know that in you they have glimpsed home.

One day I see a mirror woman. Standing in the mall, staring at me, as a pair of yellow tights saunters past between us. Then she turns and faces a shop window. If I gaze more intently a glimmer as of scales or small mirrors can be seen reflected off her skin. Only she knows that which is within me, hide it as I may from others.

A condition of exile, of being the émigré, is always one of not being known, to watch and to watch others looking at the surface of yourself, as if somehow a mirror is there, and they have to play back to themselves everything they may have heard about you and people from your city, every stereotype, every little box.

I enjoy being slotted away into the little categories, little parcels of their data. In some perverse way it excites me to be stamped and labelled and yet to know I escape detection. It is like playing a game, a game I am used to playing in the old city: something to do with slipping into selves, something to do with the uncertainty of being, of role-playing, play-acting.

It is a lonely yet exhilarating condition, to be seen and yet not seen, to have some part of you always alone. If I have always somehow been alone, being alone cannot frighten me. Not now. It used to, once. Now it is part of my psyche, part of the inheritance the old city gave to me: to be alone and to walk alone.

Whether it is a legacy to be envied or pitied I do not know. It has shaped others like myself born into the city. Like the city, we have changed. Each time our identities rewritten. I feel as if I suffer from amnesia. I am a person of no past, only a continuously changing present.

I had thought upon coming here that I would begin to live, to breathe, to form my own identity, but I am as before the actress, playing out roles and watching from a distance. And I am alone. As always. Something to do with the nature of my city, perhaps. Something to do with standing alone. Something to do with paranoia, of an 'I'-land (island) surrounded by possible enemies. It was Sartre who said *Hell is other people*. I understand that.

Without willing it or wanting to, I follow her as she moves slowly along the mall. A stream of humanity flowing and counterflowing, so many black catfish struggling. The mall is alive with catch, in spite of a pattering drizzle. I duck through after her. Variegated umbrellas bob along on human eddies. I notice other people looking at me, turning their heads, swivelling their eyes. Have I made myself too obvious? But possibly they look at me because they have always done so. I draw attention to myself against my will.

There is no way back. I have dreamt a number of times that I have returned to the city, and on each occasion I am filled with a terrifying sense of helplessness and a great anxiety to leave. Each time, I cannot leave: my plane takes off before I reach the airport, I miss the chance, I am held back, someone prevents me.

I wake up sweating in bed, relieved that it is only a dream, and that I am here. My anonymity is my freedom, my passport.

But I have lost her ... somewhere in the crowd as my eyes turned to glance at a juggler.

Ching

Roxanne has left. Let her go. I rinse the cups in the sink and look into my garden through the open window. A warm smell of flowers and dry grass.

And then, a figure standing in my garden. A woman. How familiar her face! I think to have left *them* behind.

The city rocks, side to side, cradlewise, splitting open like a fruit, warm acidic scent attracting, flush, ripening, drawing to itself: black flies and flying insects, a parade of ants. And in the seams, which have widened, they have emerged. The mirror creatures. And there, one of them stands, watching me.

Her sea-green face repels. It is the colour of water, viridian, lime-white, aquamarine. The long licking tongues of waves. Sloshing. My sense of reality is for the moment a bollard in the sea with a rope tied to it, tugging. The wake. The prow rising and falling, the boat slanted to starboard. The rising tide of hungry creatures awakened. On the prowl. Seafarers climbing onto shore. The people of a city like so much flotsam.

It is here that I see them. I had thought to leave my old city behind me, but it remains. Burnt into the skin. A look, a sound or a scent is enough to recall it.

Ching

A wild bleak wind blowing. My garden flooded from three days of rain. I celebrate the anniversary of Tang's death with a quiet dinner alone. At my age the social circle starts closing. Furthermore this is a strange land and I know few people. Those that I have met are friendly but differ from me, their inner worlds have no correlation with mine. We are polite, we talk, but they unconsciously or not steer away, finding relief in their neighbour. Why? I cannot say, but I have grown used to it. And as one grows ever older, death will be something each of us faces on our own.

Even for *him*. He has tried to run from death, wanting immortality. Yet even emperors die, some without farewell. Each one alone. He is lingering, I hear. A severe stroke.

He waits to die and I ... I wait to mourn him.

As now I mourn Tang, that good quiet man, so mild in manner, so unwise, so unsuited to fight the battle he wished to fight. It cannot have been otherwise. Death was his end, the only end, and he embraced it keenly.

He was not one to cling to life when it had already ended for him. We never had children. They would not have taken it well, their father dying in such a way. It dried up my womb, that black medicine she made me drink. I should not have trusted her, the wisewoman. Wise, indeed! I accept it. I accept all of it. My life, my fate. Who I am. It cannot have been otherwise.

★

The Chairman is dead. Even he cannot ward off death. I fold up the newspaper I have been reading. I wonder what is happening in my city now. I have lost track of its daily news. I have almost completely lost touch with my friends there. One of them has emigrated. One stopped writing and others write on an irregular basis: a Christmas card, a remembrance on birthdays, a postcard from their holidays. Once I received a postcard of the city. I fell upon it with scissors and cut out an outline following the shapes of the buildings, and when I was done, it lay in my hand like a shell. The surface was glossy and mainly dark blue.

There is that about the city which is transient, unreal. Its outline makes a picture postcard of the hyper-new: slender skyscrapers, the orange illumination of electric lights, a night backdrop limning the infinite. To the forefront will be the river. Sometimes a mere smudge, with the buildings taking prominence in the picture, but more often than not a wide expanse of blue, and the buildings like stars.

The Chairman is dead. I wonder that I do not grieve. It is the shock. I am sure that when it has time to sink in, I will weep for him. Until then I am dispassionate. Not even he! Finally death catches up with the great. He may have known that in the end the mirror creatures have the upper hand, for they hold our souls. We think we have defeated them when we are in our full powers. We think we are free, but it is only a loan of time.

I think of home. I feel a yearning for it, perhaps for a return to a place that never existed. I know there is no way back.

In the mirror, I face the mirror woman: outcast, exile, immigrant. Standing at a point of truth, knowing that there is no truth, only illusions and more illusions, that all thought is implanted, that every society carries within itself a form of oppression, that living is itself tenuous, that in the end is only silence and something other.

What is the point of speech? What is the purpose of my memories?

Words are feeble things gasping on the page like fish.

It is not what I say, for I have lied in speaking, without

intending to, because it was the easiest thing to say at the moment, it is what I know.

'What?' you say.

'Things,' I say.

I have only myself, at this point of a complex world, a small spark of fire, continuing human existence. At the end of everything I am alone. At the end, before all interrogators, and denouncers, before those who would try me and punish me for living.

I face them implacably. When I die it will be at my own hand. They cannot crush my spirit. I, Madame Mao, I stand alone.

68

Ching

'What was it for?' we say when our lives are ending. I wonder if he asked himself that question before he died. Or does an emperor disappear with an eclipse of the sun?

There was a point to it. A point to our lives.

Perhaps, in the excitement of events when they happen, things seem to have a purpose. But upon reflection there is nothing. Nothing to hang onto for comfort.

Perhaps I, perhaps Tang, perhaps even the Chairman, have tried to step beyond the palm of the Buddha's hand or to escape the strings of the director.

Perhaps we walk our little rounds upon the stage. This is where I start, and this is where I end, and which is my beginning.

They come for me. In the blackness my audience hides. In my eyes they shine the lights that swim. I tread the wood. I touch my face. It is wet. They bind my hands. So I hear them. The whisperings.

They say, 'She must have been a demon.'

I say, 'Let them criticise. Let them judge. I am the one in the arena. Only I know what I have suffered. What I have endured. The cowards! Standing at the ringside howling for blood. What do they know?'

Glossary

Ah Pek. Old Man.

Ah Po. Old Woman.

Ah Yi. Aunty (used as a term for any woman who is older than oneself or in a position of authority, whether related or not).

Ai. An exclamation.

Aiya. An exclamation.

Alamak. An exclamation.

Amah. Servant.

Attap houses. Wooden houses on stilts with high-peaked thatched roofs.

Bee hoon. Fried rice vermicelli.

Buaya. Crocodile (used here to mean a flirtatious person).

Ching Ming Festival. 'Pure Brightness' Festival, a time when the Chinese visit the graves of their dead relatives to pay their respects.

Choy sum. A leafy vegetable, sometimes called Chinese flowering cabbage.

Five-foot way. A Singaporean term for the footpath in front of shops, which is exactly five feet in width.

Ham chin peng. A deep fried dough cake with red bean paste inside.

Jagar. Security guard.

Kachang puteh. Roasted nuts of various kinds.

Kali-yuga. The age of destruction in Hindu cosmology.

Kampong. Village.

Kavadi. The portable shrine of metal frames decorated with peacock feathers, fruit and flowers connected to the skin by hooks which is carried by Hindu devotees during the Thaipusam Festival as a way of giving thanks for answered prayers.

Kiasu. Afraid to lose out to others, or not to lose face.

Kopi tiam. Coffee shop.

Kopi-guni. Coffee with milk.

Kopi-O. Black coffee.

Kopi-peng. Iced coffee.

Kris. Malay sword with wavy edge.

Kueh lapis. Multilayered, tri-coloured glutinous cake.

Lah. An exclamation.

Laksa. Yellow noodles in a spicy coconut soup with prawns, shredded chicken, bean sprouts and dried bean curd.

Lor. An exclamation.

Mamak shop. Colloquial name for an Indian-owned shop selling newspapers, magazines and sweets.

Merdeka. Independence.

Orang laut. Men of the sea (pirates).

Pao Chou. 'Repay the bitter' (a call for revenge).

Pasar malams. Night markets with roadside portable stalls selling clothes, pirated tapes, snacks, fruit, toys, anything and everything.

Peranakan. Refers to the culture of the Straits Chinese (the Chinese who were born in the time of the Straits Settlements or who intermarried with the Malays).

Pon piah. A Chinese biscuit.

Po Po. Old woman.

Pontank. To play truant.

Putat laut. A seashore tree whose fruit can be used to stun fish.

Rojak. Singaporean salad dish of sliced cucumbers, turnips, pineapples, bean sprouts and *yew char kuay* mixed in black shrimp paste, ground peanuts and chilli paste.

Roti pratas. Flat Indian pancakelike bread eaten with a curry.

Sambal. Fried chilli, onion and prawn paste.

Samfoo. A Chinese blouse.

Suttee. Hindu custom of widow burning herself on her husband's funeral pyre.

Thaipusam Festival. Hindu festival in the month of Thai (January/February) originating in Tamil Nadu honouring Lord Subramaniam.

Tiadapa. An abbreviation of *tidak apa* which means 'it doesn't matter'.

Tilak. A sacred Hindu mark on the forehead.

Triad. Chinese secret society, now often associated with organised crime.

Tudong. The Malay word for the traditional Muslim headscarf worn by women.

Wayang. Chinese street opera in Singapore.

Wei. An exclamation.

Yew char kuay. Deep-fried bread sticks.

In the Hands of the Living God
by Lillian Bouzane

£7.99 • paperback • 1 84024 216 7 • 129 x 198 mm/320 pp

The story of a courageous and impassioned woman and of dangerous games played out against a backdrop of Renaissance Venice.

At the end of the fifteenth century, Venice rules Europe through her control of the trade routes. But in a time of progress, the renowned explorers of the day are pitting themselves against each other to discover a passage through to the Eastern Spice Islands. The discovery would mean the downfall of Venice.

Mathye, an accomplished musician and lady of the Venetian court, is married to Giovanni Caboto, Columbus' rival and the greatest seaman of them all. This is the story of her struggle with love and loyalty to the man who will betray his country by sailing for the King of England. Success could bring death, both to Venice and his family.

Lillian Bouzane is an award-winning poet. She was born in Newfoundland, Canada. *In the Hands of the Living God* was long-listed for the IMPAC Dublin Literary Award and is Lillian's first novel.

Salar Jang's Passion
by Musharraf Farooqi

£7.99 • paperback • 1 84024 224 8 • 129 x 198 mm/320 pp

High farce and the spice of conflicting passions in Pakistan.

'Farooqi combines Desani's eye for absurdity, Rushdie's delight in wordplay, the gently wicked humour of Dickens and George Eliot's ability to find the right word for everything.' *Mitali Saran*

The sleepy town of Purana Shehr is happy to trundle along in a round of petty arguments over tea and frustrated fantasies. Until, that is, the arrival of the termites. In the narrow lanes and grubby markets of the Topee Mohalla neighbourhood, and against a backdrop of destruction, passions stir as the residents begin to come to life. A royal chaos ensues as boundaries are broken, old fools are made, and overhand plots are hatched. And at the eye of the storm, Salar Jang, an eccentric septuagenarian with a fortune to bequeath, embarks upon an increasingly bizarre courtship, much to the dismay of his only heir and daughter.

Musharraf Farooqi was born in 1968 in Hyderabad, Pakistan. He worked as a journalist and editor in Karachi and has since translated many Urdu classics. *Salar Jang's Passion* is Musharraf's first novel.

House of the Winds
by Mia Yun

£7.99 • paperback • 1 84024 212 4 • 129 x 198 mm/256 pp

At this world's heart are Korean women . . . laughing, wailing, spirit-cajoling, bosom-bracing, fire-breathing.

Korea, 1960s. A girl stands in the middle of a sunny cabbage patch with her mother. The air is full of butterflies (the souls of children in afternoon naps) and secrets (although they were not secrets at the time). War, Japanese rule and loss are bleeding wounds in living memory, and sadness springs in the heart of this Korean family. As a child, Youngest Daughter believed that her mother was happy with nothing but her children; as an adult, she unravels her memories and finds the threads of her past – of brutality and tenderness, of magic, of the ghosts of ancestors, of words unspoken – that weave themselves into the fabric of all their lives.

Mia Yun was born in Seoul, Korea in 1956. She now lives in New York and has worked as a reporter, translator and freelance writer. *House of the Winds* is Mia's first novel.